FALLING FOR HIS PRACTICAL WIFE

Laura Martin

MILLS & BOON

First Published in Great Britain 2021
by Mills & Boon, an imprint of HarperCollins*Publishers* Ltd,
1 London Bridge Street, London, SE1 9GF

www.harpercollins.co.uk

HarperCollins*Publishers*
1st Floor, Watermarque Building,
Ringsend Road, Dublin 4, Ireland

Falling for His Practical Wife © 2021 Laura Martin

ISBN: 978-0-263-28413-3

07/21

MIX
Paper from
responsible sources
FSC™ C007454

This book is produced from independently certified FSC™ paper
to ensure responsible forest management.
For more information visit www.harpercollins.co.uk/green.

Printed and bound in Spain
by CPI, Barcelona

To my boys.
What more can you ask for
than days filled with love and laughter?

Chapter One

Eastbourne 1815

> *Dear Beth,*
> *Do you remember when I promised I*
> *would never climb out of a window again?*
> *Well...*

Trailing a hand over the silky wallpaper, Annabelle paused for a moment and closed her eyes. It had been a busy few days, packing up the last of their belongings, organising the carts of furniture to be taken to the little cottage overlooking the sea she and her mother were renting. Annabelle had barely stopped, itemising and sorting, all the time trying to ignore the deep sorrow she felt at leaving her childhood home.

'It's a fresh start,' she murmured, taking her

fingers off the wallpaper and forcing herself to stride purposefully out of the room.

'I've changed my mind,' Lady Hummingford announced as Annabelle came downstairs to see Mr Lennox and Mr Hardy, two men from the village who had been hired to do the heavy lifting, struggling with a weighty mahogany desk. She had watched them take it out to the cart only a few minutes earlier and now it was coming back in through the front door.

Quickly Annabelle pulled down her veil, hiding her face from the men and also conveniently hiding the eye roll she allowed herself at her mother's behaviour.

'Mr Lennox, Mr Hardy, would you mind if I had a private word with my mother? If you would be so kind as to take the desk back out to the cart and then why don't you get a refreshing drink from the kitchen. You've been working so hard.' She half expected her mother to protest, but Lady Hummingford stayed quiet until the men were back outside.

'It is ridiculous to leave before the house is even sold, Annabelle. We could live here for months longer.'

'We can't afford the upkeep. We can't afford the staff. We can't even afford the wood for the fire.' Annabelle took a step towards her mother and reached out for her hand. This might be her childhood home, the sanctuary she had only left a handful of times in over a decade and a half, but it was where her mother had met her father, where they had been a family, where she had mourned him. She had to remember this was just as hard for her mother as it was for her. 'The cottage is comfortable and in a beautiful location. If you give it a chance, I think we could be happy there.'

Lady Hummingford scoffed and turned away and Annabelle clenched her jaw so she wouldn't say anything she would regret.

'What I don't understand is why Mr Ashburton couldn't pay for the upkeep of this place for a few more months until it sells rather than paying the rent on a new cottage.'

Sensibly Annabelle remained quiet. She knew exactly why. Birling View was a beautiful property, sat on the cliffs of the south downs with uninterrupted views of the sea. It had suffered from a gentle neglect over the last few years, with no money and no staff to maintain it to a proper standard. Despite this it should be easy to sell to the right person who was willing to spend some time and money restoring the house to its former glory.

The problem they'd had was that Annabelle's mother was so reluctant to leave that she would point out the flaws of the property to any interested party. Lord Warner had come to look around only last week and had seemed enthusiastic about the sale. Five minutes with Lady Hummingford and he'd scuttled away, mumbling something ominous about collapsing roofs and subsiding walls.

Mr Ashburton, the brother of the man who had just married her beloved sister Beth, had promised to help with the practicalities of selling the property. Beth and her new husband, Josh Ashburton, had sailed for India straight after the wedding, but Mr Leonard Ashburton had offered his services in overseeing the sale of the house and setting Annabelle and her mother up in a smaller property. He had quietly paid the first few months' rent on the new cottage and settled the most pressing of their debts. It was Mr Ashburton who had taken Annabelle aside and pointed out that they would never sell Birling View with Lady Hummingford still in residence, doing her utmost to put off everyone who showed an interest. Reluctantly Annabelle had agreed, so here they were, almost ready to leave their home for good.

'Have you all your personal belongings packed, Mother?'

'Yes,' Lady Hummingford said tersely. Annabelle squeezed her mother's hand, trying to show she understood the pain and turmoil, but Lady Hummingford glanced down and then stepped away without a word.

Trying not to feel hurt, Annabelle turned and walked from the room, heading out of the house to check how the loading of the cart was going.

On Mr Ashburton's advice they were leaving most of the furniture behind at Birling View. They could only fit a select few pieces in their new cottage and she knew a house as large as this one would sell better with the rooms furnished. It had been difficult to decide what to take and what to leave behind, and she suspected despite her ruthlessness they would arrive at their new cottage to find the rooms overstuffed with belongings.

Outside Annabelle was checking the ropes holding the furniture in place when she heard the clatter of approaching hooves. After a moment a carriage rounded the bend of the drive and she sent thanks to whoever was watching over her. Mr Ashburton had promised to send his carriage for her mother to travel in to their new home. When the carriage hadn't turned up earlier in the morning she had been dread-

ing telling her mother she would have to ride
in the cart with the furniture. Their own carriage had been sold months earlier and much
to Annabelle's distress the horses had been
taken by their new owner a week ago. She had
sobbed then, burying her head in her mare's
mane and soaking it with her tears.

'Ah, good,' Lady Hummingford said, stepping out into the warm July sunshine, pulling
her gloves on to her hands. 'The carriage is
here at last.'

'I need to do one final check of the house
before we go, Mother.'

Her mother toyed with the heavy set of keys,
tapping them against her leg. 'You should ride
in the cart, Annabelle. Ensure our belongings survive the journey in one piece. Heaven
knows we have little enough left.'

Annabelle tried not to let the hurt show on
her face. For years she had been dismissed and
belittled by her mother, treated as an incon-
venience and an embarrassment. It shouldn't
surprise her, this suggestion that she was better placed with the furniture, but it hurt all
the same.

'I shall wait in the carriage. Let me know
when you have finished in the house and I
will lock up.'

'Yes, Mother.'

Fighting back the tears, she ran up the steps and through the front door, closing it softly behind her and resting her forehead on the cool, solid wood. She reminded herself that this had been her choice, her decision. Before Beth had departed for India she had once again urged Annabelle to join her and her new husband as they set sail for their new life.

'You're a fool,' Annabelle muttered to herself. Right now she could be strolling the decks arm and arm with her beloved sister and instead she was running herself ragged, trying to ease her and her mother's descent into genteel poverty.

Straightening up, she squared her shoulders and lifted her chin. Now was not the time to mope. There was too much to do. Later tonight, when she was tucked in her bed in the attic room of the cottage, she could let the tears fall and allow the self-pity to flourish, but right now she needed to check they weren't leaving anything essential behind.

Walking slowly through the rooms, Annabelle tried not to remember all the happy times. The spot in the drawing room where she and Beth used to giggle together as they stabbed at their needlework and plotted minor pranks to play on their governess. The comfortable chair in the library where she had lost herself between the covers of the thousands of books she loved to read, curled up and momentarily able to forget her true place in the world. Then there was the bedroom she had shared with Beth, the heavy four-poster bed they had lain in night after night, whispering about their hopes and dreams.

It was cathartic walking through the house like this and Annabelle wished she could linger in the silence for longer, but she knew the men from the village would be eager to set off on the journey to Eastbourne and her mother was likely getting increasingly impatient.

As she began descending the stairs, she froze as she heard the heavy click of the key turning in the front door, followed by the unmistakable scratch of the key being withdrawn.

For a moment she couldn't move, unable to process what was happening, and then she flung herself down the rest of the steps, dashing across the hall to pull at the front door.

The handle wouldn't turn, the door was locked firmly from the outside and without a key there was no way she would ever be able to get out that way. Quickly she ran to the drawing room, throwing herself at the window, hammering at it to catch the attention of who-ever had locked her in.

Annabelle saw the door to the carriage close and a moment later the wheels began to turn. Her mother had locked her in and instructed the carriage to move off.

Even though she knew it was pointless, she continued to rap on the window, hoping her mother might decide to check she hadn't left her younger daughter behind.

'How could you?' she whispered, sinking on to the large wooden windowsill. The carriage was now halfway down the drive, turning the corner so it was obscured by the avenue of trees. The rational part of her brain told her it was of course an accident. From what she could work out the cart with their possessions had already left. Lady Hummingford, thinking Annabelle had exited the house and climbed aboard the cart without telling her, had locked the front door. Still, most mothers would have bothered to check before they'd locked their daughter in a deserted house.

Annabelle watched until the carriage had disappeared completely, feeling the panic begin to build. Her mother would realise eventually. It was only an hour's journey to the cottage, so at most it would be a little over two hours before she was let out. Two hours was nothing, but she suddenly had the overwhelming urge to get out of the house. She didn't want to be in this empty shell of what used to be her home.

Upstairs, on the first floor, there was a window just above and to the left of the main entrance that had never locked properly. Annabelle had used it to creep out a few times in her youth and had mostly found it was an easy climb over to the pillars next to the front door and then a small drop to the ground. If she was careful, she could be out of the house and waiting in the sunshine for her mother to realise her mistake.

Before she could talk herself out of it she hurried upstairs and tested the window, finding it swung out with a soft creak. The drop didn't look too bad even if she didn't make it to the pillars. With one final look back at the house, she climbed up on to the windowsill.

Leo entered through the wrought-iron gates at a steady trot. He was late and he hated being late. As usual his great-uncle had been reluctant to let him leave, wanting to discuss the minutiae of estate business before Leo had been able to make his escape.

His lateness wasn't the only reason for Leo's bad mood. Once again his great-uncle had brought up the subject of Leo's unmarried state, a subject Leo hated discussing. Months earlier Lord Abbingdon had declared that much of his money wouldn't pass to Leo on his death unless Leo was married. As heir, the title and estates would become his, but the money that was needed to run such large parcels of land Lord Abbingdon could leave to whomever he wanted. Leo knew it was likely an empty threat, a ploy to get him married off and producing heirs to secure the family's future before the old man died, but it was a matter that had been on his mind more and more recently. Even more so since his great-uncle's doctor had pulled him aside and told him gravely there wasn't much more they could do for the old man.

Taking a deep breath, he pushed the headache of his inheritance and his great-uncle from his mind and tried to enjoy the warmth of the sunshine of his shoulders and the fresh sea breeze. He liked this part of the country, appreciated the stunning white cliffs and rolling hills. Even the dilapidated estate Lady Hummingford had clung to over the past few years since her husband's death was charming in its own way.

'What the hell?' He couldn't quite believe what he was seeing. The façade of Birling View looked as it always did, pretty but in need of some loving care. The drive was quiet, with the carriage and cart of furniture seemingly already departed. What caught his eye and caused him to curse was the slender form of a woman climbing out of a first-floor window.

Quickly he urged his horse forward, stopping just underneath the window in question and dismounting even before Emperor had come to a complete stop.

'What on earth are you doing?'

The figure hanging from the window ledge went completely still.

'Good afternoon, Mr Ashburton,' Lady Annabelle said eventually. She turned her head a fraction and he saw the flush of colour on her cheeks, but whether it was from embarrassment or exertion he could not tell.

'I suggest you climb back inside right away.'

'I'm afraid that is impossible,' she said quietly.

Taking a step closer and peering up, he saw the full extent of her predicament. For reasons known only to her she had climbed out of the window, swinging her legs down and then turning round in an attempt to lower herself closer to the ground before dropping the last few feet. Somewhere in the process her skirt had snagged on part of the window frame and now was tethering her to the window. Where she had twisted it was impossible for her to climb back in and if she dropped her dress would tear from her body.

Suppressing the questions on his lips, Leo frowned as he tried to work out the best way to get her down.

'I think you're just going to have to tear your dress,' he said eventually.

Above him Lady Annabelle nodded, but didn't move.

'If I drop from here, the dress will hold me too close to the wall.'

He saw the problem. Her skin would be scraped against the brickwork unless she could propel herself far enough out.

'Plant your feet on the wall and push as you let go. I will stand underneath and catch you.'

It looked as though she were about to protest again, but then she simply nodded, placed her feet squarely on the wall and pushed. There was a loud ripping sound and Leo barely had time to brace himself before Lady Annabelle came hurtling through the air towards him. He caught her, but the force of her pushed him off his feet and they ended up in a tangled pile on the ground.

Lady Annabelle's pointy little elbow caught him full force in his stomach, pushing the air from his lungs and for a long moment he couldn't do anything but lie there with her on top of him, trying to catch his breath.

After twenty seconds Lady Annabelle began to wriggle, pushing herself up on her hands to look down at him. He was acutely aware of how her body was pressing into his.

'Are you hurt?' Her brows were furrowed and her eyes were flitting over him as if trying to assess for injuries.

Firmly he put his hands on her arms and rolled her to one side, groaning as he sat up.

'Nothing permanent,' he said gruffly, testing out his arms and legs. His back was jarred from the impact with the ground and his abdomen felt a little tender from where she had landed on top of him, but nothing was broken.

'Thank you for breaking my fall.' She scrambled to her feet, hands searching her hair for the veil she normally wore over her face that had become dislodged in the fall. As she realised it was missing her expression turned to one of panic and her eyes began darting from left to right, searching for the thin piece of fabric.

Leo felt it under his elbow and got to his feet, holding it out and unable to look away as she took it with relief and fastened it back into place. She seemed to relax once her face was shadowed by the veil, not noticing her skirt was ripped and open at the front, revealing her petticoats and stockings underneath.

'I'm not sure there is anything we can do to fix your dress,' Leo said, trying not to look at the slender calves that poked out from underneath her petticoats.

'Oh.' Lady Annabelle looked down in dismay and quickly gathered the material around her, grimacing as she realised quite how ripped her dress was.

'What an earth were you thinking, climbing out of the window like that?' He heard the anger in his voice, even though it wasn't his place to be angry with her. She was not his responsibility, not his sister or his wife. If she wanted to risk life and limb climbing out of windows, then really it was none of his concern.

'I was locked in.'

'Don't be ridiculous.'

From under the veil her eyes sought out his

and he saw her chin raise a notch. Lady Annabelle might hide from society, but she had a backbone and it would seem his tone had rankled her.

'Why do you think I was climbing out of the window, Mr Ashburton? It was hardly for fun,' she said frostily. 'My mother left without checking if I was still in the house and locked the front door with the only key. All the other doors and windows have been locked for days in preparation for our departure. That upstairs window doesn't lock, so it was my only option.'

'Your mother left you behind?' He knew Lady Hummingford was an unfeeling woman, but even for her it seemed a bit harsh.

'I'm sure it was an accident.' Her voice was steady, but he saw her wince underneath the veil. Quickly she turned her back to him, ostensibly looking up at the house and the window she'd made her escape through, but he wondered if it was to hide the pain she felt at being so insignificant in her mother's thoughts.

'I am sorry I was delayed,' he said quietly. 'I had meant to be here to ensure everything went smoothly.'

'It does not matter, Mr Ashburton. Please do

not feel you have to wait with me either. I'm sure my mother will send the carriage back for me just as soon as she realises what has occurred.'

He wondered if she actually expected him to ride off without a backwards glance, leaving her alone and abandoned. Leo shook his head. He knew he had a reputation for being a cold man, a difficult man to know or like, but he had been brought up a gentleman and a gentleman would never leave a lady in distress, no matter how little she cared for his assistance.

'You can ride with me,' he said, walking over to where his horse was happily munching on some grass from the lawn to the side of the house.

That made Lady Annabelle turn and face him. Although from his current distance he couldn't see the expression on her face, he rather liked to think it was one of surprise.

'Surely it'll be too much for your horse to carry both of us.'

'Emperor is strong and we can take it slowly. The ride is less than an hour.'

Still she hesitated, so he led the horse over to her.

'Let me help you up.'

Deftly he helped her on to Emperor's back, ensuring she was comfortable in the spot in front of the saddle before he mounted behind her. He felt her stiffen as his body made contact with hers, but then with a flick of the reins they were off down the drive.

Chapter Two

Dear Beth,
Have you ever, through no real fault of
your own, muddied the knees of a gen-
tleman's breeches as you both sailed to-
wards the ground?

For the first five minutes Annabelle sat stiffly
on the back of the majestic horse. It was the
closest she'd ever been to a man and the closest
she'd been to anyone save her mother and sister for a long time. Out of habit she raised one
hand to check her veil was in place before remembering Mr Ashburton was behind her and
unable to see her face even if he leaned around.

One of his arms was resting in the curve of
her waist as he gripped the reins lightly with
a single hand. The other hand was steadying
her, placed carefully above her hip. For any-

one else it might have been an intimate gesture, but Annabelle knew Mr Ashburton was only doing his duty. He was a man who took his duty seriously. When she and Josh were courting, Beth had told her how Leo was always dashing to old Lord Abbingdon's bedside, ready to take on new responsibilities as the old Viscount's health failed. Then there was she and her mother. He had promised that he would see them settled in a new home, with Birling View sold and their debts settled, and that was exactly what he was doing. Even if it inconvenienced him.

'Thank you for coming down today,' she said, turning her head slightly so her words weren't whipped away by the breeze.

'It is a good job I did, otherwise you might still be hanging out of the first-floor window.'

Annabelle ignored the comment and pushed on with her thanks. She had been raised to be polite and, even if she disliked this man sitting behind her, she would remember her manners.

'I must thank you especially for sending the carriage for Mother. I think she would have refused to leave if she had had to travel in the cart.'

'And you? I sent the carriage for both of you.'

'Mother thought it best someone travel with the furniture.' She tried not to let her voice quaver. Mr Ashburton didn't need to know how much that decision had stung her.

'Hmm.'

They were on the top of the cliffs now, following the narrow path a few feet from the edge. Annabelle felt the tears sting her eyes as she looked at the view. Twenty-one years she had lived at Birling View and, for all her living memory, she had only ventured further than these cliffs on a handful of occasions. *This* was her home, her sanctuary, or at least it had been.

'Are you unwell, Lady Annabelle?'

She realised she had taken a shuddering breath to try to suppress the tears that were welling in her eyes and Mr Ashburton with his hand on her waist had felt the movement.

'No, just a little emotional. I am practical about our need to leave Birling View, but that doesn't make it any less difficult.'

'It is your home.'

'I have many happy memories here. Memories of my father and my sister.' Her father was gone, he'd passed away five years earlier, and now Beth had left, too. She would never begrudge her sister her new life in India with the man she loved, but she missed her sorely already and she'd only been gone a month.

To her surprise Mr Ashburton pulled gently on the reins and slipped out of the saddle, holding up a hand to help her down.

'There is no great hurry,' he said quietly, 'Take a few moments.'

She blinked in surprise at the softness of his tone and then realised that he understood a little of what she was feeling. He might not have lost his home, but his brother had left alongside her sister, and neither of them knew when they would see their beloved siblings again.

Walking to the edge of the cliff, Annabelle lifted her veil and felt the warm breeze on her face. She loved the salty tang to the air and the distant call of the seagulls. Down below her she could hear the waves crashing into the cliff, churning up the water as it hit the chalk. For a moment she closed her eyes and allowed the flood of memories: playing on the cliffs with Beth, going for solitary winter walks when the wind was so cold it felt as though her eyelashes might freeze together. Tending the gardens of Birling View in her muddy boots, she and Beth giggling as they had no clue how to make a garden thrive.

Her sister always worried Annabelle's life

was too small, too insular. She'd shunned company because of the scars on her face and the spiteful comments of people when she did go out, but she had grown to love her little world and could have happily lived out her years in Birling View with just her books for company.

With a sigh she dropped her head back, startled when she felt something thump into her so hard she was catapulted back on to the grass.

In amazement she realised Mr Ashburton was lying on top of her, pinning her to the ground. He was a big man, at least six feet tall with a muscular physique. She was small, in stature and build, and completely immobilised by his weight upon her.

For a moment she was too shocked to say anything. She looked up at him and saw the concern on his face.

'You thought I was going to jump?' she murmured.

'You closed your eyes. You took a step forward.'

'I wouldn't jump. Not ever. I was just enjoying the moment.'

Mr Ashburton looked down at her, studying her face, nodding after a few seconds as if satisfied he believed her. For a moment longer he didn't move and Annabelle was acutely aware of how his body was pressed so closely against hers, then with a muttered apology he rolled off her, springing to his feet.

Annabelle gathered her ripped skirts around her, but didn't stand, and after a moment Mr Ashburton sat down beside her.

'I am sorry,' he said again, louder this time.

'Did you really think I would jump?'

'It looked as though you were about to.'

They fell silent, sitting side by side.

'My life isn't that bad,' Annabelle said quietly, wondering why she was trying to justify herself to this man who was little more than a stranger. 'Mother might be…difficult, Sea Spray Cottage isn't as grand as Birling View, I will grant you, and Beth is halfway across the world, but I don't wish to end my life.'

She felt his eyes on her and suddenly realised she hadn't lowered the veil. From the direction of his gaze she could tell he wasn't focused on the scars on her cheek, but she felt self-conscious all the same. She had lived with the scars since the age of four after she had fallen from a set of shelves she was climbing and pulled a vase on top of her. There were three red slashes across one cheek, with a fourth bisecting them. She often thought it looked as though she had been mauled by a wild animal.

Carefully she pulled at the light material until it hid her face, refusing to meet Mr Ashburton's eye even though she could feel his gaze upon her still.

'We should continue,' she said eventually, standing up and pulling her tattered skirts around her. 'Mother will be sending the carriage back for me soon and if we are quick we should hopefully be able to intercept it on the way.'

Without another word Mr Ashburton helped her back on to the horse and settled himself in behind her and, as his body brushed against hers Annabelle had to remind herself she didn't like this man very much, even if his strong arms had come to her aid numerous times today already.

The journey was a beautiful one, over the rolling hills and white cliffs before descending down the coastal path to the outskirts of the little town of Eastbourne. Nevertheless he was relieved to see the thatched roof of the cottage coming into view. Lady Annabelle made him feel uncomfortable and he wasn't sure why. She was a pleasant enough young woman, well raised and polite, and he had spent his formative years in the company of many young women of her ilk as his great-aunt had strived to prepare him for the life he would one day lead. It wasn't even the scars she was so self-conscious of, or the ridiculous veil she pulled down to hide her face. He wasn't sure what it was about Lady Annabelle that made him feel so off balance, but he would be pleased to deposit her in the company of her mother and take his leave, duty done for the day.

'Annabelle, where on earth have you been?' Lady Hummingford said as they slowed to a stop on the other side of a neatly trimmed hedge. He spotted his carriage out of the corner of his eye and the cart which would have carried their furniture. It would seem Lady Hummingford hadn't rushed to return to Birling View when she had discovered her daughter wasn't with her.

'The cart left while I was still in the house, Mother,' Lady Annabelle said with more poise than he would have been able to muster. 'Then you locked me in.'

'What on earth were you still doing in the house?'

'Checking everything was in order, as I said I would.'

'You should have been on the cart.' He noted there was no apology from the Dowager Countess, or any sign of remorse for putting her daughter through such an ordeal. 'Mr Ashburton, how grateful we are you could make it today.'

With a nod of acknowledgement he slipped off Emperor's back and then turned back to help Lady Annabelle down, making sure he lifted her away from her mother so she had a chance to arrange her ripped skirts before the older woman caught sight of her.

'You must be famished after the long ride. I will ask the maid to set out some tea.'

'Thank you.' He would rather be on his way, but Leo knew he would have to drink at least one cup before it would be polite to take his leave.

'Goodness gracious, Annabelle, what have you done to your dress? Get inside at once.'

Not for the first time in his life Leo was thankful he had been born a man. No one would dare to speak to him like that now he was an adult and he felt a twinge of admiration for Lady Annabelle as she squared her shoulders and glided slowly into the cottage instead of scurrying off.

The cottage was light and airy and, although

small compared to Birling View, it was well proportioned and well situated. Lady Hummingford led him into a bright room with three comfortable armchairs at one end and a table at the other, barking instructions to a young girl who he assumed was to live in as their maid. As soon as they sat down there was an almighty crash and a string of curses from outside. Lady Hummingford stood and excused herself, dashing outside to see which expensive piece of furniture had been dropped.

Leo had closed his eyes, weary from the long ride and the busy days beforehand. His limbs were beginning to feel heavy and he knew he was at risk of dropping off when he heard a soft cough. Lady Annabelle was sitting quietly opposite him. How she had managed to get into the room without him hearing he didn't know. She must be particularly light on her feet. She'd changed into a light green day dress with embroidered flowers up one side and he was surprised to see she had removed the veil.

He took a moment to study her: the golden blonde hair was similar to her sister's, but the bright blue eyes were all her own. She had a pretty face, with small, neat features. If it weren't for the scars on her cheek she would be considered a diamond of the Season in London. For a few seconds he was reminded of the first time he had set eyes on her, when he had visited Birling View with Josh and found Lady Annabelle creeping around after dark so she wouldn't be seen by the house party guests. He'd been struck then by the wariness in her eyes and the sense that she didn't quite fit anywhere in the world.

'I didn't mean to disturb you, Mr Ashburton, please feel free to rest if you wish. You must have had a busy day.' She spoke softly and not for the first time he wondered where she got her mild manner from.

'Are you happy, Lady Annabelle?' he asked abruptly. As he saw the surprise on her face he cursed himself for asking the question so bluntly. An idea had popped into his mind, a preposterous idea…but he hadn't been able to stop himself from pondering.

'Well…' She looked around in panic and then sat back and considered his question. 'Do you know, no one has asked me that for a long time. No, Mr Ashburton, I am not happy, but I am contented. I think that is enough.' She folded her hands demurely in her lap and then fixed him with a piercing stare. 'I will make a good life for myself and my mother here.'

'Is that what you want? To make a life here with your mother?'

She let out a low, astonished laugh. 'Within the realms of possibility, yes.'

'What do you mean?'

'There are very few options open to me, Mr Ashburton. Of those that are this will suit me well enough.'

'You have other options.'

She looked at him for a moment, then shook her head. 'Not many viable ones.'

'You could join your sister in India, or marry and have a family of your own.'

'India is Beth's adventure.'

'And marriage?' He knew he was pushing too hard, but he wanted to see her reaction.

'I know no gentlemen, Mr Ashburton. I'm a recluse with no prospects. I hardly think anyone is going to step forward and offer for my hand at this stage.' It was said without bitterness, just the gentle acceptance of someone who had resigned themselves to their fate a long time ago.

'But if someone were to offer, would you want it?'

With narrowed eyes she slowly nodded her head. 'Of course, but why torture myself with the impossible?'

Leo sat back in his chair and steepled his fingers together, his mind racing. Many years ago when Annabelle's father was alive, the old Earl had done something for Leo he would never forget. In thanks Leo had agreed to marry his elder daughter, Lady Elizabeth, when she was of an appropriate age. Six months ago they had both half-heartedly started courting, but neither had truly wanted the match. Lady Elizabeth had promptly fallen for his brother and now they were on their way to India together as man and wife. Leo was happy for his brother, but it had meant he wasn't able to fulfil his promise to the old Earl and he didn't like not keeping his word.

He looked at Lady Annabelle. She was quiet, well-bred and, apart from climbing out of first-floor windows, didn't seem to have any overtly annoying habits. Her scars had kept her cloistered inside for most of her life, but he didn't need a wife to show off to society, he just needed a wife to keep Lord Abbingdon happy and the money from the inheritance coming his way. In addition, Lady Annabelle was unlikely to refuse. The alternative was spending the rest of her days running after her objectionable mother in this small cottage.

If he asked Lady Annabelle to marry him,

he would gain the wife he needed and fulfil his promise to her father.

'I wonder, Lady Annabelle—' he said, but cut himself off as Lady Hummingford sailed back into the room.

'My apologies, Mr Ashburton, the hired help don't seem to grasp the meaning of valuable.'

'Not at all. I was just going to ask Lady Annabelle for a tour of the garden before I leave.' He turned to the younger woman. 'Would you oblige?'

Her eyes narrowed and he knew she was aware something else was afoot here, but she couldn't quite work out what.

'Of course, Mr Ashburton.'

He offered her his arm and they strolled from the room and back out of the open front door, having to stand to one side to allow two men struggling with a heavy piano past.

'What are we doing, Mr Ashburton?' Lady Annabelle turned to him once they were out of earshot of the house in a pretty little garden filled with flowers.

'It is a beautiful day—'

She shook her head to cut him off. 'I don't believe you are that eager to see the garden here at Sea Spray Cottage.'

'I have a proposition for you,' he said, trying to soften his tone. It wouldn't do to bark the marriage proposal at her, he wanted her to consider it properly at least. 'And I wanted to discuss it out of earshot of your mother so the decision you make is yours and yours alone.'

Gesturing to the little wrought-iron bench at one end of the garden, he followed her over and waited until they were seated comfortably before beginning again. He was sat to her right and she had turned her head so he couldn't see the scars on her left cheek. Lady Annabelle was very proficient at hiding herself.

'Do you know a little of my circumstance?' he said, thinking that if they were to unite it would not be an emotional attachment, so best to discuss this like a business arrangement. 'Did your sister mention to you why I was considering marriage?'

'I know you felt you owed our father a debt of gratitude,' Lady Annabelle said slowly, a slight frown on her face, 'But Beth did not tell me anything more than that.'

'I did owe your father a debt of gratitude and when I asked him how I could repay it he suggested I marry Lady Elizabeth when she was of age. Of course, that didn't quite work out.'

'Father wouldn't have begrudged Beth her happiness, even if you had the better prospects.'

He suppressed a smile as he glanced up, knowing she was adding *on paper* silently. Josh might not be in line to inherit a title and the vast estates that went with it, but he was going back to run his own shipping and transport company in India, and Leo didn't doubt he would make his fortune within the decade.

'That is indeed part of the reason I approached your sister, but I also have another rather pressing reason to want to find a wife. I'm sure you're aware that Lord Abbingdon is no longer a young man and has myriad health issues. When he passes away I will become the next Viscount and I will inherit a fair amount of land.' He paused, wondering if she was aware of where this was leading. Lady Annabelle looked mildly interested, but as though what he was saying couldn't have anything to do with her. 'The estates, of course, require a substantial amount of money to run and Lord Abbingdon has made it a stipulation of his will that I only inherit the money along with the land if I am married.'

'How strange.'

'He is adamant he doesn't want the estate passing into the hands of increasingly distant, and in his mind inferior, relatives. He thinks if I am married I will produce an heir and secure the family name.'

'I can see why you pushed ahead with courting Beth when you did,' Lady Annabelle said quietly.

'Lord Abbingdon is very sick, his doctors do not expect him to live more than a month or two, so my need to get married is even more pressing than ever.'

Lady Annabelle nodded politely, but he could see she had no idea he was about to propose to her. It was as if she had labelled herself as unmarriageable a long time ago and couldn't see past that perception.

'I have never felt the desire to marry for love or companionship,' he said, feeling the lie fall thickly from his tongue. Lady Annabelle didn't need to know anything about his past, it was all long buried along with his heart. 'I am looking for a match that is mutually beneficial. I would offer a comfortable lifestyle, the chance to be mistress of a grand house and no expectation to have to mingle with society.' He paused, watching the young woman next to him closely. 'What do you think?'

'I'm sure there are many young women who would be delighted to accept your proposal.'

'Yes, but I'm not asking them. I'm asking you.'

'Me?' Lady Annabelle almost fell off the bench as she backed away so quickly with surprise. 'You shouldn't jest about these things, Mr Ashburton.' She stood, two spots of colour rising on her cheeks and just the very first glint of tears in her eyes.

'I do not jest. Ever. Sit down, Lady Annabelle, if you would.'

She hesitated, looking over her shoulder wistfully at the cottage behind her, but something about his proposition must have intrigued her enough to stay.

'I need a wife for all the reasons outlined. You have as much as told me your prospects are poor, there is no suitor waiting for your hand. If you decline my proposal, you will likely spend the rest of your youth looking after your mother.'

Lady Annabelle grimaced and he knew he'd touched on her main reason to want to get away.

'We barely know one another.'

'We don't need to. We don't even need to live in the same house if we don't want to.'

'A marriage on paper only?'

'Not exactly. But think of it as a business arrangement from which we both benefit.'

Her eyes flitted around the garden and he could see her mind was racing.

'And children?' she asked eventually, homing in on the one area he had hoped she might not ask about. 'You said yourself you will need an heir.'

'My brother will be my heir. I'm sure he and Lady Elizabeth will have plenty of children.' It would be wrong to allow her to think there would be children. He had resigned himself long ago to a single life. He was willing to take on a wife, in name if not into his life properly, but he did not want the emotional attachment children would bring.

'I don't know what to say, Mr Ashburton.'

'Don't say anything. Not now. Take a day to think about it. I will need an answer by tomorrow afternoon. I shall stay at the Three Boars tonight and call on you tomorrow. Consider your options and I expect an answer before I leave for Kent.'

He stood, bowed over her hand formally, then took his leave, wondering if this detachment was how you were meant to feel after proposing to a woman.

Chapter Three

Dear Beth,
You will never believe what happened
yesterday. I am almost certain I must
have imagined it. And yet...

Annabelle paced around the garden, walking so quickly that every so often her skirt would catch on one of the plants that spilled in a riot of colour from the flowerbeds. Her mind was in turmoil, her stomach churning, and every time she thought she had come to a decision about Mr Ashburton's proposal she found some reason to doubt herself.

'What are you doing, Annabelle? You're wearing a track in the grass you've stomped the same path so many times.' Lady Hummingford emerged from the back door of the cottage with a frown on her face. She had been

in a foul mood all day, slamming cupboards
and letting out dramatic huffs and sighs. Annabelle had spent the morning trying to keep
out of her way, but her mother always seemed
to find her.

'Just enjoying the sunshine, Mother.' She
hadn't confided in her mother about Mr Ashburton's proposal. She knew her mother would
push her towards the union, thinking of the
money, thinking her new son-in-law could
move her out of this tiny cottage to accommodation more suiting a woman of her status.
Annabelle wanted to make her decision without the interference of her mother.

'This situation is untenable,' Lady Hummingford declared, sighing dramatically as
she perched on the edge of the little bench at
one end of the garden. 'The house is tiny, the
maid is useless and I dare not show my face
in company ever again.'

For a moment Annabelle felt a swell of com-
passion for her mother. She had been raised
to be the wife of a man of status, to have his
children and run his household. Lady Hummingford had done her part over the years and
now she should be sitting back and watching
her daughters live their own lives while she
became one of the matriarchs of society. In-

stead she had lost her husband, her home and her status.

'I know it is a lot to adjust to, Mother, but we need to give it a chance. Perhaps in a few months things won't seem so bad.'

'For you. This suits you perfectly well, hiding away in a cottage far from civilisation, not having to socialise with anyone, but for a normal person it is hell.'

The criticism only stung a little. Annabelle had become used to her mother's harsh and insulting words over the years and had found it easier to filter out the horrible parts than to get upset every time.

'I'm sure you'll still receive invitations to socialise.'

Her mother scoffed. 'Of course, I will. People love to revel in others' misfortune.'

In a flash Annabelle saw what her life would be like if she stayed here with her mother, year after year stretching out, listening to her mother's complaints, hearing why their life wasn't good enough. A marriage to Mr Ashburton might not be for reasons of love, but she would get to be mistress of her own house. It sounded as though he didn't really want a wife, aside from allowing him to fulfil the terms of Lord Abbingdon's will, but that suited her. She would get to live a life of quiet independence, away from her mother and barely bothered by Mr Ashburton.

The last of the doubts nagged at her. The most persistent of the lot was the thought that if she married Mr Ashburton she would never know the love of a husband. With a sense of determination she pushed the doubt aside. She had never planned to marry, even if she had dreamed of being swept off her feet when she was a young and foolish girl, and never went out long enough to meet anyone. This was the perfect solution, even if the idea of being married to the serious and sober Mr Ashburton made her stomach clench with anxiety. She reminded herself of the kindness he had shown her when they had first met at Birling View a few months earlier. He'd been there, half-heartedly courting Beth at the time, and had caught Annabelle creeping round after dark and, even though it was a strange thing to be doing in her own home, he had not drawn attention to it, seeming to instinctively understand her desire for privacy wasn't something easily explained.

'Lady Hummingford, Lady Annabelle, I trust your first night in your new home was comfortable.'

Mr Ashburton came walking through the garden gate, his bearing as upright as ever and his manner clipped and to the point. He acknowledged Annabelle with a formal nod, with no hint that he'd proposed to her the day before. There was no intimacy, no connection, and Annabelle felt the certainty in her decision draining away.

'It was not the level of comfort I am used to, but I slept adequately, thank you,' Lady Hummingford said, smoothing her dress down on her knees.

'And you, Lady Annabelle?' He turned his dark brown eyes on her and regarded her seriously, making Annabelle want to squirm away from his gaze. She hadn't known he was coming so early, hadn't had time to don her veil and conceal her scars. Still, Mr Ashburton didn't seem overly affected by her scars—in fact, if they weren't so obvious for everyone to see she would have sworn he hardly noticed them at all. She grimaced. It was a sign of how little he actually *saw* when he looked at her. And this was the man she was planning to marry.

'I slept well, thank you,' she lied. She hadn't slept more than a few hours, tossing and turning in an unfamiliar room, feeling completely alone without the comforting presence of her sister in the bed next to her.

'Good. Would you care to take a stroll along the promenade, Lady Annabelle? We can leave your mother to rest after her disturbed night.'

Silently Annabelle nodded, knowing words would stick in her throat if she tried to speak.

The nerves were twofold. First, she felt anxious about giving Mr Ashburton her answer when she wasn't at all sure she was making the right decision. Second, she felt nervous about going out, walking along the seafront, everyone's eyes upon her. Until recently she hadn't left the estate of Birling View for years, and although in the past few months she'd taken a few trips out, encouraged by her sister, it still felt strange to be walking among others.

'Take your bonnet, Annabelle. People will stare less,' her mother said harshly.

With her hands shaking she rushed inside to pick up her bonnet, making sure she chose one with a veil attached.

Mr Ashburton didn't comment on the face covering when she emerged, but she could see his eyes raking over it, taking in her insecurities.

The cottage was situated on the very outskirts of Eastbourne and to access the promenade they first had to walk down the narrow coastal path from the cottage to the sea. The sun was bright and the day hot, but there was a light sea breeze that whipped at their clothes and provided much-needed relief from the warmth.

'It must be hot under there,' Mr Ashburton said as they strolled stiffly side by side.

'I'm used to it.' She hadn't often worn a veil when secluded in the safety of the estate, but over the last few months she had grown used to the thin material covering her face.

'You don't have to wear it.'

'People stare,' she said quietly.

'Does it matter?'

She glanced up at him and wondered what it would be like to be as self-confident and sure of himself as Mr Ashburton. He was the sort of man who never doubted himself, never cared what others thought of him. He wouldn't hide behind a veil because of his appearance. Of course he didn't need to. Mr Ashburton was an attractive man with a strong jaw, thick dark hair and dark eyes that fooled you into thinking he might care. Annabelle had no doubt he had women falling over themselves to dance with him at the balls he must attend in London, or to sit next to him at the fancy dinner parties. Surely one of them would be a better choice than her.

'Can I ask you a question, Mr Ashburton?'

He inclined his head, then looked across at her expectantly. They were walking side by side, but not touching. Annabelle hadn't felt confident enough to take his arm as she knew was the custom when a woman walked next to a man.

'Why did you ask me to marry you?'

'For the reasons I explained yesterday.'

'I know you need a wife urgently, too, and I understand you do not feel the need to wait for a woman you have romantic feelings for, but there must be a hundred debutantes in London clamouring for your attention. Why would you choose me over them?'

'I will not do you the discourtesy of answering with meaningless platitudes or pretending we have a connection that is not there. I made a promise to your father to marry his daughter and I take my promises very seriously.'

Annabelle nodded, feeling strangely hollow. She had hoped he might say he saw something in her he admired. Even if it were just her ability to run a household or her sensible manner. This was so impersonal.

'There is another reason,' he said slowly as if not sure whether to go on. 'I am aware that the debutantes husband hunting in London have a certain expectation of married life. They are more likely to be dissatisfied with the arrangement I am offering you. They would want a more…conventional marriage. To socialise together, share a life together, have a family.'

Annabelle felt as though she had been punched in her stomach. She couldn't blame the man walking so calmly next to her—in fact, she should thank him for being so honest. He wasn't trying to deceive her into marrying him, just the opposite, he was making sure she was aware of exactly what she would be getting herself into. It just made her feel nauseous to think he had chosen her because she had such low expectations from life. Nauseous and sad.

'Does that make sense?'

'That's very clear,' she said, trying to make her voice sound as normal as possible.

Mr Ashburton stopped and reached out to take her arm, placing his fingers on the bare skin of her forearm until she stopped and turned towards him. He was very still, just his eyes moving as he searched for hers under the veil, then he let out a tiny sigh of exasperation.

Annabelle felt her pulse quicken as his hand came up and lifted the material of the veil, folding it back over the top of her bonnet so he could see her face. For one crazy moment she thought he was going to kiss her and was surprised to find her body swaying towards him. The embarrassment when she realised he just wanted to see her expression as he said the next words sent a flush to her cheeks.

'I know I'm not offering you the fairy tale, Lady Annabelle. I'm offering you the choice of a different future. You can stay here with your mother, reading your books, toeing the line. Or you can marry me and become mistress of your own house. Free to make your own decisions. In neither scenario do you end up with what most women dream of—the doting husband, the brood of children running around.'

Annabelle hated that he knew her secret weakness. She had known for many years she wouldn't get the future other young women of her birth would. There would be no dazzling debut in London, no gentlemen falling over themselves to fill her dance card. There would be no perfect man asking for her hand in marriage. She'd known none of this was a possibility for her, but she had still dreamed of it. Every so often she would torture herself with daydreams about how her life could have been if it wasn't for her disfigurement.

'Do you have an answer for me?'

With visions of both possible futures spinning in her head, she took a deep breath to still her thoughts and compose her mind.

'I will marry you, Mr Ashburton.'

'Good. I shall see to the arrangements.'

'When do you expect the wedding to be?' It felt surreal, as if she were asking about someone else's wedding, not her own.

'We need to move quickly. I shall look into getting a special licence. If not, as soon as the banns can be read.'

Annabelle swallowed hard and summoned a smile. If he was successful in purchasing a special licence, they could be married within the week. Even if it was to be a church wedding Mr Ashburton was a determined and organised man. No doubt he would secure the soonest date and she would be saying her vows within the month.

They strolled on in silence for a few minutes and Annabelle felt Mr Ashburton's impatience to get away now he had his answer. She wondered if this was what her life would be like. Fleeting meetings with her husband when he visited to sort out some detail of their shared life and then his swift departure to return to the life he truly wanted to live.

Leo knew he couldn't just abandon the woman who had just agreed to be his wife, but he had the overwhelming urge to be alone. He wanted to stride off across the cliffs and lose himself in the deserted countryside while he worked on suppressing the emotions raging inside him.

Lady Annabelle wasn't the first woman he had asked to marry him, although she was the first who had been free to give him an affirmative answer.

For a moment he allowed himself to picture Emily's face, the features blurred by the passing years. It wasn't fair to think of her now when he should be focusing on the fresh start Lady Annabelle was offering him.

'Do you wish to tell your mother while we're together or will you do it alone?' he asked, forcing his mind to more mundane details.

'I will tell her. I need to choose the right moment.'

'Indeed. Don't wait too long though. You will need to start packing and preparing for the move to Kent.'

'Where will we live?'

'My main residence is just outside Tunbridge Wells. You will reside there. I split my time between there and London.'

'Very well.'

It all felt so formal, so cold, but he knew it was for the best. Lady Annabelle was a sensible young woman, but he didn't want to give her any reason to think this was anything more than a business arrangement. He didn't want her to grow fond of him, didn't want to have to consider her emotional needs when making decisions. It would be better if she closeted herself away in Tunbridge Wells and busied herself with running the house without wanting too much from him.

'Is there anything you will need, Lady Annabelle?'

She tilted her head to one side for a moment as if considering.

'No, I don't think so. That is…' She trailed off.

'Go on.'

'It's not something I *need* as such.'

'Something that would make your move to Kent easier?'

She nodded.

'Then tell me.'

'Does your house have stables?'

'Of course.'

'Then I would like a horse to ride. I know it is a significant expense, but if I am to spend much of my time alone I would like to be able to go riding. It is one of my pleasures.'

'You do not need to justify the request, Lady Annabelle. It is very reasonable.'

Stopping for a moment, she turned to him and he could see her giving him a tentative smile from underneath her veil. It would seem his fiancée was easy to please. He supposed after leading a life as restricted as Lady Annabelle had that any little freedom was significant.

'We should return you home,' he said gently, trying not to make it seem as though he was abandoning her now he had got what he wanted. 'I need to start my journey before it gets too late.'

'Of course.' She turned at the same time as he did and their bodies collided. Lady Annabelle was small and she bounced off him, stumbling backwards, her arms flying up from her sides as she tried to regain her balance. He lunged forward with the aim of gripping her and steadying her, but his foot caught hers and for the third time in two days they landed in a tangled heap. Leo was quick to spring to his feet, bouncing back as if she had burned him with the contact. He saw the flicker of hurt on her face at his reaction to her, but stalwartly ignored it. It wouldn't do to bring emotions into their union—the sooner Lady Annabelle accepted that the better.

Chapter Four

Dear Beth,
I can't quite believe this is happening, but
today I travel to Kent to prepare for my
wedding. I keep telling myself it doesn't
matter that we've only spoken half a dozen
times, but surely I should know a few sim-
ple facts about my future husband. I don't
even know if he takes his eggs poached or
scrambled in the morning.

'**D**on't do anything to jeopardise this, Annabelle,' Lady Hummingford muttered as the
carriage began to slow. 'Smile…be polite. *Try*
to remember all the lessons I taught you when
you were growing up.'

Annabelle murmured something vaguely
positive and wondered if it would be classed as
a crime if she pushed her mother from the car-

riage. It was barely moving and no one could argue that Lady Hummingford wasn't antagonistic. The journey had seemed endless, with her mother swinging between expressing her incredulity that someone, *anyone*, would be willing to marry Annabelle and lecturing her daughter on what not to do to mess up this opportunity.

Thankfully the carriage finally stopped and a footman opened the door before her mother could say anything else.

'Lady Annabelle,' Mr Ashburton said, stepping forward to greet her. He lifted her hand, but didn't quite touch it with his lips and Annabelle was reminded of the moment he had leaped away from her when they had tumbled together on the promenade in Eastbourne. It would seem Mr Ashburton didn't like close contact, at least from her. 'And Lady Hummingford. I trust your journey was comfortable.'

She got the impression he wasn't really listening to her mother's reply as he offered Annabelle his arm.

'Mrs Westcott will show you up to your room, Lady Hummingford. I'm sure you will want to rest after the arduous journey, so you are fresh for tomorrow. Lady Annabelle, my great-uncle has requested an audience.'

'I can accompany Annabelle,' Lady Hummingford said.

'No need. Lord Abbingdon tires easily, it will be better if it is just Lady Annabelle and myself.'

Before her mother could protest Mr Ashburton had swept Annabelle away through the dark hallway and into the depths of the house.

'We'll keep the visit short,' Mr Ashburton assured her. 'Then you can rest before tomorrow.'

Tomorrow. The big day. Her wedding day. Annabelle felt her stomach do a flip at even just the thought of it.

'He is a man who does not care for niceties. He may be—' Mr Ashburton searched for the right word '—unpleasant. It doesn't mean he disapproves of you, at least not any more than he disapproves of anyone.'

'I will try not to take whatever he says personally.'

'Good. Very sensible.'

They were still downstairs when they paused outside a closed door, the wood heavy and patterned with carved flowers and berries. The man beside her—she still couldn't bring herself to think of him as her fiancé—hesitated as if wanting to say something more, then thought better of it and knocked, not waiting for an acknowledgement before pushing open the door and entering.

The room was dark, with only a small amount of sunlight filtering in through the tiny gaps in the heavy curtains. It smelt musty, the air thick and cloying, and Annabelle had the urge to run over and pull open the curtains and throw wide the windows to let some fresh air in.

It took a moment for her eyes to adjust to the gloom, but once they did she saw there was a bed against one wall, a grand, four-poster piece of furniture that would have dominated any normal-sized room, but it looked at home in its spacious surroundings. On the bed, propped up with the covers pulled up to his chin, was an old man, so thin he looked skeletal. As Annabelle moved closer she could see the waxy yellow tinge to his skin and eyes and a horribly bloated belly tucked under the blankets looking out of place with the rest of his skinny form.

'Come closer, girl. Don't dawdle in the doorway. How am I meant to see you from there?' The old man's voice was surprisingly strong and Annabelle felt herself bristle at the tone. She might be a recluse, a scarred young woman who didn't have many prospects, but she was still the daughter of an earl and didn't appreciate being spoken to as though she was one of the old dogs lying by the fireplace.

'Lord Abbingdon,' she said, channelling her mother's most superior tone, 'a pleasure to meet you.'

Next to her she felt Mr Ashburton jolt in surprise. He had expected her to cower and shy away from the crotchety old man.

Instead she swallowed hard, trying not to breathe through her nose to avoid the worst of the smell, and glided regally over to the bed. Without being asked she took the chair closest to Lord Abbingdon and raised her eyes to meet his. Without even a flicker she held his gaze, seeing his eyes move to the scars and over the rest of her body before returning to her eyes.

'My great-nephew tells me you are to be married tomorrow. If I give my blessing, of course.'

'It is important for all parties involved to be satisfied with one another,' Annabelle said serenely.

Lord Abbingdon let out a low chuckle. 'You're assessing me?'

'Mr Ashburton and I are not married yet.

There is still time to change our minds if we do not feel our families are suited.'

'Balderdash. Don't you dare go pulling out now. There must be some legal precedent. Leonard? Breach of promise or some such thing?'

'No one is changing their minds, Lord Abbingdon,' Mr Ashburton said firmly. 'Lady Annabelle is just quietly reminding you that you are not the one holding all the cards here.'

Lord Abbingdon eyed her from his position in bed. 'I thought you were meant to be meek and mild.'

'That is not what I said,' Mr Ashburton murmured, shaking his head in despair. 'I said quiet and reserved in manner. As befits a woman of Lady Annabelle's status.'

'You do have that going for you, I suppose. The daughter of an earl, albeit an impoverished one.'

'I hope I have a little more than just that going for me,' Annabelle said quietly but firmly.

'Hmm. What about children? Any problems in the family in that department?'

'Lord Abbingdon, I understand you are keen for your great-nephew to marry and sire an heir. Here I am, the woman he has selected, ready and prepared to walk down the aisle tomorrow. I am from an ancient family, there is no scandal in my past and...'

'And children?'

She saw the tension on Mr Ashburton's face and smiled serenely, smoothing down the skirts of her dress. 'The women in my family have always been blessed with children.'

'Good. That's enough, I'm tired. Get the deed done tomorrow.'

Thoroughly dismissed, Annabelle murmured a farewell and started to move away from the bed.

'Stay a moment, Leonard,' the old Viscount said, reaching out and clutching at his greatnephew's hand.

'I'll be out in just a moment,' Mr Ashburton said as Annabelle hesitated by the door.

'She'll do,' she heard the old man say as she closed the door. 'Shame about the scars, but at least she's not some vapid debutante more interested in spending your money than looking after the house and producing children.'

Annabelle quickly let go of the door handle and moved away, her fingers rising to her cheek and covering the scars as she felt the familiar humiliation whenever anyone judged her appearance.

She heard the old man chuckle and then say in a more serious tone, 'Time for you to move on, too. No more moping about that broken heart of yours.'

'You did well,' Leo said as he strode into the drawing room, finding Lady Annabelle perched on one of the chairs, staring out of the window. He was pleasantly surprised at how well his fiancée had handled Lord Abbingdon. Leo had been managing the man's difficult moods and pointed comments for years, and as such knew he respected a firm, no-nonsense response. He liked people to be direct, to stand up to him. Lady Annabelle had taken in the old man and his traits and assessed him, then adjusted her manner and words accordingly.

'He hasn't told you to call off the wedding?'

'Good Lord, no. If he was able, I think he would be out of bed by now and dancing a jig that I'm finally going to be standing up in church and saying my vows.'

'He looks very frail. Is there something wrong with his liver?'

Leo blinked in surprise. From all accounts Lady Annabelle had spent her life cloistered and secluded. She hadn't walked the streets of London, hadn't seen the drunks sprawling out on the streets with their skin tinged yellow and their swollen bellies protruding over skinny legs.

'Yes. The doctors say his liver is swollen to at least double its normal size, although they do not know why. He hasn't touched a drop of alcohol for years.'

She nodded sagely, seeming to take in the information and file it away.

'How did you know?'

'He has that appearance of someone whose liver is failing. He must be very tired.'

'Have you seen it before?'

Lady Annabelle shook her head. 'I spent a lot of time on my own at Birling View and the library was filled with books. I read a lot. There were some old medical volumes there.' She smiled to herself at the memory. 'Some winter days I would curl up in the library for hours.'

Leo felt suddenly very contented in his choice for a wife. Lady Annabelle was used to living her life alone. She wasn't going to be needy, always wanting him to be with her, always wanting company or entertainment.

'I have a decent library at Five Oaks, and a good selection at my London home, Millbrook House, but if there are any books you would like then just let me know and I will arrange to have them delivered.'

'That is very kind.'

'Are you ready for tomorrow?' He searched her face as he asked the question, but Lady Annabelle was a master at concealing her feelings. She looked serene even though he knew she must be feeling some upset at the sudden upheaval of her life.

'I think so. I have barely had to do anything.'

Leo felt a tiny flicker of guilt. He was aware most young women would want to be involved in organising at least a few details about their wedding, but he had wanted to get everything sorted as quickly as possible so hadn't consulted Lady Annabelle on a single detail. Instead he had sent a note informing her of the date of their nuptials. Quickly he pushed the guilt away. Lady Annabelle understood the need to be practical.

'Mr Ashburton, may I ask you a question?' She looked deadly serious and Leo felt his heart begin to pound. Ideally he wanted to spend a little time with Lady Annabelle before the wedding. He didn't want to give her any reason, or any chance, to pull out.

'Of course.'

'Do you have a mistress?' It was a bold question, a question many men wouldn't tolerate from their wives, but he didn't have anything to hide on that front.

'No. Would it matter if I did?'

'No, but I would like to know. I am aware our marriage will not be close in the traditional sense, but I wouldn't like people knowing things that I do not.'

'I don't have a mistress.'

'I heard your great-uncle say something about heartbreak?'

Leo felt the whole world slow. Here was his future wife asking him about the one topic he really didn't want her to know about: the woman he had once been foolish enough to love.

'Many years ago—many, *many* years ago—I was in love. The young woman in question died. It took me a while to recover from the sorrow I felt at her passing.' It was the truth, although nowhere near all of it. He'd been young and foolish, believing that love could conquer the social and familial expectations heaped upon them. It hadn't taken the world long to disabuse him of that notion.

'I'm sorry, I shouldn't have asked.'

He hadn't thought of Emily for a long time,

not properly. He had loved her and lost her, but it seemed a distant and hazy memory, pushed away by his sadness and need to forget that particularly painful part of his life.

'It is of no consequence. My great-uncle thinks, wrongly, that I have not decided to marry until now because I still mourn for Emily. He is incorrect and I have told him so on many occasions, but he will not be swayed in his opinion.'

'Why haven't you married, Mr Ashburton?' Lady Annabelle had a soft voice and calming manner about her that made him want to sit down and spill all his darkest secrets and desires. She was an expert at making herself seem unthreatening and unassuming, of blending into the background so you didn't notice her sharp eyes taking everything in. For a moment he considered telling her about the trauma of losing his parents at such a young age, then having his brother ripped from him when they were split up to live with different guardians on different continents. It made him mistrust relationships, it made him realise how fragile the world people built up around them really was.

'I haven't felt the need to,' he said abruptly. Lady Annabelle didn't need to know about his cold and emotionless upbringing or his deeply ingrained character flaws.

He felt a flicker of remorse at the rebuke, but at least on the outside Lady Annabelle didn't even flinch. He supposed after living with her sharp-tongued mother for so long meant she was used to harsh words. Still, it didn't mean he should speak to her that way.

'Please excuse me, Lady Annabelle, there are some final details to see to for tomorrow. Is there anything you need?'

'No, thank you.' Her words were accompanied by a soft smile, but he had the impression he had disappointed her. Brushing off the feeling, he bowed and quickly exited the room, hoping he hadn't said anything to make her change her mind.

Chapter Five

Dear Beth,
Is it normal to feel sick on your wedding
day? Or to want to stay in bed and hope
that no one finds you?

'How on earth can you sleep in on such an important day?' Lady Hummingford burst into the room, flinging back the curtains and sending Annabelle under the covers of her bed to hide from the bright sunlight. 'Get up, the day is wasting and we have no time at all to get you prepared.'

Annabelle peeked out from under the crisp white sheets and wondered how her mother would respond to a plea for ten more minutes in bed. She decided it would be unfavourably and, to save herself the lecture, she slowly sat up in bed, blinking away the sleep from her eyes.

It had been a long night, tossing and turning as every possible scenario for how the rest of her life could be ran through her mind. She'd fallen into an uneasy slumber as the light had started to trickle through the curtains and felt as though she had only just fallen into a deeper sleep when her mother had burst into the room.

'The maids are bringing up hot water for you to bathe in, then they will dress you and do your hair. You have two hours until we need to leave for the church.'

With a thought for her grumbling stomach Annabelle considered enquiring about breakfast, but already her mother had sailed out of the room. She felt a pang of disappointment that Lady Hummingford wasn't staying to get her ready for her wedding day herself, but Annabelle shouldn't have been surprised. Her mother had never been very maternal and didn't believe in showing affection.

In something of a daze Annabelle watched as the maids filled the bath with steaming water and set up the screen to preserve her modesty. After disrobing she slipped into the warm water, feeling some of the tension ease from her muscles. She had never had a lady's maid, there hadn't been enough money over the last few years to afford more than a couple of servants to help run the sprawling Birling View estate. As such baths had always been a bit of a chore. She and Beth had to carry the bath between them to the bedroom and then do multiple trips up and down the stairs to the kitchen to collect enough water to fill the bath. In later years they'd just kept it in a small room off the kitchen to save on the labour involved, but that was dark and gloomy and not very relaxing. It felt like a luxury to have someone fill it for her and she had to hide her surprise as one of the maids slid behind the screen and started lathering soap into her hair.

'It's an exciting day for you, my lady.' The young maid went by the name of Lottie and looked to be about the same age as Annabelle.

'Yes,' Annabelle murmured.

'A day every woman dreams of, her wedding day. I caught a peek of your dress, too. It looks absolutely beautiful.'

It was beautiful. Made of cream-coloured silk with an intricate gold embroidery covering both the bodice and skirts, it was the most beautiful piece of clothing Annabelle had ever laid eyes on. Mr Ashburton had sent a dressmaker to the cottage a few days after she had accepted his proposal and it had been thrilling not to have to worry about the cost of the dress and the service of the dressmaker for the first time in her adult life. Most of her dresses were second- or third-hand, passed down by her mother or sister, altered to fit her small frame. It was wonderful to have something of her own.

'It's so thrilling that the master is finally getting married. The house has been so quiet for so long and to think one day soon it'll be filled with the sound of children.'

'Mmm…' Annabelle murmured, closing her eyes and sinking down in the water so only her face remained unsubmerged. She didn't want to think about any of that. One day she was sure she would be able to accept her fate without feeling a flicker of pain or longing for the children she would never have, but she wasn't quite there yet.

'Stop dilly dallying and get out of that bath.' For once her mother's voice was a welcome interruption and Annabelle quickly rinsed the soap from her hair and body before standing and wrapping the large towel Lottie handed to her around her body.

Once in a dressing gown, she seated herself at the dressing table, avoiding looking in the mirror as Lottie began to brush out her hair. The golden locks were one of her favourite features, although Annabelle wasn't sure if that was because she liked her hair or if it was more that it could be used as a convenient shield to hide her scars behind.

'There are some things I need to talk to you about, Annabelle,' Lady Hummingford said, sitting down on the edge of the bed and looking pointedly at her daughter in the mirror. 'Important things.'

Annabelle felt the heat begin to rise in her cheeks, wondering if her mother really was going to try to tell her what happened between a man and a woman on their wedding night. Or at least what was meant to happen. She wished she could stop her, to explain that out of the thousands of books she had read during her years of solitude at least a few dozen had provided her with enough insight into marital relations that she really did not need this talk. Some had been very explicit indeed.

'Mother…'

'Don't interrupt me, Annabelle, you will listen to what I have to say.'

Falling silent, Annabelle wondered if she should have told her mother the whole truth about her marriage to Mr Ashburton. Lady Hummingford knew he harboured no tender feelings for Annabelle, that she was a convenient option for a bride and nothing more, but she wasn't aware of quite how separate Mr Ashburton was proposing their lives should be after the wedding. Annabelle doubted they would ever lay side by side in bed together, let alone anything more intimate.

'As a wife there are certain duties you will be expected to perform. It is important you please your husband, do as he asks. Do as he tells you.'

Annabelle knew her mother was only repeating what she had been told on her wedding day, but the advice seemed a little disempowering. She waited for more to come, for the wedding night advice mothers always seemed to impart in the novels she'd read, but Lady Hummingford just shifted uncomfortably and repeated, 'Do as your husband asks. Even if it is a chore for you.'

'I'm sure Mr Ashburton wouldn't ask me to do something that I wasn't comfortable with,' she said, the picture of innocence. Normally she wouldn't tease her mother, but she felt as though Lady Hummingford should have some better advice for her younger daughter on her wedding day than *Do as your husband asks*.

'Ah, well. There are certain duties a wife is expected to perform…'

'I'm aware I will take responsibility for running the house and overseeing the servants,' Annabelle said, giving her mother a beatific smile.

'Yes, there's that, of course, but I'm talking about more *personal* duties.'

'Like making sure the cook prepares my husband's favourite meal and that his preferred drink is always available.'

'No, I wasn't thinking about that.'

Annabelle cocked her head to one side and suppressed the giggle that was building inside her. 'What were you thinking about?'

Lady Hummingford opened her mouth a couple of times and then closed it again, standing and brushing an imaginary fleck of dust from her skirt.

'It doesn't matter. Mr Ashburton will instruct you when it is time.'

Annabelle watched as her mother sailed out of the room, then caught Lottie's eye in the mirror and they both burst out laughing.

'I shouldn't have been so cruel,' Annabelle murmured.

'She was being rather vague, my lady,' Lottie whispered, checking over her shoulder to ensure Lady Hummingford hadn't re-entered the room.

'I just wanted her to give me some useful advice, something that showed she had thought about what this is going to be like for me.'

'Mr Ashburton is a good man, my lady,' Lottie reassured her. 'He will be a good husband, I'm sure.'

Annabelle regarded the maid in the mirror. Many people seemed to be of the opinion that Mr Ashburton was a *good man*. Quite what they meant by this she didn't know. It was one of the things Beth had repeated when she had been considering marrying Leonard Ashburton, before she admitted she had fallen for his brother instead. Leonard Ashburton was a good man. He might be abrupt and cool in his manner, but underneath he was considered to be essentially good.

In silence Annabelle watched as Lottie expertly pinned up her hair and added the clips with little pearls on the end to the top and back. Then it was time to step into the dress and have the young maid pull on the ribbons that made up the corset area. The material was luxurious under her hands and the dress shimmered in the morning light.

'You look lovely, my lady,' Lottie said as she stood back to admire Annabelle in the dress. The young maid's smile froze just for an instant as her gaze travelled up to Annabelle's face and fixed on the scars. Her figure might be alluring and her hair like spun gold, but the scars would always be the thing that everyone fixed on.

'Could I have a moment, Lottie?' Annabelle asked softly, knowing it wasn't the young maid's fault her eye had caught the scars.

Lottie curtsied and hurried from the room as Annabelle sank back on to the chair in front of the mirror. She indulged herself in a moment of self-pity. The dress was perfect, her hair was perfect, the day outside was perfect. As always it was just her face. If it weren't for the scars she would probably be marrying someone who wanted her for more than just her low expectations of life.

The walk downstairs felt never-ending and by the time Annabelle reached the door she wondered if she was about to be sick. She felt strangely nauseous, as if her body were floating and swaying above the ground and all she wanted to do was pick up her heavy skirts and run past the assembled servants, out the front door and not stop until she was back in her bedroom at Birling View.

Instead she checked her veil was in place over her face and glided down the stairs as she had been taught as a young woman. She would do her duty today, play her part and tomorrow she would wake up with a husband and a house of her own.

At the front door her mother stood tapping her fingers on the wood of the door frame, even though Annabelle was punctual to the minute of her planned departure time for the church. Lady Hummingford looked her up and down and eventually nodded her approval, but didn't say anything to Annabelle.

A footman helped her up into the carriage and Annabelle arranged her skirts around her so her mother could fit on to the opposite seat, and to the waving of the staff they set off for the church.

'Mr Ashburton is keen to leave for his own house after the wedding. I understand you will return here to change and then set off for Five Oaks immediately,' her mother said as they settled back into their seats. 'He has arranged for your belongings to be packed and sent there. I will return to Sussex.' Lady Hummingford curled her lip in disgust at the thought of the little cottage. Annabelle bit her lip to stop herself from offering to speak to Mr Ashburton about her mother's accommodation. The last thing she wanted was Lady Hummingford coming to reside with them. One of her main motivators for marriage was to finally have a chance of a life of her own.

'I will come to visit soon.'

'I don't know why you would want to visit that dreary little cottage. Much better if I come to visit you.'

'I will write and let you know when Mr Ashburton thinks it will be a good time.'

'Make sure you do.'

The carriage began to slow and all too soon they were at the entrance to the church. Mr Ashburton had hinted it would be a quiet affair, just a few essential guests and the vicar conducting the service. She wasn't sure if he wanted to keep it small for the convenience of organising a smaller affair, or because he wanted to keep the wedding quiet. He didn't seem to be the sort of man who would be embarrassed by his choice of wife, but she reminded herself that she didn't really know him, not past a few superficial conversations.

As the carriage door opened she had to take a steadying breath before stepping down. In just a few minutes she would become Lady Annabelle Ashburton.

Chapter Six

Dear Josh,
Today I said my marriage vows. You
looked so happy when you married Lady
Elizabeth, I have to confess I envy your
happiness.

Leo stared up at the statue in front of him.
It was of Mary and the Baby Jesus, carved
lovingly out of a huge piece of marble and
likely had been standing in the same spot for a
couple of hundred years. It was solid, reliable;
it had been here since before he was born and
it would be here after he had died. The thought
made him relax a little, made him remember
he was just a small part of a very big world.

He hadn't expected to feel nervous. This
part was just a formality, just a few words
said to one another. In his mind he had al-

ready taken on Lady Annabelle as a wife, she was already his responsibility. This wedding shouldn't make a difference to that.

'Are you ready?' William Wilbersmythe murmured from his position by Leo's side. He wished it was his brother Josh standing next to him and felt the pang of loss heavily for a moment. It had been wonderful having his brother back in his life, albeit only for a few short months. He wished Josh hadn't had to rush back to India, but he understood the call of responsibility and Josh had a business to take the reins of.

'Is she here?'

'I think I heard the carriage.' Wilbersmythe was as close to a friend as Leo had. They'd grown up on bordering estates, attended school together and been in the same year at Cambridge. There was nothing offensive about the earnest man standing next to him, but Leo had never felt at ease letting anyone close. The only person he had ever let through his defences was his brother.

Sure enough, the doors to the church opened and Leo turned to catch sight of his fiancée silhouetted in the door for a second before she moved into the church. She was elegant, gliding down the aisle, and looked stunning in a dress of cream and gold. A white lace veil was clipped into her hair and covered her face, but as she came to a stop beside him he saw her hesitate and then take it by the edge and lift it up so it cascaded down her back instead.

Stiffly they stood side by side as the vicar intoned the words of the wedding ceremony. For years Leo had not expected to marry, had never thought he would be in this position. It was only in recent months Lord Abbingdon had added the stipulation about Leo being married to his will and even more recently that the need to marry had become pressing with the old Viscount's health fading fast. Perhaps once he had dreamed of a future with a wife and a family, but that dream had been because of Emily. When she'd died he had never thought of marriage again.

The ceremony was over in a flash. The vows said, the delicate golden band placed on to Lady Annabelle's finger and the congratulations of the vicar. He had a wife. It didn't feel quite real, but he was a married man.

'Congratulations,' Wilbersmythe said, clapping him on the back. Leo knew he should be moving, should be guiding his wife from the church to the waiting carriage, but he felt as though he were in a daze.

Beside him Lady Annabelle leaned in and took his arm and at the contact he came back to himself. She was looking up at him as if she expected him to say something to her.

'Well, that's done now,' he said quietly, knowing immediately that he had said the wrong thing by the crestfallen look on Lady Annabelle's face. She hid it well, recovering her composure in a matter of seconds, but the hurt had been real and visible. He had to remind himself that this might not be a love match, but she was still his wife and would expect a little warmth and emotion from him.

He was about to try to salvage the situation when she turned her head away from him and pulled on his arm so they walked rapidly up the aisle of the church and into the sunlight outside.

'Congratulations,' Lady Hummingford said, kissing her daughter on the cheek, her posture stiff.

The whole scene was rather awkward and Leo was surprised to see Annabelle lower the veil over her face again, only understanding at the last moment when he saw the moisture of tears in her eyes. It was her wedding day and she was holding back the tears.

* * *

'We should start our journey to Five Oaks,' Mr Ashburton said. 'The journey is only an hour, but it will be good to get settled in.'

Annabelle nodded, not trusting herself to speak. Her throat felt as though it was swelling and she knew if she tried to utter a word it would come out raspy and garbled. So much had changed in a matter of a few hours. A very underwhelming few hours. For some reason she had expected something more, but Mr Ashburton had summed it up perfectly when he'd said, *Well, that's done now.*

After bidding farewell to her mother, she climbed up into the waiting carriage followed by her new husband. They had returned briefly to Willow House to change out of their wedding attire into more comfortable clothes for travelling and to bid farewell to Lord Abbingdon, who had not been able to make the wedding.

They sat in silence for a few minutes as the carriage picked up speed on the open road.

Eventually Mr Ashburton cleared his throat and waited for her to look at him before speaking.

'I will see you settled at Five Oaks, then tomorrow I must return to London.'

'So soon?'

'Mrs Barnes, my housekeeper, will ensure you have everything you need.'

Annabelle nodded. She wasn't even sure she was upset, but it did feel a bit as if he was dumping her in the house and fleeing as soon as possible.

'I will be away a week, perhaps a little longer.'

She wondered if he planned on getting to know her at all. She had never envisioned long walks in the countryside arm in arm, or cosy evenings by the fire, but she had thought he would perhaps want to spend a few days together, to introduce her to her new life.

Quietly Annabelle sighed. Perhaps it would be better this way. She could find her place at Five Oaks without worrying what her new husband thought all the time. By the time he returned she would be at least partially settled in.

'Is something amiss, Lady Annabelle?'

'We are married, Mr Ashburton—perhaps you could call me Annabelle?'

He nodded stiffly and for a moment she thought he wasn't going to reciprocate the offer to use first names. 'My given name is Leonard—' he paused, hesitating for a moment '—but my brother, my family, call me Leo.'

It sounded too familiar, too relaxed for the stiff man sitting across from her, but it was better than calling her husband Mr Ashburton all the time.

Content with her small victory at becoming a little closer to Leo, she sat back and stared out of the window of the carriage. 'Gosh, look at the sky.'

Gone was the brilliant blue, cloudless sky of an hour earlier. The clouds had rolled in and outside was darkening quickly.

'It is all that heat, we're well overdue a summer storm.'

Annabelle leaned forward, looking with interest at the heavy clouds and almost exclaiming in delight as the first flash of lightning lit up the sky.

'You like extremes of weather?'

'I find storms fascinating. There was a book in the library at Birling View that detailed the most extreme weather conditions ever recorded. One was a storm that caused thirty shipwrecks in the English Channel alone.' Slowly she sat back in her seat after catching sight of Leo's expression. He looked both surprised and indulgent, as if he were an older brother listening to his younger sister's unimportant ramblings.

'I hope this storm isn't enough to make the record books,' he murmured.

Watching as the rain started to fall in earnest, she occupied herself by counting the seconds between the lightning flashes and the peals of thunder.

The storm was short, at least overhead, but the rain continued even once the thunder and lightning had passed on. In the heavy rain the carriage slowed and Annabelle spared a thought for the unfortunate coachman sitting exposed and the horses having to tramp through the thick mud on the roads. She wrapped her arms around herself, shivering as the rain brought a chill to the air that hadn't been there before.

'Have my jacket,' Leo said, shrugging it from his shoulders and holding it out.

'I couldn't. You'll get cold.'

'I insist.'

After another moment's hesitation she took it, slipping her arms into the sleeves and catching a hint of her husband's scent. She was just about to thank him when the carriage jolted unexpectedly and she almost flew from her seat. Leo shot out an arm to catch her, gripping her thigh through her skirt.

'Are you hurt?' he asked as the carriage settled to a stop.

'No.' Her voice was shaky and her heart was pounding in her chest from the shock of the sudden movement, but other than that she was fine.

'Good.' He glanced down at his hand on her leg and slowly removed it, as if worried she would collapse on to the floor. The pressure from his fingers had been strangely comforting, but she was made of sterner stuff than he gave her credit for. She wouldn't crumple at a few jolts in the carriage. 'Wait here while I see what is happening.'

Before she could hand him back his jacket he had jumped from the carriage and she heard the faint murmurings as he discussed the situation with the coachman. Annabelle peered through the window, trying to make out what had happened without getting too wet. They were in the middle of nowhere, some tiny country lane in the depths of Kent. If the carriage had lost a wheel or broken an axle, help would be a long way away.

She sat back as Leo reappeared, shaking the water from his head as he climbed back in. He was soaked through, his white shirt almost transparent and sticking to his body.

Momentarily she was distracted by the outline of his biceps in his shirtsleeves and had to force herself to pay attention to what he was saying.

'The wheels are stuck in the mud. It's surprisingly thick given it's been such a dry summer until now.'

'Do you think the horses will be able to pull us out?'

Leo grimaced, running a hand through his wet hair and spraying her with raindrops.

'Not with us in it.'

The rain was still pelting down in force and Annabelle could see what one minute out in the downpour had done to her husband, but she wasn't so precious she would insist on staying in the dry while the coachman struggled with the horses in the storm.

'I'm happy to step down,' she said, giving the brightest smile she could muster. It would be a matter of minutes and it couldn't be that far to Five Oaks where she could change her clothes and get dry.

'Are you sure? We can sit it out if you would prefer.'

'Nonsense. I'm sure with the carriage lighter the horses will have us on our way in no time at all.'

As she stepped out of the carriage she regretted her decision immediately. At least until she saw the unfortunate coachman covered in mud and straining to push the carriage from behind, soaked to the skin. For a long moment they watched as the horses strained and the coachman pushed, but the mud held tight to the wheels. Now she was outside Annabelle could see a little better what had happened. It would seem they were crossing a ford, the road dipping lower with a constant trickle of water crossing it even in the summer. Somewhere upstream a bank must have collapsed in the rain, sending a torrent of mud down that had collected on the road and then sucked in the carriage wheels.

'It's not moving,' she murmured, surprised to see Leo stride forward and add his shoulder to the back of the carriage. As he pushed she could see every muscle in his body tense and tighten and she couldn't help but wonder how he kept such a perfect physique. She knew many men of his class fenced or boxed, but she couldn't see her conservative husband enjoying either of those sports. Perhaps there was a side to him she couldn't imagine yet. For a moment she remembered how his body had felt on top of hers when he'd launched himself at her on the clifftop and felt herself grow hot inside. It was the first close contact she'd ever really had with a man and she wondered if it was acceptable to admit she found her husband attractive, even if he had made it very clear their marriage would not be a physical one.

Little by little the carriage inched forward and Annabelle held her breath, hoping it would suddenly jolt free. It seemed to be almost there, but the men were slipping in the mud and the horses struggling with the prolonged effort. The rain was easing a little, but she was already soaked to the skin and she didn't fancy walking a few miles to the nearest village to seek sanctuary. She glanced down at her cotton dress, already splattered with mud, the hem sodden. A little more mud wouldn't make much of a difference to it, already it was probably unsalvageable. At least she had changed out of the expensive silk dress after the wedding.

After shrugging off the last of her indecision she hurried forward and planted her feet squarely in the mud, feeling it ooze over the top of her thin shoes immediately.

'What are you doing?'

'Helping.'

'Go back to the road.'

She didn't respond to his order, instead braced her hands against the back of the carriage, gritted her teeth and began to push with all her strength. At first she slipped and slid, but after a minute she managed to lodge her feet against something solid and push against the carriage. The muscles in her arms began to ache and her feet had gone numb and Annabelle felt foolish for believing that her petite form could make a difference. Still, she wasn't going to give up and redoubled her efforts alongside the two men, almost shrieking in delight as the carriage jolted forward and then rolled out of the mud and on to the other side of the ford.

Annabelle hadn't been expecting the sudden movement and felt her feet dislodge and start to slip from under her. Leo's hands reached out for her and he grabbed her by the dress, but the momentum of the movement added to the slippery ground underneath their feet meant that he lost his balance and went tumbling into the mud and water of the ford, pulling her on top of him.

They were both drenched to the skin, their summer attire no match for the storm or the mud, and Annabelle felt herself flush as their bodies pressed together. With their clothes soaked by the rain it was as if nothing was separating them. His skin was cool to the touch and the muscles underneath firm and absently Annabelle trailed her hand over her husband's chest, fascinated by the outline of his pectoralis major muscles. She loved anatomy books, had spent hours looking at the intricately drawn pictures and could name every muscle in the body, but never had she seen such a perfect living illustration as Leonard Ashburton.

Grimacing, Leo took her by the arms and hoisted her off him, setting her on her feet before scrambling to get out of the mud himself. With a growl of distaste he looked down at his sodden garments, covered in mud to the waist.

Annabelle couldn't help herself—she giggled.

Leo turned to look at her with an eyebrow raised and Annabelle clamped a hand over her mouth, but he looked so ridiculous standing there with his superior expression, his face covered in splatters of mud. The laugh burst through her hands and soon she was giggling so much her stomach muscles began to hurt.

'Please, share the joke, Annabelle,' he said, his voice witheringly serious.

She pressed her lips together and tried to

compose herself, but couldn't maintain a straight face for more than a few seconds.

'I think the chill has gone to your head,' Leo muttered, taking her by the elbow and escorting her back to the carriage. Up front the coachman was checking the horses and the bindings, but it wasn't long before they were ready to leave.

'I'm getting your beautiful carriage muddy.' Annabelle looked around in despair, finally able to put the comical sight of her husband from her mind.

'I think that is the least of our worries. The carriage can be cleaned.'

'As can we.'

Leo looked at her for a long moment and then nodded. 'I suppose you are right.'

Chapter Seven

Dear Josh,
Do you remember that story our tutor
used to tell us about the monster from
the swamp? Today I fear I resembled that
monster more than just a little.

Leo had to suppress a groan as they drew up outside Five Oaks. The staff had assembled outside the front door, ready to properly welcome their new mistress to the house. Their new mistress who looked as though she had spent the day wallowing in the swamp. Not that he looked any better. His trousers were uncomfortably heavy with the weight of the mud and his white shirt was soaked through and splattered.

'The staff are outside,' Annabelle said, the horror apparent on her face.

'Mrs Barnes is a traditionalist. She will want to welcome you to your new home.'

Annabelle's hand drifted to her head, but the veil that had covered her face must have been dislodged while she was in the mud, pushing the carriage.

'I don't suppose it matters,' she muttered almost imperceptibly to herself. Leo was about to step down from the carriage when he noticed a glint of tears in his wife's eyes. Annabelle had struck him as a strong person, not the sort of woman to fuss or swoon at the slightest provocation, yet here she was almost crying at the thought of greeting her new servants looking as though she'd been bathing in mud.

Stiffly he reached across the gap between them and took her hand, noting with a grimace how she flinched at his touch.

'Annabelle,' he said, trying to soften his voice as much as he could, 'how you look does not matter. You are the mistress of this house and a few splatters of mud are not going to change that.'

She gave a tiny nod and he squeezed her hand.

'I'm not going to lie to you and say they won't gossip and talk about this over their dinner, but what does it matter really?'

'My mother always said having the respect of the staff is vital.'

'She isn't wrong, but when they look at you they are going to see a woman standing tall despite being covered in mud, who helped push our carriage loose instead of standing feebly by watching.'

He saw her posture straighten a little. Her shoulders dropped and her chin raised up a notch.

'Come on. Let's face them together.'

He jumped down from the carriage, turning back to help her, only appreciating how caked in mud she was as she unfolded through the doorway. Her dress had been a simple cotton garment, perfect for such warm weather, but now was soaked through and muddy up to the waistline. He doubted even the most fastidious of maids would be able to restore it. He would have to organise for a dressmaker to visit to provide her with a few new pieces for her wardrobe to make up for it.

Looking up, he saw all of the servants transfixed by Annabelle. The maids and footmen were wide eyed and even Mrs Barnes looked shaken by his new wife's appearance.

'Lady Annabelle, may I present your new home.'

All the servants managed to curtsy or bow and Mrs Barnes stepped forward to take charge of the situation.

'This is Mrs Barnes, the housekeeper.'

'A pleasure to meet you, Mrs Barnes, I hope you'll share all the secrets of Five Oaks with me.' Despite her wobble in the carriage Leo was surprised to see his wife smiling serenely at the housekeeper as if she were totally in control of the situation. He felt a flicker of respect for her. Annabelle might have been shut away for years from society and the public eye, but she had been raised as the daughter of an earl and had the knowledge of how to act even if she hadn't put it into practice before. For a moment he just watched her before remembering he was also standing covered in mud and soaked to the skin.

'A bath, perhaps, sir?' Michaels, his valet, murmured as he approached.

'Might be a good idea.' The thought of sinking into a tub of hot water sounded like absolute heaven. 'Fill one for Lady Annabelle in her bedroom as well.'

He strode over to Annabelle who was asking the names of the maids and repeating them, trying to commit each name and face to memory.

'Come inside and we can clean up. I'm sure Mrs Barnes can introduce everyone properly tomorrow.'

She was shivering, the movement almost imperceptible, but he drew her to him all the same. Not that his skin had much warmth to share, but he pressed her hand into the crook of his elbow and led her inside.

'It's a beautiful house.'

'Yes, I think so. When I started to run the estates for my great-uncle he let me choose one of his properties to have as my own. Five Oaks isn't as grand as some of his other estates and residences, but it has something special about it.'

He could see she was eager to explore and he felt an unfamiliar urge to show her round, to take time to answer her questions about his home that was now hers, too. It would have to wait. If she stood shivering in that sodden dress much longer, she would catch a chill and spend the first week of her married life in bed.

'The maids will fill a bath in your bedroom for you.'

'And you?'

For an instant he couldn't help but imagine sinking into a hot bath with his new wife. He had to cough to cover his surprise—he hadn't

thought of anyone in that way for a long time—
and quickly tried to think of something other
than Annabelle stepping from her dress and
beckoning him to come join her in the bubbles.

'Michaels, my valet, will see I have a bath
in my quarters.'

She nodded, seemingly unaware of his mo-
mentary discomfort, and he hurried her up the
stairs.

'This will be your bedroom.' Unceremo-
niously he opened the door and ushered her
inside. It had been designed originally as a
guest room, large and spacious with a lovely
view over the gardens. There was a room more
suited to the lady of the house, but it had an
adjoining door to his room and he had thought
it best they avoid any confusion and stay further apart.

'It's lovely.'

'Good. Glad you like it.'

He turned to leave, but was stopped by
Annabelle's delicate hand restraining him.

'Where is your bedroom?'

'Just down the hall.' There was no good
reason for him to feel guilty about putting
his wife in the guest bedroom, but he did all
the same. He was sure she would understand,
would appreciate the clear boundary between

them, but still something made him feel as though he were doing something underhand.

'I shall see you for dinner.'

Leo gave her a final tight smile and then left the room, closing the door quietly behind him. As soon as the door clicked shut Annabelle burst into tears. If someone had asked, she wouldn't quite be able to put into words why she felt so lonely and abandoned, but she did.

She couldn't even flop down on the bed and bury her face in the soft pillows. Instead she stood shivering and waiting in a strange room in a strange house, left here by her husband of only a few hours who couldn't wait to get away from her.

'Don't be weak,' she murmured to herself. She'd known exactly what sort of marriage she was getting into. Taking a deep breath, she swiped the tears from her cheeks and reminded herself that she didn't mind being alone, enjoyed it even.

There was a quiet knock on the door and then one of the maids entered.

'Kitty, isn't it?'

The young maid beamed at her from under a mop of beautiful ginger curls.

'Yes, my lady. We're just filling the bathtub, my lady. Would you care to come to the bathroom?'

'You have a bathroom?'

'Oh, yes, my lady. Mr Ashburton had it put in two years ago, I've never seen anything quite like it.'

Kitty led her down the hallway to one of the many heavy wooden doors and opened it as if showing Annabelle into a holy chapel.

It was impressive. Cool marble covered the floor and a stand that would hold a basin of water was just inside the door. At the other end of the room was a full-length mirror, and then the bath hidden behind a moveable screen. There was steam coming from the bath as the servants brought in big pails of water.

'Mrs Barnes had thought you might want to bathe before dinner, so she was already heating the water up.'

Kitty helped her undress behind the screen and then Annabelle stepped into the bath and gasped at the heat of the water.

'Is it too hot, my lady?'

'Not at all. It's lovely.' Slowly she sat down, marvelling at how the warmth of the water turned her white skin pink. Already she could feel her core warming up and she sank down so everything but her head was submerged.

'Would you like me to help you wash now or would you like a few minutes to yourself first?'

'Could you come back in ten minutes, Kitty?'

'Of course, my lady.'

The door shut and Annabelle was alone. She closed her eyes and allowed her mind to wander, to become enveloped by the heat. She felt exhausted, both physically and emotionally. For the past four weeks, almost ever since agreeing to marry Leo, she had barely slept, pacing her room at night wondering if she'd made the right decision.

'No turning back now,' she muttered to herself. Perhaps she would sleep better now there was no option of changing her mind.

As the water enveloped her Annabelle felt herself begin to drift off into a doze, floating in that magical state half between being awake and asleep. The time must have flown by because before she knew it the door was opening again and there were faint footsteps approaching the bath.

'What the…?'

Annabelle's eyes shot open as she heard Leo's voice and saw him standing at the edge of the screen. For a moment she was too shocked to do anything, but then it hit her that she was lying in the bath completely naked, her dignity covered only by a few scant bubbles. Frantically she threw her hands across her body to cover herself, slipping down in the bath as she did so, her head dipping underwater and making her inhale a mouthful of bathwater.

She surfaced, feeling the strong tug on her arms as her husband hauled her from under the water.

'Thank you,' she muttered, although she knew she would have been completely fine on her own. It was only a bath after all.

Stiffly Leo turned around, shaking his wet arms.

'I think there has been some confusion,' he said. 'Michaels said the bath was ready.'

'Kitty showed me in here a few minutes ago.'

'Ah.'

'I'm in your bathroom, aren't I?'

'Yes.'

'I can leave.'

'No. Five Oaks has three bathrooms in total. I expect I have a hot bath waiting in one of those. Unless...' He trailed off and for a moment Annabelle thought he was going to suggest getting in with her. She was surprised to find her first reaction was an illicit thrill rather than complete horror.

'Unless?' she asked, her voice barely more than a whisper.

'We are newlyweds. Perhaps the servants misinterpreted our request for a bath as one bath rather than two.'

Annabelle was glad Leo's back was still towards her so he couldn't see her face, couldn't see the mortification as she realised *he* would never be the one to suggest a shared bath.

'That might be it. I'm very happy to get out and let you have the bath.' She stood, the water splashing over the sides in her haste and splattering on the back of Leo's trousers.

'No need. You enjoy it. I'll find Michaels and see what has happened.'

Without another word he strode from the bathroom, using one of the doors at the far end of the room. Annabelle had assumed the two facing doors at the far end were cupboards, but it seemed one led straight into Leo's bedroom.

As the air cooled her skin she sank back into the bath, only to hear the door open again.

'Only me,' Kitty called out brightly. 'I've got clean towels and I'm here to help you with your hair whenever you're ready.'

'Where do those doors lead, Kitty?' Annabelle pointed at the two doors at the far end of the room.

'The one on the right goes to the master's bedroom and the one on the left to the mistr—' She trailed off without finishing the word.

'The mistress's bedroom?'

'Yes, my lady.'

'I've never seen anything quite like it. Or known a house to have three rooms dedicated to bathing.'

'Mr Ashburton did a lot of renovations when he took over the house, my lady. I understand bathrooms are what all the big houses have in London.' Kitty spoke wistfully as if London were a magical place she could never imagine visiting.

'It is a very modern concept.' Perhaps all the big houses in London did have bathrooms, she wasn't any better placed than Kitty to know.

The mistress's bedroom. The room adjoining Leo's. Most certainly not the room she had been given.

Silently she listened while Kitty chatted away as she lathered the soap into her hair and then helped her to wash it off. Even as she stepped out of the bath into the soft towel her eyes kept flicking to the door at the end of the room.

Chapter Eight

Dear Beth,
Have you ever felt as if you've made a
monumental mistake?

'Mr Ashburton has sent word he isn't feeling very well so won't be joining you for dinner,' Mrs Barnes said with a sympathetic smile.

'Oh.'

'I expect he'll be better in the morning and can show you around your new home then.'

'Yes. Of course.'

Annabelle sat at one end of the long dining table as the evening meal was brought to her. She knew it was delicious, but she barely tasted it, going through the motions of eating rather than actually enjoying it.

After dinner she wandered through the downstairs rooms, lighting a candle as the light faded to illuminate the grand drawing room, a cosy library and Leo's study. There were other rooms, but Annabelle felt the pull of the library and soon found herself perusing the shelves by candlelight.

As she ran her fingers along the spines of the books she felt some of her melancholy slip away. She would stop waiting for Leo to be present, to be part of her life—he had already told her that wasn't how their marriage would be. Instead she would build her own life here. Tomorrow she would ask Mrs Barnes to show her the house and introduce her properly to the servants and tonight she would choose a book and read until her eyes felt heavy tucked into her comfortable bed.

After she had picked a book about Roman history she ascended the stairs and was about to go into her room when she heard a faint moan followed by a fit of coughing. She paused with her hand on the doorknob, listening intently and feeling bad for her unkind thoughts towards her husband. Perhaps he was really ill and not just wanting to avoid her.

The coughs subsided, but there was another faint moan and Annabelle realised she wouldn't be able to go to bed without checking everything was well with Leo. Quickly, not giving herself time to change her mind, she hurried along the hall, stopping outside Leo's bedroom to listen. Sure enough a few seconds later there was another groan followed by a long coughing fit.

Annabelle tapped quietly on the door and after hearing no answer deliberated for just a moment before pushing it open and peering inside.

'Leo, are you unwell?' she called, not yet stepping into the room.

There was a groan in response and then her husband mumbled something incomprehensible from the bed.

Pushing the door open a little wider, Annabelle entered the room, allowing her eyes to adjust to the darkness. It was pitch black in here, the heavy curtains drawn across the windows blocking out the moonlight that had illuminated the hall.

'Annabelle?' Leo muttered as she approached the bed.

'I heard you cry out.'

In the candlelight he looked flushed and tousled, as if he had spent the last hour tussling with the bedclothes.

Tentatively she reached out and felt his brow

with her fingers, exclaiming as she felt how hot he was.

'You're burning up.'

'It's just a little chill.'

She thought of how soaked he had been, how caked in mud. A little chill could turn dangerous.

'Do you need anything?'

'Water.'

Looking round the room, she found the glass of water by his bedside and held it up to his lips, being careful not to spill any on him as he took a few sips.

'I'll be fine tomorrow.' She could see his body shaking as he was overcome with shivers.

She hesitated, wondering if she should stay or do anything more, but knew from experience that when you felt that ill you just preferred to be left alone.

'Do you need the doctor?'

'No. I'll be fine in the morning. Just need to get rid of this fever.'

'Would you like me to sit with you?'

'No, get some rest. It's been a long day.'

Annabelle reached out for his hand where it was lying on top of the covers to the side of his body and laid hers over his for just a second.

'I'll come check on you in the morning.'

He didn't reply and she could see he had already drifted into an uneasy sleep.

Annabelle watched him for a moment to ensure he seemed comfortable and then quietly left the room.

She had slept well. The bed was comfortable and all her fears and worries about the wedding had dissipated. Probably in a couple of days when the reality of her situation hit her she would struggle to sleep again, but for now she was just glad she was better rested.

'Did you want your breakfast in bed, my lady, or in the dining room?'

'Is Mr Ashburton up and about?'

'No, I think he is still in bed.'

'I will check on him first, then take my breakfast in here, thank you, Kitty.' There was a little table and a chair positioned by the window with fabulous views out over the gardens. The light was pouring in through the window now Kitty had pulled back the curtains and Annabelle thought it looked like the perfect breakfast spot.

Pulling on her dressing gown, she padded along the hallway to her husband's bedroom. This time she didn't hesitate to knock on the door, but there was no answer, not even a groan.

Quietly Annabelle slipped into the room, her breath catching in her throat as she saw her husband's dishevelled form in the bed. He was sleeping uneasily, tossing and turning from side to side, his arms throwing the covers from him one second and pulling them back across him the next.

'Leo?' Annabelle whispered, not daring to approach the bed at first. There was no answer. 'Leo,' she called a little louder.

When he didn't respond she made her way to the side of his bed and placed a hand on his brow. He was burning up, his skin hot to touch and flushed. The coolness of her hand must have soothed his warm skin as he settled a little under her touch.

She watched his breathing, counting the rate and frowning as she realised it was much faster than it should be. She could hear a dry raspy sound at the back of his throat, but no coughs as there had been the night before.

Decisively she crossed to the corner of the room and pulled the bell to summon one of the servants. Leo was a fit and healthy man, there was no reason he shouldn't rally within the next twenty-four hours, but she could do a lot to help his body cope with the fever that had gripped it.

Michaels, Leo's valet, appeared and regarded his master with concern.

'Mr Ashburton is still quite unwell today,' Annabelle said quietly, drawing the valet away from the bed. 'Could you ask the maids to bring up some cool water and a towel and a jug of water for him to drink when he awakes?'

'Of course, my lady. Is there anything else you need?'

'Not for now, thank you, Michaels. We may need the doctor later if he doesn't settle, but we will see how he goes throughout the morning.' The valet hurried off and Annabelle looked around the room, wondering if she was interfering too much.

'Nonsense,' she muttered to herself. Leo was unwell, he needed someone to ensure he was well cared for. She would do the same even if she were not his wife and the wedding ring on her finger gave her even more reason to be here.

As quietly as she could, she lifted the heavy armchair from the corner of the room to the side of the bed so she could see if he woke and needed anything. A couple of minutes later Michaels re-entered, carrying a heavy bowl of water and followed by Kitty and another young maid carrying towels and a jug of drinking water and a glass.

'Anything else you need, my lady?'

'Could you bring my breakfast here in about half an hour, Kitty, and a book from the library, I don't mind what, to read while Mr Ashburton is sleeping?'

Michaels stayed as the two maids left, lingering near the door. 'I can stay with him, my lady, if you would prefer.'

'Thank you for the offer, Michaels, but I'm happy to sit with Mr Ashburton. I will ring if he needs anything.'

The valet left and once again she was alone with her husband. Annabelle busied herself by setting up the bowl of cool water on the little table next to the bed and the pile of towels just behind it. She took the first towel and dipped the corner in the water, squeezing out the excess before gently dabbing it on Leo's brow. Just as he had settled when she had placed her cool hand on his forehead the night before, he sighed now at the relief from his burning skin with the cooling towel.

She had just dipped the towel back into the water and squeezed it out for a second time when Leo's eyes flicked open and focused on her for a moment. It seemed to cost him a lot of energy to even look at her and after a weak half-smile he settled back on to the pillows and drifted off into sleep again.

Annabelle thought of the times she and Beth had been unwell. Beth had lain in bed for four weeks when she was ten, coughing and coughing until blood stained her delicate hanky. Annabelle, although only nine herself, had refused to leave her sister, crawling into bed beside her and holding her hand as the fever raged. Then when Annabelle was twelve she had fallen from a tree branch where she had been sitting and reading and broken her leg. The doctor had come and inspected it, declared there wasn't much to be done and either she would walk again or she wouldn't. For six long weeks she had to stay in bed and Beth had been her constant companion, making her laugh with titbits of gossips and reading to her to distract from the pain. It had been her sister who had helped her stand for the first time and who had clapped her hands in glee when she had taken her first faltering steps.

As she dipped the towel in the bowl again and again, dabbing it gently on Leo's forehead, she felt the lump form in her throat as she thought of her sister. She missed Beth so much it hurt physically, as if she had been stabbed in the heart. She wished Beth was here to tell her what to do, how to approach married life, how to make the best of things. Instead she was completely alone.

She sat down, draping the towel over the side of the little table so it could be used again later, but as her bottom touched the seat Leo's hand shot out and grabbed her. Annabelle stifled a shout, realising he was reaching for her in his sleep, and gently took hold of his hand, stroking it and murmuring soothing sounds under her breath.

Leo dreamed. Some of the dreams were fantastical with dragons and giant rats and people who could fly like birds, while others were more based in reality, distortions of memories and events that had once happened. Every so often he would claw at consciousness, trying to bring himself out of the restless sleep, only to be pulled back down into the depths of his dreams.

Every time he tried to surface Annabelle was there, dabbing his brow with cool water, stroking his hand, and on the last occasion dozing peacefully in the chair by his bedside, a book rested on her chest. The spot beside him was never empty and he felt strangely reassured by the presence of his wife, the almost stranger.

He wasn't sure how much time had passed when he finally woke properly. The daylight was streaming in through the curtains and there was distant birdsong drifting in through the open windows.

'Water,' he croaked, pushing himself up on the pillows so he was at least half-sitting. Annabelle jumped at the sound of his voice and scrambled to her feet. She smiled at him tentatively as she passed him the glass of water, supporting the bottom so he wouldn't spill it all down his front. 'Thank you.'

'It's nice to see you awake.'

'How long have I been sleeping?'

'A day and a half. It is Monday morning.'

He grimaced. His head was still pounding and his body felt hot, but he didn't feel anywhere near as uncomfortable as he had when he'd tumbled into bed on Saturday evening. Then he'd been shivering uncontrollably and the room had been spinning. He'd assumed it was a chill from getting so cold and wet in the storm, but it had developed into a full-blown fever.

'How do you feel?'

'Tired.'

'You should rest some more. But have another few sips of water first. You must be dehydrated.'

He obeyed and took a few more sips of water before settling back down on to his pillows. It wasn't often that he got ill; he was a healthy young man and could count on one hand the number of times he'd had to spend more than a few hours resting from a malady. Still, normally when he got a fever he would crawl into bed and rest, tended just by Michaels or a designated maid. They would come and go quietly, bring him his meals or change his sheets, but no one had ever sat by his bed like Annabelle was. She looked perfectly content just to *be* with him. Armed with her book— he squinted at the cover: on crop rotations for the arable farmer, of all subjects—she looked as though she were planning on staying until convinced he was better.

'You don't have to stay,' he said quietly, hoping that despite his words she would. It was peculiarly comforting to have her sitting there beside him.

'I'll stay while you rest. Beth always sat by my bedside when I was ill, I know how reassuring it is to have someone there, just in case you need something.' Although he would never admit it out loud, he envied her childhood. Those precious years spent with her sister as her constant companion. He would have coped much better with the loss of his parents if Josh hadn't been ripped from him a mere few weeks later. Two mourning little boys shouldn't have been separated, but his great-aunt had been adamant she was only taking Leo in, the eldest and heir to Lord Abbingdon. Josh had ended up with an old friend of their father's as his guardian, soon to travel to India. Not a conventional upbringing, but from what Josh had told him it had been filled with love. Unlike his own.

He closed his eyes, unable to stop himself from smiling as Annabelle laid her hand lightly on his where it rested on the covers as he drifted off to sleep.

The next time he woke she was dozing in the armchair, her feet up underneath her and her head tucked into the crook of her elbow on the armrest. She looked young and innocent, and although he was desperate for more water he hesitated to disturb her. Now he could see it was beginning to get dark outside, the sun falling towards the horizon.

Shifting in bed, he levered himself into a half-sitting position, waiting for the pounding in his head to begin as he moved. There was a mild ache, but nothing like the constant headache that had made him want to squeeze his eyes shut every time he'd woken in the last couple of days.

He adjusted his position and reached out for the glass of water on his bedside table, his fingers gripping it momentarily before a coughing spasm made his arm jerk and the glass go flying. He could only watch in horror as it flew at Annabelle, spilling the cold water over her chest and the glass settling in her lap.

She awoke with a cry of surprise, sitting up and almost dislodging the glass, catching it at the last moment before it fell to the floor and shattered.

'I'm sorry, I knocked it as I coughed.'

Annabelle looked down at her sodden dress and his eyes followed the direction of her gaze. He watched as she took one of the towels from his bedside table and began dabbing at the water, unable to tear his eyes away as she distractedly pulled at the front of her dress, revealing a flash of creamy skin underneath.

'There were easier ways to wake me,' she murmured and Leo saw the faint smile tugging at her lips.

'You *don't* like to be woken with a dousing by a glass of cold water every morning? I'll keep that in mind.'

'Was that a joke, Leo? Are you feeling very unwell?'

'I have been known to crack a joke or two in my life,' he said, sinking back on to the pillows. He found rather than tiring of her presence he was enjoying having her here, teasing him. It wasn't what he had expected to feel.

'One or two in thirty-odd years is a such a lot…'

'Thirty-three,' he informed her. 'And I think you'll find it is three jokes in thirty-three years now.'

She grinned at him, not the tentative, shy smiles she had given him before, but a proper face-changing smile. He liked it, liked the way it made him feel to be the one to make her smile like that.

Pouring him another glass of water from the jug, she handed it to him and looked over him with the regard of a professional nurse.

'You look better. May I?'

When he nodded she placed her small hand on his forehead and held it there for a moment.

'Much cooler. I think the fever must have broken.'

'I recover quickly,' he said as he pushed himself up in the bed again. It was hard to stay propped up with the number of pillows behind him, he just kept slipping down. 'I'll be back to normal by tomorrow.'

'There's no need to rush. It was a horrible fever. You were delirious at one point.'

'Was I? I hope I didn't say anything too shocking.'

'You muttered non-stop for at least half an hour. I can recommend delirium for other newly married couples who have yet to become better acquainted.'

They fell silent as he drained his glass of water and Annabelle refilled it for him.

'Do you feel completely better?'

'I still have a mild headache and my muscles feel as though I've run from here to London, but I feel much better than I did.'

'I'm glad. Do you want to sleep some more?'

He felt restless, as if he wanted to fling back the bedcovers and pace about the room, but he knew it wouldn't do anything for his aching muscles.

'Not just yet.'

'I could read to you. Or we could talk—' she paused, biting her lip '—or I could leave you in peace if you prefer.'

He surprised himself by shaking his head. 'Stay. It is nice to have some company.'

Chapter Nine

Dear Josh,
I never knew how reassuring it is to have
someone nurse you back to health when
you are unwell.

The next two days passed in a blur. Although
he felt much better and was recovering quickly,
the fever returned twice and he still needed
more sleep than usual. He was pleasantly surprised to find he looked forward to Annabelle
knocking on his door in the morning and slipping into his room. She bustled around opening his curtains and letting in some fresh air,
bringing him fresh flowers to sit on his windowsill. She spoke quietly, making him smile
at her wry observations of the household she
had joined, and she wasn't afraid of allowing
the time to pass in silence either.

The irony of the situation wasn't lost on him. He'd been adamant he wanted to lead a separate life from Annabelle, to continue as he had before he was married, but he'd failed at the first hurdle.

By the fourth day of his illness he felt much better and rose early, planning on joining his wife downstairs for breakfast.

'Good morning, Mr Ashburton,' Mrs Barnes greeted him as he descended the stairs. 'Are you feeling better today?'

'Much better, thank you.'

'We have all been so worried about you.'

'It was just a chill. I am fully recovered now. Thank you for your concern.'

'Lady Annabelle is taking her breakfast in the dining room this morning, sir.'

'Wonderful.' He moved through the hall, but paused when he saw Mrs Barnes linger as if she had more to say.

'Lady Annabelle has been dedicated in her care to you,' the housekeeper said, keeping her tone light in a way that made Leo realise she had something she felt was very important to say. 'She sat up with you all night the second night you were ill.'

'She's a very kind young woman.'

'Yes. I wonder, Mr Ashburton, if you have considered moving her into the bedroom for the mistress of the house. It is the best proportioned room in the whole of the upstairs and a beautiful room. She is going to be living here after all.'

He raised an eyebrow. It was a very forward suggestion from his housekeeper, but he had always valued honesty from his staff and had encouraged them over the years to voice their opinions while still respecting his authority.

'Has Lady Annabelle said she isn't comfortable in her current room?'

'No, no, nothing like that. It was just a thought I had, sir.'

'I will consider it. Thank you, Mrs Barnes.'

His housekeeper did have a point, Annabelle should have the bedroom designed for the mistress of the house. It was almost next to his, separated only by the bathroom in between which had doors from either bedroom and allowed easy passage from one room to the next. He hadn't wanted to move her so close to him in case it gave her the wrong idea about the expectations of the marriage, but he could see now she might have taken it as an insult that he didn't think her worthy of the best bedroom.

The problem was, if he moved her now, it might give even more of the wrong impression that he had moved her because his expectations of the marriage had changed. Running a hand through his hair, he deliberated. Perhaps he would not suggest the move, but find some other way of thanking her for her care these last few days.

Annabelle gave him a sunny smile as he entered the dining room. She wasn't wearing a veil and he was glad she didn't feel a need to in her new home. He was aware she normally wore one out and about, but at Birling View she had felt comfortable enough to go without and he wanted her to be as relaxed here.

'Good morning. It's lovely to see you up.' She spoke softly as always and watched him over the rim of her teacup as she took a sip of tea.

'I feel much better. Thank you for keeping me company these last few days.'

In between his numerous naps she'd read to him, told him funny stories about her childhood and even helped him with the estate accounts he'd been worrying about getting behind with. She was an easy companion. Years of living with her mother meant nothing much fazed her. Even the few times he'd been unintentionally sharp with her she had shrugged it off with good grace.

'Will you be returning to London today?'

'Ah, yes, I'm not sure.' He had planned to leave the day after their wedding, but the fever had stopped him. Now he was recovered he could ride for London today or tomorrow, but he felt an unexpected reluctance to leave.

'Perhaps it might be better to wait a couple more days. I know it isn't the longest journey, but you don't want to feel unwell on the road. Unless your business is pressing.'

'Not pressing, no.' He felt a little guilty. There was no real reason for him to return to London. He had everything he needed here to keep up with estate business, but had decided before the wedding he would make a swift exit the day after they were married to keep some distance between him and his new bride. It seemed a callous move now that he thought about it. 'I was thinking—' he said, stopping to clear his throat '—that it is customary for newlyweds to go on a honeymoon. I know ours isn't a conventional marriage, but there is no reason we cannot have a few days away together.'

Annabelle looked shocked and for a minute seemed unable to speak.

'That would be lovely,' she said eventually. 'This is the farthest I've ever been from home, from Eastbourne, so it would be lovely to see somewhere else.'

'Good. I will make the arrangements.'

'Where will we go?'

He deliberated. The honeymoon had been a spur-of-the-moment suggestion. He'd travelled around most of England and Wales over the years as well as frequent trips to the Continent. He liked the countryside, unspoilt and quiet, without many people to ruin it.

'Dorset is beautiful and not too far to travel. Devon and Cornwall are probably my favourite areas but the journey can take days and days.'

'Dorset sounds wonderful. *"Nymphs lightly tread the bright reflecting sand, And proud sails whiten all the summer bay."'*

'A poem?'

'Charlotte Turner Smith. She wrote it about Weymouth.'

'She's a novelist, isn't she?'

'She was. She died in 1806. We had many of her books in our library including a wonderful book of her poems. Very atmospheric.'

'You really did spend a lot of time in that library, didn't you?'

'It was that or tackle the gardening.' She

pulled a face. 'I love a beautiful garden to stroll around, but I fear I was not born to be a horticulturalist.'

'Your mother didn't hand over any of the running of the house to you?'

'No. She insisted on overseeing everything herself.' She dabbed her mouth delicately with her napkin before setting it down on the table beside her plate. As she rose Leo realised he was sad she was leaving, sad to be losing her company over breakfast, he'd grown so accustomed to it over the last few days.

She smiled at him and touched her fingers to his shoulder as she passed him and he felt himself stiffen. Something had happened to him while he was unwell, something had altered inside him.

'You're a fool,' he muttered to himself. Suggesting honeymoons and considering moving Annabelle to a room closer to his—all because he realised he actually quite liked his wife. He still needed to be careful, still had to ensure there was a boundary between them. It wasn't that he thought his wife was madly in love with him, he wasn't as conceited as that, but he had seen how she had been living with her mother, deprived of warmth and companionship. *He* couldn't be the one to offer her that.

It would just end in disaster, with Annabelle hurt and hating him. He didn't know how to care for someone, at least no one apart from his brother and he'd loved him since childhood, and he knew he wasn't going to be able to learn at the age of thirty-three.

With a scowl on his face he finished his breakfast. The idea of a honeymoon was souring, but he had suggested it now and would have to go through with it. He had seen how happy the proposal had made his wife.

Chapter Ten

Dear Beth,
Today I go on my honeymoon. I would
say it is a joyous occasion, but my new
husband has been so grumpy since we set
off that he looks as though he has swal-
lowed a bad-tempered owl.

Cautiously Annabelle peeked out from under
her veil at her husband, wondering if the fresh
air was improving his mood. He'd been nothing short of grumpy these past few days and
had gone back to avoiding her for long peri-
ods of time. After he had recovered from his
illness she had thought there had been a shift
in their fledgling relationship—he'd seemed
more relaxed, happier to be in her company.
He'd even suggested this honeymoon with no
prompting whatsoever from her. Then it had

been as if something had flipped inside him and he'd returned to being distant and cool.

The last three days they'd spent travelling in comfort by carriage to Dorset. Annabelle had read the pile of books she had brought with her, written two letters to her sister and spent hours staring out of the window at the passing countryside. On three occasions she had tried to start conversations with her husband and had been quickly and abruptly shut down.

Unperturbed, she had this morning decided to suggest they ride the last twelve miles of the journey, thinking it might improve Leo's mood to be in the sunshine and fresh air.

So far she was calling it a cautious success. He had smiled once, commented on the beauty of the countryside twice and had enquired as to her comfort on three occasions. It was progress.

'You're smiling,' he said, looking at her with his brows slightly furrowed.

'And you're frowning. I think mine is the more appropriate reaction to our surroundings.'

'I'm not frowning.' He settled his face into a more neutral expression.

'Well, you're not now, but you were. You frown a lot.'

She tapped her horse with her feet and trotted off before he could react. It was clear Leo had lived for a long time without close human companionship. She might have been a recluse, but she'd had the love and company of her sister. The little she knew of Leo's upbringing was third-hand, so perhaps inaccurate, but she gathered he was raised by a great-aunt who didn't really want him and most certainly didn't like children. No wonder he didn't know how to interact with others all that well. Not that she pretended to be an expert on that front.

'I don't frown a lot,' he said, catching up with her.

'You're frowning again now.'

Relaxing his face again, he grumbled something under his breath.

'It can't be far now,' Annabelle said, steadfastly ignoring whatever it was he was grumbling about.

'A few more miles. Did you want to rest before we push on?'

'My legs do ache a little.' In truth, she could ride for another five hours without stopping—she loved being on horseback with the wind in her hair and the ground falling away under her horse's hooves—but it was such a pleasant day she was determined to make the most of it.

They stopped in the shade of a tree, Leo carefully looping the horses' reins over a low branch. They were strong animals, healthy and well fed, the best they could hire from the inn they had stayed at the night before. Annabelle hadn't been privy to the negotiations, but she hoped Leo had arranged for them to keep the horses while they were honeymooning in Dorset. It would be lovely to get out on horseback every day.

Annabelle sat down on the grass, leaning her head back against the trunk of the tree and closing her eyes. After a moment she felt Leo sit down next to her, close but not close enough for their bodies to be touching.

'Tell me about where we will be staying.'

'It's remote. I hope you don't mind that.'

'Of course not.'

'There's a tiny village called Kimmeridge and just a little further on a beautiful bay with views in both directions of the Dorset coastline. Our cottage is outside the village, five minutes from the bay.'

'A cottage?' She opened her eyes in surprise. She had just assumed they would be staying in an inn or something similar. A cottage was intimate, private.

'Yes. I have a friend who has a property

nearby. He is in residence at the moment and offered us use of his guest rooms, but I thought you would prefer something more private. The cottage is at the edge of his estate.'

'That sounds...lovely.' For a moment she considered how she felt. A cottage did sound lovely, they wouldn't have to worry about anyone else, but she did feel a flicker of uncertainty around Leo's motivations. He knew she felt uneasy in company and that made the gesture of a private cottage thoughtful and considerate, but she wondered if it was a completely altruistic decision. Her scars made people stare—even when her face was covered with the veil people peered and whispered, trying to make out what she was hiding underneath. Perhaps the cottage was as much for his benefit as hers.

'You would prefer somewhere else?'

'No.'

She felt his eyes on her and forced herself to smile. She was overthinking things. Whatever the motivation she would be happier in a cottage than staying elsewhere.

'I've never been on holiday before,' she said, lifting up her veil and tucking it over the top of her bonnet.

'I haven't been on holiday with someone else since I was eight.'

Before. She was fast learning everything in her husband's life was split into before and after. Before the illness that had killed his parents and after it.

'You can remember holidays with your family?'

For a moment she thought he was going to get up and walk away, but instead he settled back against the tree, his hand brushing her leg as he lifted it to run it through his hair.

'Yes. Every year we would go to some seaside town. One year Lyme Regis, which is not far from here, another year Brighton. Father would teach us to skim stones from the beach and Mother would paddle in the shallows.'

'They sound like happy memories.'

'They were good times.'

She chewed her lip, wondering how to ask him more about it. He had hardly spoken of his family before. All she knew was through Beth.

'Where was your favourite?'

'Probably Lyme Regis. It's tiny and has the most magnificent cliffs. Every day we would walk the two miles from our accommodation into the town to buy fresh bread and cheese and then picnic on the beach. There were these ancient curios to collect from the beach and we spent the whole week with bare feet on the sand.'

Annabelle stayed silent, hoping he would say more.

'I was six, I think, and Josh four. I can remember him running at the sea, fully clothed, so excited to see it. He fell in face first and got completely soaked and our father had to go in to haul him out. They both collapsed on the beach, laughing.'

'Your father didn't mind getting wet?'

'My father's temperament was much like Josh's is now. He was relaxed, warm, didn't let the little things bother him. My mother was similar, she always had a smile and a kind word for everyone.'

Annabelle wondered if he was remembering with an orphan's nostalgia or if his parents had been as they were in his memories.

'I was always the odd one out.'

There didn't seem to be a diplomatic way of asking if he had always been so distant or if it was something that had developed as he was growing up. A life without love, deprived of the people who care for you, must have had a profound impact on Leo's character.

He glanced at her. 'Josh and I were the most

opposite you could imagine, but we loved each other like only siblings can.'

'I can't imagine being forced to grow up without Beth,' she said quietly, reaching out and placing her hand gently on top of his. 'She gave me love and strength even when life seemed too difficult to bear.'

For a long moment he looked down at their hands, hers on top of his, then he stood abruptly, turning away so she couldn't see his expression.

'We should get moving if we want to reach the cottage by lunchtime.'

Annabelle tried not to let her disappointment show. Every time she felt as though her husband was opening up, revealing a little of himself, he pulled away and returned to the distant man everyone thought him. Instead of wallowing, she summoned a sunny smile and remounted, trying to ignore the spark of excitement that ripped through her as her body brushed against Leo's as he helped her up on to her horse.

'Stop it,' she muttered to herself. The last thing she needed was to feel attracted to her husband. If he got any hint of that, he would run to the other end of the country. She was aiming for pleasant companionship, nothing

more, so steadfastly she tried to ignore the first flares of desire deep inside her.

'Did you say something?'

'No. How long do you think until we reach the cottage?'

'An hour or two at the most. I don't think it is far now. Can you press on and we will eat when we get there?'

'Of course.'

The carriage was meeting them at the cottage, taking the longer but wider roads, but still it would probably arrive after them. Lunch would be later, but Annabelle didn't mind. She never had much of an appetite when it was hot like this.

The rest of the journey took an hour and a half, although they rode slowly down the country lanes, allowing the horses to pick the pace as the sun rose higher in the sky and the day grew warmer. Annabelle looked around her in interest as they passed through the tiny village of Kimmeridge. It had a shop and an inn and not more than twenty houses clustered round the centre of the village. They were certainly remote.

Another ten minutes later they saw the cottage, perched on the top of a hill with views down to the cliffs below and the sea beyond.

It was whitewashed and quaint, small in size but well maintained. To one side there was a fenced-off area she assumed was to be used as a paddock for the horses with a shelter at one end. The rest was open countryside—the rolling hills of Dorset were right on their doorstep.

'It's beautiful.'

'It is, isn't it.'

'I thought nowhere could compare to my wonderful South Downs, but I feel a little foolish making that assumption when I haven't seen anywhere else. This is just as stunning, in a different way.'

They dismounted and saw to the horses first, removing the saddles and bridles so they could take a long drink from the trough and then run free in the paddock. Only once the horses were settled happily in the shade did they turn their attention to the cottage.

It was even smaller than Annabelle had first thought—she doubted there could be more than four rooms inside. As they opened the door she found herself holding her breath in anticipation. Having never thought she would marry, she hadn't ever considered what her honeymoon might be like, but ever since Leo had suggested a trip away her imagination had run wild.

The cottage was small but cosy inside, with one room downstairs that offered comfortable armchairs and a small dining table and a kitchen at the back. The stairs led up directly from one side of the downstairs room.

'It's smaller than I imagined,' Leo said, a frown on his face.

'It's perfect.' For her it was. There was nowhere for any servants to stay so it would be just the two of them. She swallowed, hoping it would bring them closer together rather than pushing them apart.

'Let's take a look upstairs.'

She could tell there was something wrong by the way he went completely still in front of her at the top of the narrow staircase.

'Is there a problem?'

'Yes.'

Slowly he stepped aside and Annabelle caught a glimpse of the room beyond. It was light and airy, with a large window on each side that let in the light and allowed unparalleled views of the sea. The bedroom, the *only* bedroom, took up the whole first floor and in the middle was a comfortable-looking bed.

It was a large bed, plenty big enough for two.

'We can still enquire if there are rooms available at the inn.' Leo's voice was gruff and Annabelle felt her world swaying. Surely she wasn't so repulsive he couldn't even bear to share a bed with her. It wasn't ideal, of that she was aware, but they were married, there was nothing scandalous about sleeping chastely side by side in one bed. It was so big they probably wouldn't even brush against one another.

'Whatever you think best,' she said, turning away, wishing she hadn't taken her bonnet off as they'd entered the cottage and could still hide behind the veil. Her cheeks were flushing red and she knew if she thought about it too much the tears would flow.

'There is only one bed, Annabelle,' he said and she could tell he was making an effort to soften his voice. 'I wouldn't want to make things uncomfortable.'

'Whatever you think best,' she repeated and turned and hurried back downstairs, the air in the cottage suddenly seeming humid and close.

Outside she took a few deep steadying breaths, thinking Leo would likely follow her in a minute or two. When he didn't emerge she walked over to the edge of the paddock and leaned on the fence, watching the horses munching on the grass.

* * *

It was ten minutes before Leo came out of the cottage. She heard his footsteps and felt his presence behind her, but didn't turn around.

'I'm not very good with people,' he said eventually, coming to stand next to her and lean on the fence. 'I never have been. Often I say the wrong thing. People think I am cold, arrogant.' He sighed and she shifted so she could see him out of the corner of her eye. 'Perhaps I am.'

The silence stretched out between them for a while and for once Annabelle didn't try to fill it or ease the awkwardness.

'I think I said something wrong in the cottage, something that upset you, but I do not know what.'

Annabelle stared out at the horses and wondered if she should be honest with the man who told her so little of his thoughts and feelings.

'I am your wife,' she said eventually. 'Perhaps ours is not the most conventional of marriages, but we are married. There is no reason we cannot stay in this cottage together, even with only one bed.' Quickly she glanced up at him, but as usual it was difficult to read his expression. 'I know I am not pleasant to look at, but all we would be doing is sleeping side by side.'

'Annabelle…' he said, reaching out for her hand, but she stepped away.

'I didn't realise I was so hideous you couldn't bear to be close to me even for a short while.'

'That's not it at all.' He waited until she looked up and met his gaze, which took a long time, but she sensed he was more stubborn than her and eventually gave in. 'I don't find you hideous. Good Lord, you're *not* hideous.'

She scoffed. 'I know what I look like.'

'Annabelle, you're a very attractive young woman who happens to have a scar covering one cheek. That scar isn't the sum of you.'

'It is what everyone sees.'

'I won't pretend I don't see it, but it isn't all I see. And I certainly don't think you're hideous. That's ridiculous.'

'You reacted pretty strongly when you saw there was only one bed.'

'I'm new to this, too,' Leo said with a frustrated little sigh. 'I've never been married before. I've never had to consider the needs of someone else so often before. We are not having a normal marriage and I thought that would mean it would be awkward to share a bed. Most women…' He trailed off.

'Most women would get the wrong idea?'

He mumbled something and she felt a laugh bubble up from deep inside.

'Do not fear, Leo, I don't find you so irresistible I might fall in love if my hand brushes yours in bed one night.'

'I wasn't thinking that.'

She could tell it was exactly what he was thinking. For so long he hadn't married as he hadn't wanted anyone to get close and even now he was doing all he could to keep her at arm's length.

'I am aware of what this marriage is and what you wish it to be, Leo.'

He remained silent so Annabelle pushed on.

'But we are both reasonable people. Our lives are intertwined now, however separate you wished you could keep them. I am planning on living to a ripe old age so we have many years ahead of us and at least some of that time will be spent together. I think it will be much more pleasant if we can find a way to develop a comfortable companionship, a friendship even.'

'You're being very reasonable,' he said with just a hint of suspicion in his voice.

'I am a very reasonable woman.'

'I don't have many friendships. I'm not that sort of person.'

'There was Mr Wilbersmythe at our wedding.'

'We're not exactly close.'

'And the friend who is letting us use the cottage.'

'Again, I don't see him all that often.'

'I won't pretend I am a social butterfly,' Annabelle said wryly. 'I probably have fewer friends than you, but I do think we can build something good out of our marriage. It doesn't all have to start and end with the question of convenience.'

'So you're happy to share a bed.'

'I am.'

'And you're happy to spend the week alone with me in the cottage. The servants will have to lodge in the inn in Kimmeridge.'

'It sounds delightfully peaceful.'

'Then we shall stay.'

Chapter Eleven

❧❧❧

Dear Josh,
Do you remember that holiday in Dorset?
The one when we spent the whole week
on the beach?

It was still light outside when Annabelle started yawning and rubbing her eyes, although he watched with fascination as she persisted with her book for another ten minutes even though he could see by the movement of her eyes she was having to read the same section over and over again because of her fatigue. The day had been tiring, with the early start from the inn and a brisk walk across the hills once they had settled into the cottage. They'd eaten dinner at the inn in Kimmeridge and then strolled back as the heat of the day finally began to subside.

'It's been a long day.'

Annabelle yawned again and then smiled sleepily at him. 'Yes. I think I might go to bed. I know it is early, but I can barely keep my eyes open.'

'A honeymoon is meant to be restful,' he said and then was hit with images of what else a honeymoon was meant to be. He shifted uncomfortably and tried not to look at his wife as she stood and headed for the stairs.

'Would you mind helping me with my dress? Normally the maid would unfasten it for me.'

'Of course.'

He followed her upstairs, his eyes drawn to the bed they would soon be sharing in the centre of the room.

'It's just a few fastenings at the back and a bow to untie at the waist.'

Her dress was pale yellow with a white sash around the middle. Simple yet elegant.

His fingers felt clumsy as he unfastened the dress, pulling at the bow at her waist last and seeing the material fall open to reveal the creamy skin underneath. Not since Emily had he helped a woman undress and he felt a pulse of suppressed desire.

Quickly he moved away, descending the stairs with a cursory *goodnight* to his wife.

He didn't desire her, no matter what his body was trying to tell him. He would not be a slave to purely physical desires.

Downstairs he tried to concentrate on his book but found he couldn't read more than a sentence at a time before he was distracted by the creak of the floorboards as Annabelle moved around above him, readying herself for bed.

He poured himself a brandy and took a few gulps, looking up as there was a rustling of sheets as his wife settled herself into bed, then silence.

Leo tried to lose himself in his book again, but in a way the silence was worse than the creaking of the floorboards. Now he knew she was in bed, lying between the sheets, her honey-blonde hair spread out on the pillow.

Stop it, he told himself firmly. He would not start fantasising about his wife. Earlier he'd been worrying she would get the wrong idea if they shared a bed together, but her cool reserve was showing him up. Annabelle was holding up her side of their bargain of what was expected from the marriage. She had quite sensibly suggested seeing if they could become friends, companions in life. Never had she once hinted she wanted anything more.

Yet here he was, thinking about that strip of creamy white skin on her back and what it might be like to slip into bed next to her.

He'd been too long without a woman, that much was clear. After Emily he hadn't wanted to get close to anyone else, including a mistress, but perhaps that option would be safer than desiring his wife.

With a growl of frustration he stood and began pacing around the room. It was wholly unsatisfying, his strides interrupted by the furniture and the small size, but he knew he wouldn't be able to sit still. Nor was it an option to go out for a walk now the sun had set. It was completely dark outside, the rural location meaning there wasn't a light for miles.

Maybe he should just go upstairs and join Annabelle in bed. That way he would prove to himself it was just the thought of having her so close to him that was unsettling. In all likelihood as soon as his head touched the pillow he would realise her presence in his bed was not something to make a fuss about.

He hesitated at the bottom of the stairs, but then blew out his candle and made his way up. A good night's sleep was exactly what he needed. The last few weeks had been busy and he was still recuperating from his feverish illness. Things would seem a lot more normal in the morning.

He slowed as he reached the top of the stairs, listening to Annabelle's steady breathing. Wondering if she were asleep already, he peered into the darkness, but it was impossible to see anything without a candle to light his way. Leo was used to getting undressed in the dark. He often dismissed his valet before dinner, preferring to see to his own clothes at the end of the night rather than have Michaels waiting for him.

Quickly he undressed, hesitating as he stepped out of his breeches. Normally he didn't wear much to bed, but tonight he would have to make a change to his night-time wardrobe. Annabelle was outwardly serene about them having to share a bed, but he doubted that would continue if she woke up next to a naked or near-naked man.

He didn't have anything suitable for his top half, but he fastened a pair of cotton drawers around his waist before slipping into bed. He collided with Annabelle's body with a loud exclamation and she mumbled something before rolling over. It would appear they both liked sleeping on the left side of the bed.

As he circled the bed and got in on the right

side he felt Annabelle shift and wriggle in her sleep. He hadn't woken her, but he had definitely disturbed her, and he stiffened as she burrowed into the side of his body. Her body was warm and inviting and he felt something he hadn't for years as she flung an arm across his body.

For a long time he lay there, listening to his wife's breathing, not wanting to move, not wanting to disturb her. So much for hardly knowing she was there. The bed might be big, but they were still very close, very intimate. When she did finally roll away, leaving a few inches' gap between them, he almost rolled with her, wanting to preserve the closeness. Instead he closed his eyes firmly and turned over in the other direction.

Annabelle awoke early, drifting out of sleep as the birds began their dawn chorus in the trees and the pale first light started to filter through the window. She felt warm and contented, as though she had slept better than she had in quite a while.

For a long moment she kept her eyes closed and her head on her pillow, not wanting to disturb her sister in the bed beside her. Finally she turned over and let her eyes flutter open, only to let out a suppressed exclamation of surprise as she remembered it wasn't Beth she was sharing a bed with.

Slowly she backed away, shuffling across the bed to put a more decent amount of room between her and her husband. Really she should get up and leave him to sleep, but she'd never been one to jump out of bed in the morning and even the knowledge that she was sharing that bed wasn't enough to force her out yet.

He seemed to be sleeping peacefully, lying on his side with one arm flung above his head, claiming the pillow as his own. At some point in the night he had kicked off most of the sheets, revealing a muscular torso which was surprisingly tanned for a man she couldn't imagine ever being shirtless in public. She had the irrational urge to reach out and run her fingers over the dark hairs on his chest, to feel the smoothness of the skin beneath.

Annabelle swallowed hard. She had always known her husband was a good-looking man, attractive in all the conventional ways. When he was awake, and often scowling, he seemed more formidable, but asleep he lost much of that sternness and looked younger somehow.

'I wonder...' she murmured, wondering what sort of man he would have been if he hadn't lost his parents and been separated from the brother he loved so dearly. Likely he would still have been serious—she'd always thought a person's character was ingrained from birth, but the events of their life did have an impact. If Leo had grown up in a loving family, with the parents and brother he had such fond memories of, she doubted he would be so keen to hold everyone at arm's length.

He shifted in the bed, flinging a leg over the covers and rolling a little further towards her. Annabelle gave a little gasp of surprise as he shot out an arm and pulled her against him. They were lying face to face, only an inch or two between their lips, and Annabelle could feel the tickle of his breath on her cheek. Their bodies were even closer, his arm exerting a gentle but firm pressure on the small of her back, holding her flush against him.

Annabelle felt something unfamiliar blossom inside her and for a moment she had the urge to lie there with him, to enjoy his touch, and not pull away.

'I missed you,' he murmured in his sleep, his hand slipping down to her buttocks. Annabelle froze as he began caressing her, knowing she should roll away, but her body was asking for one more second, one more touch. She hadn't realised how much she craved being touched, how much she wanted human contact, and Leo's fingers were doing something wonderful in the way they were tracing small circles down her back and across her buttocks.

'God, I've missed you, Emily.'

Annabelle stiffened and then felt the flood of shame rip through her. It wasn't her that Leo wanted, of course it wasn't. It was the woman he was still in love with. Someone beautiful, someone he desired. Not the wife he had chosen because she wouldn't expect much from their life together.

Unable to suppress a sob, she pulled away, leaping up from the bed so violently she knew it would wake Leo, but in the moment not caring. She just needed to get dressed and get out of the room.

Quickly she grabbed a garment from the wardrobe and, refusing to look at the bed, slipped it over her head.

'Annabelle,' Leo said, his voice thick with sleep.

Ignoring him, she pulled the dress down, not caring that she still had her nightgown underneath. Then she grabbed a bonnet with a veil attached and fled down the stairs.

'Annabelle,' she heard him call after her.

She paused downstairs to sort out her dress, wriggling out of the nightgown and rudimentarily fastening her dress so she didn't look a complete state. When she heard Leo start to move around upstairs she jammed her bonnet on her head, pulled the veil down over her face, slipped on her boots and ran out of the door.

The grass was still wet and the morning cool and she wished she had stopped to grab a shawl or a wrap for her shoulders, but she wasn't going back now.

Walking quickly to warm herself up, she headed away from the cottage and towards the sea. The tears felt hot on her cheeks and she didn't want to examine the mixture of shame and disappointment that was raging inside her.

'Stupid, stupid girl,' she told herself. Of course Leo hadn't been reaching for her this morning. He had never once indicated he found her attractive—how could he when her face was marred by such ugly scars? Again and again he had reminded her theirs wouldn't be *that* sort of marriage, from allocating a room far from his at Five Oaks, to his over-the-top reaction to seeing there was only one bed at the cottage. Even so, when he'd pulled her towards him she had felt as if it were right, as if it was how they were meant to be. 'You don't even like him.'

It was a lie. She was growing fond of her husband. He still could be cool and formal sometimes, but she was beginning to see that was a façade to keep people distant. If you got to see the real Leo underneath, he was different.

She didn't stop walking until she reached the cliffs, forcing herself to stop thinking and instead appreciate the stark beauty of the bay. The cliffs were about twenty feet high above a rocky beach below. The bay curved in a shallow crescent and the cliffs at the back were dark and layered. There were a few paths down over the rocks to the beach that looked well trodden and she could see why it was a favourite of locals and visitors alike.

Later she would go down to the beach and paddle her toes in the water, but right now the water would be icy where it had cooled overnight. Instead she picked a spot on the cliffs on a soft patch of grass and sat, watching the sun rise higher in the sky and the gulls swooping over the water searching for their breakfast.

She had been sitting for about half an hour when she heard Leo approaching from behind her. Her legs were feeling a little stiff and she had been planning on returning to the cottage soon anyway, much of her shame and upset having drained away as she sat in the stillness of nature.

'Annabelle,' Leo said softly, coming to sit next to her. 'Do you mind if I join you?'

She shook her head and he sat down next to her, close but not quite touching. Wordlessly he handed her a napkin wrapped around one of the sticky buns they had remaining from the provisions left in the cottage for them when they arrived. He had another in his hand and bit into it, eating it slowly and in silence.

'I thought you might want some breakfast,' he said once he had finished his, looking out at the sea rather than at her.

'Thank you.'

'You took off at quite a speed this morning.'

She pressed her lips together, wondering why she felt angry with him. He hadn't even been awake when he'd pinned her with his arm and mistaken her for another woman.

'Did something happen?'

'You were talking in your sleep. I didn't want to disturb you.'

'Did I say something to upset you?'

Closing her eyes, she considered for a moment. Her instinct was to reassure him, to tell him nothing had happened. Always she had been driven to put other people's comfort over her own, but she was fast realising she needed to stand her ground in her marriage or it would end up like her other limited relationships. Both her mother and her father had taken advantage of her docile personality in many ways and if she wanted her future to look different from her past she was the one who would have to change it.

'You reached out for me in bed and called me Emily.'

'Ah.'

'You were half-asleep, so I know I cannot be angry with you.'

'And yet…?' He let the question hang, but Annabelle didn't rush to fill the silence.

They sat side by side for another minute, then Leo turned to her with purpose.

'I'm sorry,' he said, waiting for her to look at him before continuing. 'Emily was the only person I have shared a bed with before. I suppose in my half-asleep state I felt a presence in the bed and my memory filled in the blanks.'

She nodded, acknowledging the apology. He really hadn't done anything wrong, not consciously. It was just her wanting something that wasn't going to be.

'I don't know why it upset me so much,' she said quietly.

'I can't imagine being called someone else's name in bed by your husband is pleasant for anyone, no matter the circumstances.'

'But ours are not normal circumstances and I know you must love Emily very much.'

He looked at her as if he was considering her words for a while and then shook his head.

'You think I'm still in love with Emily?'

'Yes. It's not a problem, of course, not even really any of my business.'

'Why would you think that?'

'It really doesn't matter, Leo. I think I was just surprised by what happened this morning, that is all.' She was starting to feel uncomfortable, as if she were prying somewhere she had no right to be.

'I'm not still in love with Emily,' he said quietly. 'I loved her and lost her, but it was many years ago.'

'What happened?' The question slipped out before Annabelle could stop it. She was curious to know about the woman who had meant so much to her husband even if it had been years ago.

He stood and Annabelle thought he was going to leave without saying anything more, but then he reached out his hand and when she placed her fingers in his he pulled her to her feet.

'Do you mind if we walk? I find it easier to talk if my body is moving.'

Chapter Twelve

Dear Josh,
I never told you about Emily, did I? I sup-
pose I was ashamed of my behaviour.

'I spent much of my youth alone,' Leo said as they strolled along the cliffs. The area was deserted, with no one else in sight, and it seemed a fitting setting for their conversation.

'Your great-aunt wasn't present?'

He grimaced. 'She took me in, provided me with somewhere to live, an education, but she didn't consider it her duty to spend time with me. From the age of eight until I went away to school I was mainly cared for by servants.'

Sometimes he still woke up with the all too familiar dread in his stomach, thinking he was still an eight-year-old, alone in the house, frightened and desperate for love. It had been an awful time. He'd been reeling from the loss of his parents and the separation from Josh and, instead of having someone hold him close and tell him everything would be all right, he'd been met with coldness and indifference.

'My great-aunt was more interested in me when I had grown a little, when I was a young man she could mould into the sort of person she thought would be fit to inherit the title.'

Next to him Annabelle remained silent, but he could feel her eyes on him, pitying him. He didn't want her pity but, given what had happened this morning, he felt he needed to explain about Emily, to show her there wasn't another woman in their marriage, not even the phantom of a dead person.

'I was twenty, in my second year of university. I had friends at school, friends at university, but no one close. I had become accustomed to holding everyone at arm's length. Then I met Emily.' He closed his eyes for a moment, trying to remember exactly how they had met. 'At first I didn't really notice her. She was married, a little older than me, and quiet. We were at a small gathering and I just ended up sitting next to her.'

'You started talking?'

'Not at first. I remember sensing the sadness

in her, without her ever saying a word. She sat there not speaking to anyone and the longer we sat side by side the more intrigued I became.'

'You saw a kindred spirit?'

'Perhaps.' He paused and looked out at the view and then motioned to one of the little paths leading down to the beach. 'A while later we both found ourselves out on the terrace, keen to be away from the noise of the party.'

Carefully he took Annabelle's hand and helped her over a rocky patch, releasing it as they got down level with the beach. It was low tide and there was a great expanse of rocky beach ahead of them, but he knew from experience the tides here changed quickly and before too long there would only be a narrow strip by the cliffs they could walk along.

'We talked a little, she was very easy to confide in. I told her of my restlessness at university and then as the night wore on about my parents and the loneliness I felt. She hinted at her unhappiness in her marriage.' He shook his head—from so little they had dreamed so much. 'She lived close to where you are from, just on the outskirts of Eastbourne. Her husband owned a small estate. I was in Cambridge, it seemed impossible that we would ever see each other again.'

Impossible, but somehow it had happened, three times that summer and a fourth just before Christmas.

'But you did,' Annabelle said quietly. She was a good listener, unobtrusive, letting him know she was listening without feeling the need to interject with comments or experiences of her own.

'But we did. She had an awful marriage. Her husband was a drunk, he hit her, humiliated her. I hated it, but she begged me not to say anything, not to do anything. It would just make things worse. I would travel to Brighton and rent a set of rooms and when her husband was in London she would make the trip to stay with me for a few days.' He ran his hand through his hair. They had been intoxicated with one another, young and foolish, not able to see that one slip, one wrong move, and Emily's life would become even worse than it already was. 'I was selfish. I loved her, but I didn't think of what was best for her. I told myself that I was making her happy, giving her hope, but I should have stayed away. She was married and I couldn't change that. Her only hope of survival was to keep her husband happy and hope he mellowed towards her.'

'What happened?'

'He found out. Of course he did. He beat Emily badly and locked her in her bedroom for three days without food or water. Eventually one of the servants took pity on her and let her out and she ran.'

They paused, halfway down to the sea, and Leo glanced at his wife, wondering if this would make her think less of him. He still felt ashamed by the way he had acted, the way he hadn't thought through the consequences of their affair.

'She ran across the fields for four miles until she reached your father's house.'

Annabelle spun to face him as understanding dawned in her eyes.

'She was the woman my father helped, the one you owed him a debt of gratitude for.'

'Yes. She hammered on your door in the middle of the night and your father let her in, beaten and filthy. Even though by law he could not come between a man and his wife, he locked the door behind her and refused to open it. Of course it helped that your father was an earl. Emily's husband couldn't push too far.'

'This would have been thirteen years ago?'

'Yes.'

Annabelle nodded, her eyes focused out to sea.

'Do you remember her?'

'I remember something. A commotion in the middle of the night. My mother arguing with my father, strict instructions not to go into one of the guest rooms. I was only eight, though.'

'Your father kept her safe until I arrived three days later. I took her back to Cambridge with me and for two weeks we thought perhaps her husband had given up and gone back to drink himself into a stupor.' He couldn't believe his naivety now, his stupidity. 'I went out to lectures one morning and when I came back to my lodgings they were ransacked and Emily was gone.' The feeling of panic, of desperation was still raw when he thought back to that day.

'What did you do?'

'I followed them back to Sussex, but couldn't gain admittance to her husband's estate. Two days later he announced she had drowned in the bath.'

Annabelle turned to him, her eyes wide with horror. 'Her husband…?'

'I believe so. I think he killed her and then made it look as though she had drowned.'

'Did he get away with it?'

'In a sense. I kicked up a fuss, but it was my word against his. None of the servants would come forward to confirm he beat her, hurt her. Six months later he drank himself to death.'

For a long moment Annabelle was silent, staring out to sea as she tried to digest everything he had just told her. He'd been living with the truth of the matter for thirteen years and often he still felt as if it were a bad dream.

'I can't imagine how you coped.'

'I buried myself in my studies, then in the running of the estates for my great-uncle. I mourned Emily—for a long time I mourned her.' He waited until Annabelle looked up at him before continuing. 'I loved her, but it was a very painful period in my life. I loved her and mourned her and over the years have worked out how to live with my guilt for not protecting her better.'

'You weren't the one who hurt her.'

'No, but she may have still been alive if I had kept my distance and put her welfare above my short-lived happiness.'

Gently Annabelle placed a hand on his arm and for once he was glad of the contact. For so long he had been without the touch of another, even a gentle pat on the arm felt filled with warmth.

'I don't want you to pity me,' he said a little

sharper than he intended. 'I just felt it best you understand. I loved Emily, but I am not still in love with her. I am a different man now from the one I was then.'

His wife still didn't look entirely convinced and he felt uncomfortable under her gaze. Quickly he pulled away, turning back towards the cliffs.

'I do understand,' Annabelle said as she hurried to keep up with him. 'Thank you for telling me, I know it must have been hard.'

Gruffly he mumbled 'yes' under his breath and set the pace quicker for the walk back, hoping it might discourage further conversation.

He believed his own words when he said he didn't still love Emily. He had loved her, with the burning intensity of a man who has been denied love for so long trying to cram it into such a short period, but she had been dead a long time. It wouldn't do to let Annabelle think that he would be more emotionally available if he could deal with his grief from losing Emily, it just wasn't true.

'That is why I wanted a marriage without the need for feelings, for an emotional connection.'

He could feel her eyes boring into him for a

minute before she spoke. 'I think you are being naive,' she said eventually. 'A marriage doesn't have to be about love, but there will always be some emotion involved. I don't think you can live with someone else in your life for that long and not feel *something*.'

Leo nodded slowly. 'You are right, of course.' He had become so fixated on trying to ensure his wife didn't think he would one day love her he had forgotten that she was human, too. 'Have I treated you poorly?'

'No. You haven't. You've been kinder to me than anyone except Beth has been for a long time.'

He wasn't sure if that was a compliment or if it should be taken as more of a comment on the world they lived in.

They walked side by side for a while to the base of the cliffs before heading up the rocky path and back to their cottage. He had the sense Annabelle wanted to say something, but even as they walked over the fields she remained silent.

Chapter Thirteen

Dear Beth,
I have a little predicament. Do you have
any advice on how not *to desire one's*
husband?

It was mid-afternoon, the day hot and heavy,
the heat even more unbearable than the pre-
ceding weeks. They had eaten an early lunch
brought up to the cottage by the maid staying
in the inn in Kimmeridge and since then Annabelle hadn't been able to summon up the
energy to do more than sit on the bench in the
shade in the little garden and read her book.
Not that she'd been able to concentrate much,
her mind kept flitting back to what Leo had
told her earlier. Everything was beginning to
make sense, even his feeling of obligation towards her father.

'I'm going to walk to the beach,' Leo said from his spot on the other side of the garden underneath a tree. 'See if there is any more air by the sea.'

'I'll come.' Annabelle hauled herself up and pulled at her dress which was sticking to her legs through her petticoats. 'I wish women weren't expected to wear so many layers.'

'Take some off,' Leo suggested nonchalantly, not even looking at her as he spoke.

'I can't.'

'Why not?'

'Well...'

'Who will know if you're wearing a petticoat or whatever you call the shirt thing you wear under your dress? Or the tight thing that goes over the top to hold everything together.' He motioned with his hand to get his point across and Annabelle giggled.

'You're not an expert in women's clothing, are you?'

'No. Never needed to be. There are too many ridiculous layers if you ask me. Are they all necessary?'

'Not in heat like today.' It would feel liberating to remove even just her petticoat or stay, anything to feel less as if she were being suffocated by material in a baker's oven.

'I can wait,' Leo said, sitting back down and closing his eyes as he leaned his head against the tree trunk.

Annabelle hesitated, then ran inside, heading to the bedroom to remove a layer or two. The material of her dress was thick white cotton, held around the middle with a pink sash. She was worried without her stay she would look shapeless and the dress would hang off her petite frame like a sack, but once she had divested herself of her petticoats, chemise and stay and regarded the look in the mirror she couldn't honestly say she noticed much difference. She did feel lighter, though, and less trussed up. Downstairs she hesitated as she went to grab a bonnet to keep the sun from her face and then decided against the one with the veil attached. She was growing used to Leo's eyes on her and it wasn't as though there were many other people around.

'Ready?' he asked as she re-emerged.

'Ready.'

By the time they reached the beach Annabelle was sweltering and she wondered if she would have been better staying in the shade by the cottage, but as they neared the sea a soft breeze started to blow up. It was only gentle, but just enough to move the air around them so it didn't feel quite so unbearable.

'I'm going to paddle,' she announced, knowing full well Leo wouldn't join her. Her husband wasn't as tense as first impressions would indicate, but she knew there was no way he would pull off his boots and paddle his toes in the sea with her. She decided it didn't matter, she was going to do it anyway.

'The rocks will be slippery.'

'I'll be careful.'

'You could cut open your foot.'

'I've been paddling on rocky beaches for my entire life.'

Sitting down on a large rock, she began to pull off her boots and stockings, glad to wriggle her toes in the fresh air. It would feel blissful to dip her feet in the cool water even for just a few minutes. Carefully she gathered up her skirt, holding it at mid-calf-level. Not so high as to be viewed scandalous, but high enough it shouldn't get soaked by the seawater. Not that there was anyone else on the beach to judge.

Feeling Leo's eyes on her, she picked her way over the rocks to the sea and found a flat rock to stand on, sighing as the water lapped at her toes. It was heavenly. A day of scorching hot weather and nothing could cool her down quite like a dip in the sea. She had a hankering for one of the secluded coves at Birling View where she and Beth would often go and swim as children, wearing only their shifts and shrieking at the icy water as they went in, but soon forgetting their initial protests as they swam and dived and laughed.

'How is it?' Leo's voice made her jump, he was standing closer than she imagined, just out of the reach of the gentle waves.

'Glorious. Are you sure I can't persuade you to join me?'

'I do not paddle.'

'Why not?'

He considered the question, as if it were the first time he had been challenged on one of his behaviours.

'I never have,' he said eventually. 'At least not since…'

She knew what he meant without him having to say it. Not since his parents had died.

'I insist. I won't have you missing out any longer.'

'Annabelle…'

Deciding to ignore him, she pulled him by the hand to the same rock she had sat on and crouched in front of him to unlace his boots. They were hard to tug off and she almost went sprawling across the beach when the first one came loose. Leo's hands shot out to steady her and she smiled up at him. With the other boot deposited on the rocks she slipped her hand into her husband's and together they picked their way to the water's edge.

'Don't tell me that's not refreshing.'

'I have to admit it isn't a bad sensation on such a hot day.'

'And nothing terrible has happened just because you've decided to dip a toe in the English Channel.'

Leo grumbled something incomprehensible, but Annabelle could tell he was enjoying himself. The frown on his face was relaxing and he gripped her hand with his as if happy to be sharing this moment with her.

They carefully moved a little deeper, so the water was at ankle height, Annabelle adjusting her hold on her dress to avoid it getting wet from the spray. She saw Leo glance down at her bare calves, but he didn't say anything and Annabelle refused to feel anything but wonderful freedom paddling in the sea.

'Thank you,' she said quietly after a few moments of enjoying the sun on her face and the water between her toes.

'What for?'

'For taking me away from my old life. If you hadn't proposed to me, I would be stuck in that cottage in Eastbourne, running around after my mother. Instead I'm here.'

Next to her Leo shifted uncomfortably and cleared his throat. Annabelle fought the urge to roll her eyes at her husband.

'If you tell me one more time that this isn't how our lives will normally be, I swear I might scream, Leonard Ashburton,' she said quickly.

He looked at her for a long moment and then laughed. 'I suppose I have been being a bit over the top.'

'Just a little. If I promise never to fall in love with you and never to expect you to spend all your time with me, do you promise to stop reminding me what sort of marriage we agreed upon?'

'That sounds like a fair deal.'

'Good.' She grinned and, feeling more light-hearted than she had for a long time, brought her foot down in the water and splashed him. 'Now I know you're not the sort of gentleman to retaliate.' She looked him squarely in the eye and splashed him again.

He looked down at the water splatters on his trousers and she held her breath as she waited to see how he would respond. When he brought his own foot down in the water to splash her, she felt something lighten inside her. She cried out as the water flew up her legs. It was refreshing, but cold all the same. Dancing away, she kicked out and splashed him again, dodging backwards and enjoying the rare sight of a broad grin on her husband's face.

Annabelle hiked her skirt a little higher, not caring that her knees were exposed, then leaned down and used her hands to splash out at Leo. As she stood back up she felt her feet slipping on the rock she had positioned herself on, sliding forward and out from underneath her. In a desperate attempt to keep her balance she dropped her skirts, instantly feeling the weight of the water as they became sodden. Leo reached out for her, gripping her hands, but it was too late. With a big splash she fell into the sea, landing on her bottom and pulling Leo off balance so he landed half on top of her.

For a moment neither of them moved and then to her surprise Leo burst out laughing. His laugh was contagious and soon Annabelle was giggling away, too, unable to move from the sea, her hands slipping on the wet rock every time she tried to push herself up, only to collapse again in a fit of laughter.

Only when they did finally fall silent did

Leo seem to realise their position. His legs were pressed against hers in the most intimate manner and one hand was on her hip. For a long moment his eyes came up to meet hers and Annabelle felt certain he was about to kiss her. She felt her lips open instinctively, ready to welcome him, even though she'd never been kissed before. When he shifted away from her she felt a crushing disappointment.

'Let me help you,' he said, his voice gruff. He managed to stand, his trousers clinging to his legs and buttocks as he moved out of the water, and Annabelle couldn't help but stare. Strong hands pulled her up, helping her to find her feet. 'That was refreshing at least.'

Annabelle couldn't find the words to reply. She was still stunned by her response to him. Despite his conventional manner she had gradually grown fond of her husband over the last few days together and she couldn't deny he was an attractive man, but her response when she thought he might kiss her had shocked her. She was ready to welcome him, to pull him to her and never let go.

'Shall we head back to the cottage?'

She nodded, taking his arm when he offered it to help her over the rocky beach. As they pulled on their shoes before ascending the narrow path on the cliffs she kept reliving the moment and felt herself blush. For a second she had thought he wanted to kiss her, she had forgotten her appearance, the way her scars made people's stomachs turn.

'Ready?'

'Yes,' she said, following him up to the clifftop. As they started to stroll back across the fields Annabelle felt some of her equilibrium returning. Leo was quiet and it allowed her to reason with herself, telling herself it was only natural she be drawn to Leo. He was the first person other than her sister or mother she had spent a substantial amount of time with and he was looking out for her in his own way. It was likely she had just mistaken gratitude for something more.

Halfway back to the cottage they slowed as a group of four men started heading towards them. They looked hot, filthy from a day working in the fields, and as soon as she saw them Annabelle's heart sank. She hated that she responded like this to people, hated that her experiences had taught her to think the worst of men she didn't know, but they were loud and rowdy and she knew their eyes would soon fall upon her face.

Wishing now she had worn her bonnet with

the veil, wishing she had anything to hide her face behind, she looked down, hoping they would just walk on by without saying anything cruel.

As they passed the men fell silent and Annabelle felt their eyes on her. They said nothing directly to her and did not start speaking again until they were almost out of earshot, but still she heard snippets floating on the late afternoon breeze.

'Did you see those scars?'

'Wonder what happened?'

'Wouldn't show my face.'

She bit her lip to stop herself from reacting and dipped her head even lower, meaning to pick up her pace and get back to the cottage as quickly as possible.

'Annabelle,' Leo said softly, stopping and waiting until she stopped with him. 'Don't listen to them.'

'I'm not.'

'They don't know what they're talking about.'

'I really am not bothered, Leo.' It was a lie, of course it was a lie. Over the years she had become accustomed to people whispering behind their hands about her, giving her second glances as if trying to work out what had happened to mar her otherwise pretty face. Even though she had barely mixed with anyone except her mother and sister and the few servants left at Birling View in the past few years, there had always been someone who had slipped past her defences. The farmer who owned the land next to theirs visiting to enquire about a lost sheep, the boy who had come to sweep their chimneys, even the dressmaker her mother had brought to the house years ago when they could still afford new dresses. All of them had stared and then looked away in embarrassment, and then, when they thought she wasn't looking, stared again.

'I can see it in your eyes,' he said, taking a step closer to her, his hand coming up and resting on her cheek without the scars. 'I can see the hurt and the pain.'

'I'm used to it,' she said, trying to shrug off his concern. She *should* be used to it by now, should be stronger than this.

'You shouldn't have to be used to it.'

'People aren't going to change, become more sensitive, no matter how much I wish it. It is I who needs to change.'

'No,' Leo said, his fingers moving ever so subtly on her cheek. 'Don't change.'

She took a shuddering breath and looked up

at him, feeling herself lost in the deep brown of his eyes.

'You're a beautiful woman, Annabelle, and anyone who can see only the scars is a fool.'

For a moment she felt beautiful, seeing herself reflected in his eyes, and then he stepped away, leaving her once again unkissed and again completely confused. When he offered her his arm she felt like screaming, like begging him to tell her exactly how he felt. Only a few hours earlier he'd been trying to keep her at arm's length, then the afternoon had passed in such a fun, companionable time, and then there were the moments on the beach and again just now where she would swear he had looked at her as though he wanted to kiss her. But he hadn't and now they were walking back in silence to the little cottage where they would share a bed, but not touch. Annabelle wasn't sure whether to laugh or cry.

Chapter Fourteen

Dear Josh,
Sometimes I wish I had your way with
words. To be able to reassure Anna-
belle with just a sentence or two...that
is powerful.

'Lord Wilstow and his wife have invited us for dinner,' Leo said, fingering the note and glancing up at Annabelle. She had been quiet since their brush with the young men who had looked at her with such horrified fascination, but he had been too lost in his own confusion to draw her out. He'd meant it when he'd said she was a beautiful woman. When he looked at her he barely saw the scars, he noticed instead the bright blue of her eyes, the curve of her lips as she smiled and the way the sun glinted off her hair making it look like molten gold. All throughout their acquaintance he'd been aware of those features, but suddenly it was as if he *saw* her for the first time. His body had reacted to her and he'd had the urge to pull her towards him and kiss her until neither of them knew where they were.

'We should go. They've been so kind giving us the use of this cottage.' He heard the trepidation in her voice and wondered what it would be like to always dread meeting new people. He wasn't one to socialise a lot, but he never had to feel nervous about it when he did so. Wherever he went he was welcomed, people wanted to talk to him, to be part of his circle, more than he wanted often, but he didn't worry about what people would say about him. He knew he was seen as serious and aloof, but that was how he portrayed himself, and he certainly didn't mind being thought of that way.

Annabelle had spent years shut away at Birling View, first by her mother who was ashamed of having a daughter so scarred, and then by herself when she realised how cruel the world was to someone who didn't look quite like everyone else. Gradually she was becoming more comfortable in his company, eschewing the veil most of the time if she thought it was just going to be the two of them. He wanted to make her feel comfortable enough in herself that she didn't care what other people whispered behind their hands and could walk down the street with her head held high, ignoring the stares.

'We don't have to go if you don't want to.'

She took a deep, shuddering breath and shook her head. 'No, we should go. I'm sure it'll be a pleasant evening.'

'I don't know his wife, but Wilstow is a good man. A kind man.'

She nodded and gave him a slightly forced smile.

'They can give us some tips on what to do for the rest of the week.' It surprised him that he wanted to stay for so long. He'd been non-committal initially on how long they were going to stay for, but he didn't feel the need to rush back to Kent. With a shake of his head he marvelled how he was actually enjoying the honeymoon he'd never planned to take with the wife he'd never intended to spend any time with.

'I'll ride to Kimmeridge and get Michaels to deliver a note to Wilstow,' he said. 'Do you want me to bring your maid back here to help you get ready?' They would be tight for time, but he didn't want to rush her when she was clearly so nervous about going. If she wanted an hour with the maid, dressing her hair and choosing the perfect outfit, then he wasn't about to take that from her.

'No, I can get myself ready. I always used to help Beth when she was going to a dinner party or a dance.'

'Did she help you?'

'I never had occasion to need it.'

Leo regarded her for a moment, a ridiculous thought crossing his mind. 'This isn't the first time you've been invited for dinner, is it?'

'Yes. I mean I went to London for Beth's wedding, of course, and we had dinner there, but I've never been invited to dinner by anyone else.'

No wonder she looked so nervous.

'You really never went out while you lived at Birling View.'

'Not at all. I never left the confines of our estate save to take the track down to the nearest beach when I was younger to swim with Beth.'

He sat back in his chair and tapped his fingers on the arm.

'We really don't need to go if you would prefer.'

'I'm your wife now. I am aware we will not

be socialising together much going forward, but I am sure there will be a few occasions when I need to be able to comfortably converse with your friends.'

He hadn't really considered it. The future seemed hazy and uncertain to him. When he had first had the idea to propose to Annabelle he had thought they would lead completely separate lives, interacting only every few months when he returned to Five Oaks. Now he didn't have visions of them waltzing through London ballrooms together, but he was finding he enjoyed her company more than he ever thought possible. It wasn't too hard to imagine spending companionable evenings with her sitting by the fire or mornings on horseback showing her the estates he ran for his great-uncle. His mind threw up a picture of more intimate pursuits, of lazy mornings spent in bed together and long afternoons under the covers.

Quickly he stood, forcing himself to think of something else, anything else. He was happy that he was becoming fond of his wife, that they could spend enjoyable time together, but he didn't want to desire her and, more than that, he didn't want to ever fall in love with her. He truly believed love was more trouble than it was worth. Everyone he had loved he'd lost and he knew he never wanted to experience the heartbreak of losing someone he loved again.

He had the urge to turn around and take Annabelle into his arms, to whisper that she would fit right in tonight. More than that—she would shine. Instead he clenched his fists to keep his arms by his sides and stepped away, moving to the table to pen a quick reply to Wilstow.

An hour and a half later Leo was sitting on the bench in the little cottage garden, enjoying the peace of the summer's evening. The air was still, the silence complete except for the twittering of a few birds. He realised for the first time in a long time he felt content. He hadn't thought of his great-uncle or his responsibilities for over a day which was a record for him—normally his duties of running the estates occupied at least part of his brain at all times. It was a beautiful evening and he felt at peace with the world.

'Do I look acceptable?'

He hadn't heard Annabelle come up behind him. She moved so quietly and gracefully he often didn't know where she was by the sound of her footfall alone, but this time she had completely surprised him. Slowly he turned and allowed his eyes to rake over her.

His wife might not have attended many social events in the past, but she certainly knew how to dress correctly for the occasion. She had chosen a deep red silky dress with a delicate lace trim around the neckline and short sleeves. A simple necklace made up of a gold chain and a single pearl hung around her neck and she had matched it with pearl drop earrings. Her hair was swept back and pinned into place and instead of the veil he knew she wished she could hide behind she had pulled loose some strands and curled them so they bounced in front of her ear and obscured at least some of the scar on her left cheek.

'You look more than acceptable. You look lovely, my dear.'

Annabelle was unable to stop her fingers drifting to her cheek, trying to cover the scarred skin, and Leo paused a moment and wondered what his wife's life would have been like if that single incident, that single moment where she had climbed the shelves and pulled the vase on top of her, hadn't happened. In all likelihood she wouldn't be here with him, she probably would have had her debut with her sister and would be searching for a suitor to enrapture.

'I wasn't sure about a veil,' she said, looking at him with a quiet pleading in her eyes.

Leo stepped towards her, aware he needed to handle this carefully. 'You look lovely without the veil. I prefer you without it. I like to be able to look into your eyes and see you looking back at me. I like to see you smile and laugh and even frown—' he paused, taking her hand '—but I do not want this evening to be uncomfortable for you. If you would prefer to wear a veil, then I would not begrudge you it.'

Silently she considered, her eyes searching his, seeming to check for the truth of his words.

'I will leave it behind,' she said, her fingers digging into his hand.

He was about to say something more, but at that moment the carriage arrived from Kimmeridge to take them to Lord and Lady Wilstow's residence.

'Shall we?'

Annabelle nodded nervously, not saying a word as they settled back on to the seats of the carriage and it moved away, their little cottage, their little sanctuary, disappearing from view.

Chapter Fifteen

Dear Beth,
You would be so proud of me, attending
a dinner party all without the comfort of
my veil. I do have to admit to curling my
hair so that it hung carefully over one
cheek...nevertheless it is progress!

Annabelle felt sick as they stepped out of the carriage twenty minutes later in front of a grand house with a pair of footmen in pristine livery welcoming them. Her hands were shaking and she felt as though she might bring up her lunch and embarrass herself even more. Carefully she arranged the curls that hung down over her cheek, wishing now she had brought the veil. She had felt it would be an embarrassment to Leo, but now she just wanted something to hide behind.

As the door opened she wondered how many ways she could make a fool of herself tonight. Leo had assured her it would only be them and Lord and Lady Wilstow in attendance, but she didn't doubt the Wilstows had many friends and tales of Leonard Ashburton's strange wife would soon reach the ears of the *ton* in London.

'Ashburton, it's been too long.' A large, affable man grinned and he shook Leo's hand with vigour. Annabelle warmed to him immediately, he had a friendly, open face and a smile that seemed to welcome you in. Beside him stood a petite woman, dwarfed by her husband and even smaller than Annabelle herself. She was strikingly beautiful with copper-red hair and perfectly symmetrical features. Her eyes though, unlike her husband's, were cold and flicked over Annabelle as if assessing her, before freezing on the scars on Annabelle's cheek.

'Meet my darling wife,' Lord Wilstow said, gripping Lady Wilstow about the shoulders and presenting her as if she were a fine piece of art for their appreciation.

Leo bowed over her hand and murmured a greeting and Annabelle caught a glimpse of the man her husband must be in society. She knew he preferred the quiet life in Kent, but he did attend the balls and dinner parties in London. He knew how to greet people, how to behave, it was as natural to him as riding a horse. Suddenly she felt very unrefined.

'May I introduce my new wife, Lady Annabelle.'

Lady Wilstow's eyebrows shot up on hearing Annabelle's title. Lord Wilstow was less perturbed and took Annabelle's hand in his own as if they were old friends.

'Delighted to meet you, Lady Annabelle. We never thought Ashburton would ever settle down, it is wonderful to meet the woman who persuaded him.' As Lord Wilstow pulled her into the house and out of the shadows he caught sight of her scars. 'Good Lord, what happened to your face, my dear?'

Annabelle froze, her mind completely blank, her tongue feeling as though it were attached to a heavy weight, unable to move. She felt her cheeks start to redden and knew with horror soon her blush would make the scars look even more angry just as everyone was looking at them.

'A childhood accident,' Leo said brusquely, 'Nothing more. Now, are you going to show me this house of yours?'

Surreptitiously Leo gave her a squeeze on the arm as he passed and Annabelle felt herself relax just a little as if he had grounded her.

'Why don't we leave our husbands to catch up?' Lady Wilstow said, her voice sweet and syrupy, but still there was the coldness in her eyes. 'Come through to the drawing room, dinner will be about twenty minutes, we can get to know one another in the meantime.'

Annabelle forced herself not to reach out and grab Leo, not to look at him with pleading in her eyes. She was now a wife, not just a recluse, and she would have to get used to people close up. She felt Lady Wilstow seemed aloof and was sure she had glimpsed a cruel streak, but she was very aware she didn't have anything to set a standard of behaviour by. Perhaps all wives of the *ton* acted like Lady Wilstow, perhaps it was expected of them. Feeling completely out of her depth, Annabelle allowed her new companion to lead her into the drawing room.

It was still light outside and as yet the candles hadn't been lit. The drawing room was opulent without being garish and Annabelle had to admit it was a comfortable room to be in. The chairs were upholstered in creamy white material, contrasting beautifully with the golden gilt frames dotted around the room and the golden fixtures. Glass doors were thrown open, giving unparalleled views of a neat garden and a glimpse of the sea beyond that. It was a beautiful house in a beautiful position.

As she sat Annabelle felt her body shift without her thinking so her scarred cheek was turned away from Lady Wilstow.

'You have a lovely house, Lady Wilstow.' It seemed as safe a subject as any and she hoped they might be able to keep on such mundane topics until Leo and Lord Wilstow reappeared.

'Thank you, Lady Annabelle. It was in such a state when I first arrived, I've spent years on updating the decor to something more modern, something more tasteful. Lord Wilstow is a darling man, but he had no idea about how to decorate a house.' Lady Wilstow's lip curled as she leaned forward to confide this last piece of information. 'Of course I *much* prefer to spend my time in London, but Lord Wilstow insists we spend at least some of the summer months in the country and it isn't as though there is much going on in the capital at this time of year.' She cocked her head and regarded Annabelle for a moment. 'What are your plans for the upcoming Season? Will you be in London?'

Annabelle hesitated for just a moment, but she could tell Lady Wilstow picked up on her uncertainty. 'We haven't finalised our plans yet.'

'Of course, a lot of husbands *do* go to London without their wives, you shouldn't feel too bad about it.'

'Mr Ashburton prefers country life,' Annabelle said, looking down at her hands, wondering how this woman she didn't know had been able to make her feel completely insignificant in a couple of sentences.

'How did you meet? Your wedding will be the talk of the town once word gets around. The elusive Mr Ashburton finally settling down.' Lady Wilstow peered at her intently as if trying to work out what Annabelle had that numerous others didn't.

'Mr Ashburton is a family friend,' Annabelle fibbed. 'And his brother married my sister a few months ago.'

'Ah, yes, I remember. The dashing younger Mr Ashburton—he set a few hearts racing while he was in London. Hasn't he returned somewhere hot and uncivilised?'

'India. Hardly the end of the world and I think they are just as civilised as we are.'

Lady Wilstow's eyebrows shot up at Annabelle's gentle rebuke and Annabelle swallowed, realising her mistake. The woman sitting next to her clearly didn't like to be challenged.

'So tell me, what happened between you and Mr Ashburton? I hear it was rather a rushed marriage.' It was rude and both she and Lady Wilstow knew it, but Annabelle felt a sense of calm descend over her.

'Mr Ashburton proposed, I accepted. Once that had happened we had the banns read, but didn't feel the need for a lengthy engagement like many do.' Lady Wilstow flushed and Annabelle felt a little pang of remorse, but that soon evaporated when her companion flashed her teeth in something akin to a smile.

'You'll have to forgive me for all the questions, but it is a slightly unusual match. All the ambitious mamas and well-connected fathers were pushing their daughters in his direction, but he eschews the popular choices for someone who has never spent a Season in London.'

Annabelle let the words hang there, wondering if Lady Wilstow would realise how rude she was being if Annabelle gave her time to digest her own words.

'I suppose you are the daughter of an earl, but still I wouldn't have put money on the delectable Mr Ashburton settling down with someone so unknown.'

Thankfully she was saved from having to say any more by the return of Leo and Lord Wilstow. The men were deep in conversation, both looking serious, but Leo broke off when he saw her expression and crossed the room to her side.

'Is something amiss?' Leo murmured as he joined her, leaning in close so their hosts wouldn't hear.

Annabelle wanted to tell him how uncomfortable she felt, how much she wished they could just leave and never have to see the prickly Lady Wilstow again, but instead she forced a smile and reassured him. 'Everything is fine,' she whispered, feeling completely off balance by the evening so far.

Taking a deep, steadying breath, she focused again on Lady Wilstow, redoubling her effort to be the perfect guest, the perfect illusion of the perfect wife. She didn't want all of society talking about her, partly for her sake, but also for Leo's. He shouldn't have to be embarrassed by his choice of wife, so it was her duty to be as normal as possible, to not let on this was her first social experience outside either of their families.

'Dinner is ready, my lady,' a footman said, leaning down to speak quietly into Lady Wilstow's ear.

'You're just in time,' she addressed her husband and Leo. 'Shall we go through to dinner?'

The dining room was just as beautifully decorated as the drawing room, the dark wood furniture complementing the wood-panelled walls and a table that could easily seat thirty. Their places were set at one end, with Lord Wilstow taking the seat at the head of the table with Annabelle to his right and Leo to his left. Lady Wilstow took the seat next to Leo's.

'How are you finding the cottage?' Lord Wilstow asked as they settled into their seats and a delicate salmon and beetroot dish was placed in front of them.

'The setting is wonderful, thank you for the use of it.'

'I know it's small, but perfect for a honeymoon, eh? Last thing you want is servants fussing around you, disturbing the intimacy.'

Leo murmured in agreement and Annabelle felt her cheeks flush and looked up to see Lady Wilstow's eyes on her, curious and probing.

'That's what I always wished we'd done for our honeymoon, something cosy and private. Instead we stayed in this huge hotel in

Brighton. There was no peace, we hardly had any time just for us.' Lord Wilstow winked at his wife who steadfastly ignored him, spearing her fish with her fork and lifting it to her lips.

'I hear you're from the seaside, born and bred, Lady Annabelle. How does my beloved Dorset compare to your Sussex?'

'It is beautiful, Lord Wilstow. I love my home—' she faltered, catching herself as she remembered Birling View was no longer her home '—where I grew up. There is something striking about the South Downs, about the white cliffs and the rolling green hills that back them...' She paused and smiled at her host shyly. 'I didn't expect to like Dorset as much as home, but there is something dramatic and striking about it in a completely different way to Sussex.'

'Well said, Lady Annabelle. You grew up just outside Eastbourne, did you not?'

'Yes, on the cliffs between Eastbourne and Seaford.'

Out of the corner of her eye Annabelle saw Lady Wilstow lean in to Leo and place her hand on the table next to his, just so her fingers brushed against his.

'My husband could talk about the coast for hours.'

Leo glanced down at her fingers aligned with his own and after a moment moved his hand away abruptly.

'It's not only the views, although they are spectacular from here all the way down to Lyme Regis, but for the past few hundred years they have been digging all manner of creatures from the rocks. The big museums think they are the preserved bones of creatures from thousands of years ago.'

Across the table Lady Wilstow let out a soft but still audible sigh.

'My darling wife thinks I'm quite mad, of course, but I think there's nothing more thrilling than getting down among the rocks, having a good old look at what can be dug out. So far I've only found fragments, but one day I hope to find something completely intact.'

'You always were fascinated in natural history, Wilstow.' Leo smiled. 'I visited the area when I was a boy and I can remember finding a few fossils then.'

'The richest pickings are further down the coast, near Lyme Regis and Charmouth, but I have found a few little bits and pieces, the odd witch's finger or snakestone, right here on the beach in Kimmeridge Bay.'

'We'll have to keep our eyes open.'

'I'll show you my collection later, so you know what to look for.'

'Enough about your rocks, my dear,' Lady Wilstow interjected abruptly. 'You forget that our guests are newly married. I would personally love to hear about the proposal and the wedding.'

Lady Wilstow looked expectantly from Leo to Annabelle as Annabelle pushed her beetroot around her plate. She knew if Leo told their hosts now it was purely a marriage of convenience with no emotion involved in the proposal or wedding, then she would be known for ever as the wife he didn't care for. It might be the truth, although she knew he had softened towards her the last few weeks, but she felt a hot flush of shame at the thought of everyone knowing she had only been chosen because Leo thought her expectations of married life would be low.

'I've known Lady Annabelle's family for a long time,' Leo said slowly and Annabelle felt some of the tension seep from her as he caught her eye and gave her the quickest of winks. 'But when my brother married her sister we renewed our acquaintance.' He smiled and shrugged, 'We realised we suited each other very well, very well indeed, so I asked Lady Annabelle to marry me.'

'Was it terribly romantic, Lady Annabelle? They say the quiet ones are often the most romantic.'

'Don't bombard the poor girl, Letty,' Lord Wilstow said, shaking his head in apology.

'*Every* woman loves talking about her engagement, Wilstow,' Lady Wilstow said, a hint of contempt in her voice. 'So tell me, Lady Annabelle, how did he propose?'

Annabelle considered for a moment, then returned the false, sickly sweet smile her hostess was bestowing on her. 'It was more romantic than you can ever imagine. Picture a pretty cottage garden, filled with summer flowers, a sea breeze rippling through the air. We strolled arm in arm for a while and then my darling husband led me to a bench and outlined all the reasons we should be together, all the reasons we couldn't live without one another.'

Across the table Leo choked on his beetroot, taking a gulp of water to wash it down. Lady Wilstow was regarding Annabelle suspiciously, her eyes flicking between Leo and Annabelle as if she wanted to challenge them, but knowing it would be too rude even for her.

'You look surprised, Mr Ashburton, surely you remember your own proposal?'

There was a long pause and Annabelle wondered if Leo was going to expose her as a liar.

'Of course, I just didn't realise my wife remembered all the details. We were so excited, you understand.' He delivered the comment in a voice that hinted at none of the emotion he spoke of, but it was enough to shut Lady Wilstow down.

'And the wedding?'

'An intimate affair. Just our close families and a couple of friends. Wilbersmythe was there—you remember Wilbersmythe from Cambridge?' He addressed his friend and Annabelle breathed a sigh of relief as the two men took over the conversation, reminiscing about friends and acquaintances from their university days. It allowed her to enjoy the main meal in relative peace, although she felt Lady Wilstow's eyes on her every so often, assessing and judging, trying to work out how Annabelle had ended up married to a man like Leo.

You are the daughter of an earl, she told herself. She had every right to be here, every right to marry Leo. A few scars and a slightly awkward social manner didn't detract from the fact this was the life she had been born into, even if she hadn't been raised for it. She just needed to keep reminding herself of the fact.

'Shall we retire to the drawing room?' Lady Wilstow asked as the footmen whisked the empty dessert plates away. 'Leave the men to their brandy.'

Knowing the evening was almost over, Annabelle inclined her head graciously and followed her hostess from the room. As she rounded the table Leo reached out and took her hand.

'I won't be long,' he murmured and for an instant Annabelle believed the lies she had told earlier in the evening about what she and Leo meant to one another.

'I'm surprised Mr Ashburton has agreed to brandy,' Lady Wilstow said as they settled once again in the calming cream and gold room. 'When we were on honeymoon Lord Wilstow barely let me leave the bedroom.' She chuckled, but there was little mirth in the sound and Annabelle wondered why she resented her husband so. It was apparent in the little gestures, the annoyed looks. It would be easy to think that Lady Wilstow was just unpleasant and would dislike anyone, and her husband seemed on the surface completely the opposite. In addition, Leo seemed to be a good judge of character and he liked this man, but she was aware no one knew what went on behind closed doors in a marriage.

'We have all the time in the world,' Annabelle said, surreptitiously checking the clock. It was just beginning to get dark outside, the sunset late in the evening at this point in the summer. She wished they were sitting on the little bench in the cottage garden, enjoying the sunset together, rather than here making small talk with the Wilstows.

'Will your main residence be in Kent? I know Mr Ashburton has the house in London...' Lady Wilstow sipped at the strong coffee a maid had brought in soon after they sat down.

'I'm not sure what our plans are yet.'

'You haven't had a Season in London before, have you? I'd remember.'

Lady Wilstow's eyes flicked to Annabelle's scars and she had to grip the handle of the coffee cup hard to stop her trying to cover them.

'No.'

'But your sister did. That is how she met the other Mr Ashburton.'

'Yes.'

'Is there a reason you didn't accompany her for the Season? You must be of age, otherwise you wouldn't be married to Mr Ashburton...'

There had been so many reasons she hadn't spent the last few months of the previous Season in London with her sister. Mainly, though, it hadn't even been a consideration. Annabelle didn't leave the estate. Therefore her mother had never even considered taking her to London.

If only you could see me now, Beth, she thought, smiling to herself. Beth had always urged her to go out, to join her at one of the local dances or dinner parties. She'd worried Annabelle was shutting herself away, denying herself a future. In the few short months since Beth had left Annabelle had said goodbye to her beloved family home, got married and now was socialising, pretending she had been doing this all her life.

'If I'm honest, I prefer country life. A Season in London never appealed.'

'That will have to change now. Unless you plan to live separately from your husband, of course.'

'As I said we haven't finalised the details.'

'Some men do prefer it that way. The obedient wife at home, looking after the house and children, then the men are free to do what they like with whomever they like while they are in London.'

Annabelle tried not to react. The thought of Leo keeping a mistress in London made her feel sick. She knew he didn't have one at present, but despite their wedding vows she wasn't going to be the one keeping him warm at night. It wasn't unfeasible that he would search out a mistress when he returned to London.

It shouldn't matter, but Annabelle realised with a jolt that it did. She might have gone into this marriage knowing it was a convenient way for them both to get what they wanted, but that wasn't all it was now. She was starting to care for her husband, to want to share her life with him, not live completely separately. Annabelle acknowledged, too, the attraction she felt for Leo, even though nothing would ever come of it.

She was saved from having to say anything more to the odious Lady Wilstow by Leo reappearing in the doorway.

'Are you happy to head back to the cottage?'

She tried to hide some of her enthusiasm, but sprang from her seat with such vigour she knew it would appear rude.

'Wilstow has described a shortcut through the woods. If you fancy a stroll back to the cottage, it should be no more than half an hour. I thought we could go while there was still a little light. Just say if you would prefer the carriage.'

'A walk sounds just perfect.'

'Good. Then we must take our leave, Lady Wilstow. Thank you for your hospitality.' He turned to his friend and shook his hand, Wilstow clapping him on the back.

'Enjoy your honeymoon and I'll see you in London in a couple of months.'

Chapter Sixteen

Dear Josh,
What is it about walking through the
woods on a moonlit night?

The sky was a wonderful palette of pinks and reds, holding on to the last of the light of the setting sun. The moon was already out—a pale yellow circle that looked almost full.

'Did you have a nice evening?' Annabelle asked as she slipped her hand through his arm.

'It was good to see Wilstow again. How about you? Was it as bad as you imagined?' He watched her as she screwed up her face while formulating her reply.

'Lady Wilstow was a little…confrontational. She clearly couldn't see why you would marry me when by her account you had women falling over each other to impress you in London.'

Leo scoffed and shook his head. 'I would hardly say they were falling over themselves.' Annabelle looked at him with interest in her eyes, so he continued. 'I suppose I was considered a *good catch* by the matriarchs of society, I received all the coveted invitations, had mothers pushing their daughters at me, but you know my reputation. I'm seen as cold, aloof. The young women themselves often didn't want to spend more than a minute or two in my company before one of us was making an excuse to get away.'

'You're not cold.'

'I am aware of my personality faults.' He shrugged. He knew it was inevitable after the way he had been raised. 'Have you ever met my great-aunt, the woman who raised me, Miss Culpepper?'

'No, although I know Beth visited her with you and your brother that one time.'

'She's regarded as a dragon by society and she's not much better in private. My upbringing after my parents died was not warm or loving, but I was clothed, fed and educated.'

'It must have been hard for such a young boy to be brought up like that, all alone.'

'Yes.' He shrugged, feeling Annabelle press in closer to him for warmth as the sun finally dipped beneath the horizon. 'I honestly think my life would have been much different, that I would be a different person, if Miss Culpepper had taken in Josh as well, if we'd been kept together.'

'It must have made saying goodbye to him for a second time really difficult.'

Leo nodded, remembering embracing his brother for the last time on the docks in London before he boarded the ship for India a few months ago. His leaving this time hadn't been unexpected, Josh had always planned to return after only a short visit to take up his place running the shipping and transport company, taking over from his guardian, Mr Usbourne. Still, even though it was planned it didn't mean it didn't hurt any less.

'I loved him fiercely when we were boys. We did everything together.' He shook his head and smiled, remembering the happy times when he and his brother had been part of a family. 'When he came back I felt at ease with him immediately, something that doesn't normally happen. Even though we'd spent twenty-five years apart, communicating by unreliable letters that had to survive a journey halfway around the globe, I felt as though I knew him, as though he understood me perfectly.'

'Have you written to him?'

Leo gave a self-deprecating smile. 'Probably more than I should. They're not even around the cape of Africa yet and I've written at least six letters.'

'I write every week, sometimes three or four times.'

'You must miss Lady Elizabeth very much.'

'I do. For all of our childhood we were the best of friends—I suppose she was my only friend really. We did everything together and she never made me feel bad for wanting to stay inside, to stay hidden away. She would try to persuade me out, try to tell me it didn't matter what I looked like, but when I said no she would just adapt her plans and make sure she told me all about it afterwards.' Annabelle sighed. 'She's the best person I know and I want her to be happy, I think she will be happy with your brother, they seem perfect for one another.'

'They do,' Leo agreed. He'd seen the attraction, the love between Josh and Lady Elizabeth even before his brother could admit it to himself.

'Beth was always so selfless, so generous. And I would never begrudge her happiness, but sometimes I do wish she was still here, that she could have married Josh but stayed here so I could have her in my life. I feel awful for thinking that way, I know this is her adventure, something she has always wanted to do, but I feel it all the same.'

'It's not selfish—you love your sister so wanting her in your life is natural.'

Annabelle paused and looked up at him, her eyes searching his.

'Do you think? I just want her to be happy, but I wish she could be happy near me.'

'Look at us—' Leo laughed '—pining for our siblings, hating being the ones left behind.'

They strolled in silence for a few minutes, taking the path into the woods that Wilstow had described to Leo earlier in the evening. The path underfoot was dry and clear, but difficult to see in the darkness where the moonlight was obscured by the trees. Once or twice Annabelle stumbled and Leo brought her closer to him to better steady her.

He was surprised to feel so easy in her company, to be able to admit how much he was hurting from losing Josh for a second time. Normally he kept everything very tightly bottled up inside and it felt liberating to have someone to share it with. Annabelle understood only too well what it was like to wave goodbye to the person you cared about the most.

'I remember about four years ago, when Beth was just starting to attend the local dances, she would come home every evening and tell me minute by minute what had happened and who had danced with whom. Even though she must have been exhausted she would pull me into her arms and she would show me all the steps just so I could feel a part of it.'

'I forget sometimes that you have never attended a ball or a dance.'

'I used to lie in bed once we finally collapsed as the sun was beginning to rise and pretend it was me who had gone out and danced and laughed and enjoyed the evening.'

'Have you ever danced with anyone but your sister?'

'No.'

Leo paused, knowing he was heading down a reckless path, but not wanting to stop. He was enjoying being with his wife, enjoying her company, enjoying *her*.

'Come over here.' Quickly he led her into a small clearing, surrounded by trees, but the space in the middle was covered only with grass and the moon shone down from above.

'What are you doing?'

'It may not be a ballroom, but dance with me here.'

'Here?' She laughed, but he could see her eyes searching his in the darkness, wondering if she dared accept.

Leo felt his heart soar as she stepped forward into his arms and he held her gently, guiding her in the steps of a silent waltz. A couple of times she faltered, but a gentle pressure on the small of her back and she was twirling around their makeshift dancefloor. Every so often her body would brush against his and Leo felt pulses of desire run through him. She looked stunning in the moonlight, the silver rays glinting off her hair and her eyes shining with happiness. He had the urge to pull her closer, to bring her body to his, to lean down and kiss her.

He could tell by the way she looked up at him she felt it, too, although as always her expression was tempered with a hint of disbelief. Annabelle never felt good enough for anything, even her husband's desire, and he wished he could make her see there was so much more to her than just the scars from a childhood accident.

Round and round they spun, Leo hearing the

music from a thousand ballrooms in his head, though none of the dances he'd shared in any of those felt anything like this.

Finally they paused, in the middle of the clearing, their bodies close and Leo's arms wrapped around Annabelle. They were both breathing hard from the exertion and as they caught their breath Leo reached out and tucked a stray strand of hair back behind Annabelle's ear, letting his fingers linger for longer than was needed, feeling the velvety softness of her neck beneath his hand.

'Thank you,' Annabelle said. 'That was the best dance of my life.'

'It was my pleasure. I didn't know I enjoyed dancing so much.'

His fingers traced down her neck and then cupped her cheek and Leo knew he was going to kiss her. It felt inevitable, as though the last few days had been building to this moment.

Slowly he leaned in, seeing the disbelief in Annabelle's eyes, knowing the only way to make her believe was to actually kiss her.

Her lips were soft and sweet, and he had to hold himself back, to make himself kiss her tenderly, reminding himself it was his wife's first proper kiss. He felt a rush of desire as her lips parted, welcoming him in, and her body melted into his.

Gently he ran his hand down her back, pulling her ever closer and in a moment of clarity he wondered why he had waited so long for this.

It was so hard to pull away, to look into Annabelle's eyes and see how she responded to him, but he didn't want to force anything, to overwhelm her. There was confusion in her expression, mixed with disbelief, but overshadowing all of that was desire. She looked bereft as he pulled away, reaching out as if to hold him to her, and Leo happily obliged. He kissed her harder this time, feeling her hands come up and tangle in his hair, her body firm and insistent. The image of tumbling Annabelle to the ground right here in the clearing came into his mind and refused to leave, but Leo held back, enjoying the kiss instead.

When they came apart neither said anything and Leo could see Annabelle needed a moment to work out what had just happened. He felt the same. Somehow he'd gone from wanting to keep his distance to wanting to spend his entire evening kissing his wife in a very short space of time. There was something enchanting about Annabelle, something that reeled him in and made him forget all the reasons he didn't want to get close to anyone.

'I'm confused,' she said eventually.

'Me, too.'

They looked at one another and then Annabelle smiled shyly. 'Thank you for the dance,' she said and then reached out for his hand. 'And for the kiss.'

Leo was distracted watching her mouth as she formed the words, unable to focus on what she was saying and instead just wanting to kiss her again. He knew he needed to think about his actions rationally, but for once he just wanted to follow his heart, to satisfy his desires. With great effort he offered her his arm and they continued through the woods, walking in silence until they emerged from the trees into the open fields.

They had gone a little off course, but out in the open Leo could just see their little cottage in the distance. It would be a twenty-minute walk along the cliffs before turning inland for the stroll back to their cottage.

As they started along the cliffs Leo could tell Annabelle wanted to say something to him, but was trying to find the words. When she was running through something in her head she often wrinkled her nose and furrowed her brow, making her look younger and completely innocent. Patiently he waited for her to work out the right way to phrase things, enjoying being with her on such a warm summer's night.

'Did you kiss me out of pity?'

Leo stopped abruptly, shocked by her question.

'Don't be ridiculous.'

'It's not ridiculous. I'm trying to work out why you kissed me. I know you danced with me out of pity, because I've never danced with a man before. I think it is fair to assume you kissed me for the same reason.'

'I wouldn't kiss you just because I pity you.' He turned to Annabelle, waiting until she looked up from the ground and met his eye. 'Do I come across as a man who would do something like that out of pity?'

'You're a good man, whatever you think of yourself. A caring man.'

'I don't think kissing a woman because you pity her is a good or caring thing to do.'

'I'm just trying to understand.'

'What is there to understand? I danced with you because I wanted to and I wanted to give you that experience. I kissed you purely because I had the overwhelming urge to kiss you.'

'Oh. But…'

'No protestations. I know exactly why I kissed you.'

'You can't have wanted to.'

'Why not?' He should have felt amused that she was trying to tell him what he did and didn't feel, but instead he felt a deep unease, that Annabelle wasn't going to be able to see that he did find her attractive.

Without speaking she gestured broadly at her face and Leo felt a pang of sorrow for his wife. For so many years her mother had treated her like a damaged piece of furniture, hiding her away, teaching her that she was second-best. No wonder she didn't think anyone could see past her scars. Her own mother, the person who was meant to love her unconditionally despite any flaws, hadn't been able to—why would she expect any more from anyone else?

Taking a deep breath to slow down his thoughts and calm his voice, he reached out and took both of her hands in his own.

'When I look at you, do you know what I see?'

She shook her head.

'I see your beautiful eyes, the way your face lights up when you smile, the way you frown when you concentrate. All the little details that make you unique.' She was looking at him as if she didn't quite believe him. 'Of course I see your scars, they are part of you, but it isn't *all* that I see. In fact, it isn't much of what I see.'

Annabelle opened her mouth as if to say something, but then closed it again without uttering a word. He could see the glint of tears in her eyes and realised she had probably never heard a compliment from anyone other than her sister before.

Standing on tiptoe, she stretched up and brushed her lips against his in the gentlest of kisses, pulling away after a couple of seconds and watching him warily to see if she had overstepped. Leo felt the desire surge inside him and suddenly it felt more important to show his wife how beautiful he found her, how desirable, than to maintain his stance on keeping his distance.

Folding her into his arms, he kissed her, this time not holding back. His hands slid from her neck to shoulders to back, making her moan with pleasure as he pulled her to him.

'Let's get back to the cottage,' he said, wanting to be back at their lodgings before sense returned and he changed his mind. Silently Annabelle nodded and hand in hand they began to run across the fields.

Out of breath, Leo kissed Annabelle against the door of the cottage as he fumbled for the key, both of them tumbling inside laughing as the door finally gave way. They landed on the floor and Leo kicked the door shut behind him, then focused on the woman underneath him. Even in the darkness he could see she was flushed and breathless, her chest rising and falling quickly both in anticipation and from the exertion. As he kissed her again he felt her hips push up instinctively, brushing against him, and he felt the wonderful coil of anticipation start to unravel.

Quickly he pulled her to her feet, both of them half stumbling up the stairs in their haste. In the bedroom they didn't bother with candles, the moonlight streaming in through the window enough to allow them to undress. Leo tugged at the fastenings of Annabelle's dress, hardly able to wait to push it down over her shoulders. It felt as though he'd been waiting for this moment for so long, as if it had been inevitable even though his conscious mind hadn't wanted to admit it.

'Help me,' Annabelle said, her voice ragged as she wriggled from the dress. Underneath she wore a ridiculous number of layers for the hot weather, but Leo was determined now and soon had pulled off everything except the last layer of cotton chemise. He slowed, taking a step back to regard his wife, her eyes shining with anticipation, her body almost trembling with nervous energy.

Ever so gently he ran a hand over the cotton, feeling the warm skin underneath, savouring the anticipation of what was to come. He felt Annabelle press towards him, moving her body underneath his hand, and he felt a thrum of desire as his fingers danced over her breasts, catching on her nipples. Looking into his eyes, Annabelle gripped the hem of her chemise and pulled it off over her head and then his fingers were on skin and she was gasping beneath his touch.

As he teased and caressed Annabelle worked on loosening his cravat and lifting his shirt off over his head. When her fingers slipped into the waistband of his trousers he let out an involuntary groan and he saw her smile in the darkness, enjoying the effect she had on him.

He kissed her, tumbling her backwards on to the bed and then beginning to explore her skin with his lips, trailing kisses down her neck and across her collarbones before grazing his teeth across her nipple and making her arch her back and beg him for more.

Leo lost track of time as he kissed and caressed, slowly working his way down his wife's body, wanting to know every inch of her skin. He loved the way she gasped and moaned as he touched her, loved the way she pressed into him as he teased bit by bit.

'I want you, Leo,' she murmured and Leo knew he couldn't hold back much longer. Lifting himself on top of her, he pressed in gently, using all of his self-control to inch forward, waiting for her to meet him before pushing all the way in. He looked down at his wife and wondered why he hadn't spent all of the honeymoon doing this, why he had wasted so much time, then she pushed her hips up and they found a perfect rhythm.

As Leo felt his climax building Annabelle tensed and cried out underneath him and that was enough to send Leo over the edge. For a long moment he held himself above her. Then, as she reached out and looped an arm around his waist, he fell on to the bed beside her and without thinking pulled his wife in to his chest.

They lay there in silence for a long time, Leo feeling an unfamiliar satisfaction. Tonight he would not think about the consequences of what they had just done, he would not think about how this had changed their relationship irrevocably. Tonight he would just enjoy the warm glow of happiness he felt surround him and the feel of his wife's body pressed against his.

Chapter Seventeen

*Dear Beth,
I never imagined anything could feel this
good.*

Annabelle woke gradually, first aware of the
brightness in the room and the warmth of the
sun on her face. As she opened her eyes she
became aware of Leo's body next to her, one
arm flung possessively across her waist, the
sheets covering his lower half only just pre-
serving his modesty.

Immediately she remembered the events of
the previous evening. The waltz in the woods,
the kiss and then the second kiss on the cliff-
tops that had led them back here and the frenzy
of their desire for one another as they had tumbled into bed. She couldn't quite believe it and
if it wasn't for Leo lying completely naked next

to her she might have thought she had dreamed the whole thing.

As she tried to keep completely still Annabelle felt a flutter of nerves in her stomach. Leo had been clear in his desire the night before, had even told her he found her beautiful, but what if he regretted it in the light of day? He'd told her so firmly that theirs would not be a physical relationship, yet here they were, having spent a wonderful evening together. She didn't want him to regret it, didn't want him to push her away and return to the distant man she had first known.

'I'm falling for you,' she murmured ever so quietly. It was liberating to acknowledge the truth out loud. She had been trying to fight it these last few days, but she was finally ready to admit she was falling in love with her husband. There was so much more to him than the formal, cool-mannered man the rest of the world saw. He hid his kind and caring side by trying to keep his distance, but when he drew you close he was thoughtful and considerate.

'Good morning,' he said as he opened one eye. 'Good lord, that's bright. Did we forget to close the curtains?'

'I think our minds were on other things.' Annabelle felt her heart pound in her chest as she waited for his reaction and felt a flood of relief when he grinned at her.

'More important things.'

He stood, not seeming to notice his nakedness, and crossed to the window, pulling the curtains across. The room was still bright, but the glare of the early-morning sun was gone and Annabelle could open her eyes fully. She watched as her husband walked back across the room, seeing him completely naked for the first time in the light.

She felt the start of a blush as he caught her staring and raised an eyebrow. Shifting under the sheet to pull it closer around her, she felt the first fluttering of hope. He didn't seem regretful or ashamed of what they'd done the night before. If anything, she thought he was looking at her as though he would like to repeat it.

'Good morning, Lady Annabelle,' he said as he joined her in bed again.

'Good morning.'

'Did you sleep well?'

'It was the best night's sleep I've had for a long time.'

'Clearly sharing a bed suits us.'

'Clearly.'

He traced a finger down the bare skin of her

arm, the only part of her except her face on the outside of the sheet.

'I could go and see what we've got left for breakfast,' he said, not making any effort to move. 'Or…'

'Or?'

'We could spend a little longer in bed.'

Annabelle couldn't control the smile that blossomed on her face and reached out hesitantly to pull Leo towards her. They kissed and touched, and Annabelle felt like screaming out with desire when Leo moved on top of her. As he looked down she tried to turn her face away so he wouldn't be able to see her cheek with the scar.

'Stop,' he said ever so gently, using one finger to tilt her chin so her head was squarely in the middle of the pillow. 'I don't want you to turn away from me while we're together. You have nothing to be ashamed of.'

'You don't want to have to look at my scars.'

'I want to look at you. All of you.'

They made love slowly, taking the time to enjoy one another even more than they had the night before, and when they had finished Annabelle cuddled into Leo's chest, trying to stop herself from building her hopes for the future too high.

'What would you like to do today?' Leo kissed her on the top of the head and stroked her back with his fingertips, sending shivers of pleasure through her.

'I don't mind. It looks like another glorious day.'

'I was thinking we could ride down the coast, head towards Charmouth or Lyme Regis, the places Wilstow was talking about last night.'

'The places where they've found those fossils.'

'Yes. What do you think? They had a few examples in one of the collections when I was at university in Cambridge and I can remember the beach at Lyme Regis from when I visited as a child. It was fascinating.'

'I think it sounds like a wonderful idea.' Annabelle felt her heart soar. She wouldn't have cared what they did today—her main fear was that in the cold light of day Leo would regret the intimacy of the night before and return to being distant and formal with her. Instead, here he was suggesting they spend the whole day together while holding her in his arms.

'We might have to find somewhere to stay over. I'm not sure if we will make it there in one day.'

'I'm sure there will be somewhere we can stay.'

'Michaels should be here soon with fresh food from the village. I will send him ahead to Lyme Regis with the carriage, that way if we wish to return back here in the carriage that will be an option.'

'I hope he brings something good for breakfast. I'm ravenous.'

He grinned at her and then kissed her. Annabelle cuddled in tighter, wondering how she could preserve this moment, preserve this feeling. She still didn't quite believe it was real.

Annabelle must have dozed because she woke to hear Michaels knocking on the door of the cottage and Leo gently extricating himself from underneath her, shaking his arm where she must have been sleeping on it.

'I'll go.' He pulled on his trousers from the night before and descended the stairs, disappearing out of view. Annabelle stayed where she was for another minute then got up, pulling on a simple cotton dress for now, not wanting to don her heavier riding habit too early in this heat.

'We have fresh bread and jam,' Leo said, gesturing to the delicious-smelling loaf sitting on the little table. 'And Michaels is going to saddle up the horses for us and then ride ahead with the carriage. He'll make enquiries about somewhere to stay in case we decide to reside in Lyme Regis for a night or two.'

'Perfect.'

They sat down to breakfast together, enjoying the crusty bread and sweet jam and Annabelle wondered if she could freeze her life right now in this moment. She wanted everything to stay exactly as it was. Soon they would have to have a discussion about what their future held and she was scared that Leo's vision might not match her own. Hopefully they might get a few more days of happiness before any decisions had to be made.

An hour later they were ready to depart. It would be a long ride along the coast, but there was no rush. If they didn't make the whole journey in one day they could stop at Weymouth or another little coastal town and continue on tomorrow. Michaels had taken a change of clothes and some personal items in the carriage and Leo had put their lunch in a saddlebag on his horse.

For the first half an hour they rode in companionable silence, enjoying the varied coastline, both lost in their own thoughts. Annabelle was reflecting on how different her life was from the one she'd imagined for herself just a couple of months ago. Then she couldn't see a way out of the drudgery and frustration of living with her mother, always at Lady Hummingford's beck and call and always having to listen to her venting her frustrations about her lot in life. She felt a little guilty for leaving her mother behind and once they were settled back in at Five Oaks she would think about arranging a visit, but if she were completely honest she was enjoying a few weeks without the constant criticism and intrusion in her life.

They had stopped for a late lunch, allowing the horses to rest and enjoying the peace of the warm afternoon. Annabelle hadn't spent a whole day in the saddle before, despite her love of riding, and her muscles felt sore and stiff as they ate their little picnic. Leo, seeing her wince as she shifted position, instructed her to lie down on the blanket and after checking there was no one else around rubbed the back of her calves and thighs until she felt the muscles relax and the tension release from them. She wished they were somewhere more secluded, somewhere Leo would be able to lift up her skirts without the risk of being seen, but for now she had to be content with enjoying the massage.

The sun was getting low in the sky when they reached Weymouth and they decided to stay overnight, finding a pretty little inn on the outskirts with rooms to spare.

The next morning they rose early with the plan of pushing on to Lyme Regis and hopefully having some time to enjoy the little village before the end of the day.

'Tell me more about your holiday to Lyme Regis when you were a boy,' Annabelle asked as they spotted the little village in the distance. It looked quaint, picturesque, with the buildings huddled around the seafront and the sun glinting off the water.

Leo smiled at the memory, taking a moment before he started speaking, and Annabelle had the impression he was just enjoying thinking about the happy times. It felt premature, their emotional relationship was so fresh and new, but she hoped one day she could help him build more happy memories.

'Our holidays were always the most anticipated event of the year. My parents would pore over maps and books about the English seaside or beauty spots. It would be months in the planning.'

'Were you involved?'

'Very much so. My mother would sit with us at bedtime and show us the pictures in the books of the places we might go. Josh and I would give our opinions and then the decision would be made.'

'It sounds as though your parents loved to travel.'

'They did. Before I was born they did a tour of Europe together. They went as far as Greece and were planning on hopping on a boat and exploring further, but my mother fell pregnant and they decided to return home.'

'I can't imagine a life like that,' Annabelle said wistfully. She'd read about the world in all its glory in numerous books in the library at Birling View, spending hours looking at the beautifully drawn atlases and taking in all the details of traveller's accounts and local traditions. Often she'd had to share those books with Beth, who she knew dreamed of travelling the world and writing about her experiences. Annabelle's dream had been a little more sedate, she'd wished just to see more than the confines of the estate and to have someone to share her travels with.

'They planned on taking Josh and me abroad when we were a little older. They talked of travelling to Egypt and perhaps even further afield.'

'Have you travelled much?'

Leo grimaced. 'Not as much as I had hoped to as a young man. First there was university and then Lord Abbingdon wanted me to take on more and more responsibility with the running of the estates. I took two short trips to Europe a few years ago, one to Paris, the other to Rome, but even though I arranged adequate supervision of the estate managers while I was away Lord Abbingdon griped about it for months and it rather took the shine off.'

Annabelle regarded her husband with curiosity. She had assumed that he was free. He was a man, wealthy in his own right and the heir to one of the richest men in England. Soon he would have a title and a place in Parliament, too. Despite all this he was still not free to do what he wanted. He had responsibilities, people relying on him, and a deep sense of duty. She wanted to suggest they might take a trip together one day, but couldn't summon up the courage. Only a few days ago he'd still been proposing they lead completely separate lives—she didn't want to jeopardise what progress they had made by moving too quickly.

'So, Lyme Regis?'

'It was Josh's choice. We had this huge book about the south coast and there was a picture of the bones of some ancient creature that had been found in the rocks. He liked the look of it and begged for us to go there that summer. We spent hours on the beach searching for curios, Josh came back with quite a collection.'

'I'm excited to see this beach I've heard so much about.'

'We can head there this afternoon. I think at low tide you can walk for miles, although never having lived by the sea I get a bit apprehensive when the consequence of getting it wrong is being dashed against the cliffs.'

They reached the outskirts of the village, heading down the main street for the inn, advertised by the swinging sign hanging from the side wall.

'The Stone and Shell,' Annabelle read out, looking at the freshly painted inn with brightly coloured flowers planted in neat borders outside.

'Looks perfect.'

Leo arranged a room and found Michaels who had arrived the day before with the carriage. His valet took over getting the horses looked after and Annabelle went to change, keen to be in some fresh clothes after the long hot ride. She chose her lightest dress of white cotton with a light pink ribbon around the middle. It was simply cut with the bodice part shaped and tighter and the ribbon sitting directly below her breasts, then the rest of the dress falling away into a long, straight skirt. There were no frills or ruffles or anything to add weight and therefore heat to the dress.

Leo changed, too, shrugging off his jacket and even rolling up the sleeves of his shirt. He looked happy and relaxed and Annabelle wondered if they could stay on honeymoon for ever. She wanted desperately to broach the subject of their life together when they returned home, but was afraid the answer might not be what she hoped for. Instead she resolved to just enjoy the moment, enjoy this unexpected bubble of happiness.

Chapter Eighteen

> Dear Josh,
> How can a mere few days change your
> life? I fear thinking about the future as
> everything has changed and it seems so
> fragile, so precarious.

Annabelle was quiet as they strolled through Lyme Regis arm in arm, enjoying the gentle hustle of people on holiday and locals. It was low tide and there was a wide stretch of beach visible with a few couples walking in the distance on the foreshore and some children playing in the sand. The back of the beach was rocky, covered in fallen stones and boulders from the cliffs behind, but the sand further down looked soft and beautiful.

'Would you care to go down to the sea?'

'That would be lovely.'

They walked in silence, Leo glancing at his wife every now and then wondering what was troubling her. She'd seemed so happy, so content on the ride over, and he wasn't aware anything had happened to change that.

'This is glorious,' Annabelle murmured, turning her face up to the sun. He realised she was wearing just a normal bonnet, not one with a veil attached. In fact, she hadn't felt the need to wear the veil at all for the last few days. He was surprised at how happy that made him feel, especially as she didn't seem self-conscious as they walked on the sand. He hoped she was finally realising not everyone would stare and, even if people did, it didn't matter as long as she knew she was beautiful.

'Let me show you where we used to search for fossils when we came on holiday when I was a boy.'

Leo took her hand and pulled her along the beach, feeling more carefree than he had done in years. It was liberating to have a few days away from his responsibilities, but more than that he hadn't realised how much he had missed having someone to share the little moments with. Of course he could have come to stay in Lyme Regis or any other seaside destination on his own, but it would have felt hollow, lonely. With Annabelle by his side he had someone to show the things he enjoyed, to discuss the day's events with and perhaps even to reminisce in years to come.

At the thought of the future he felt some of his excitement fading. He didn't want to think past these next few days. Here on honeymoon he could see how he and Annabelle fitted together, but when they returned back to Kent, or, even worse, London, he couldn't imagine how their lives could be. He'd never planned to allow Annabelle in, to make her an active part of his life. When he had pictured the role of a wife before they were married he'd thought of her running the house at Five Oaks, perhaps hosting the occasional local family if she was comfortable with it. They would pass one another, barely needing to interact, both happy in their solitude.

That clearly wouldn't work now. He couldn't go five minutes without wanting to touch her, to see her smile, to hear her opinion on something or other. Even so, he couldn't imagine her slotting into the life he must lead. It wasn't what he had promised her when he proposed and he wasn't sure how to go about discussing the changes.

'Look, can you see at the bottom of the

cliffs, where some of it has crumbled and broken away?' Leo pointed, deciding to push all thoughts of the future from his mind and just enjoy the here and now for a few more days. 'That's where you find the fossils. They get washed from the cliffs or fall with the rocks as the cliffs get battered by the sea and weather.'

'I'm not sure what I'm looking for.'

They came away from the water's edge, heading back towards the cliffs, both with their eyes cast downwards, looking for anything unusual.

'Here,' Leo called out after a few minutes. He bent down to pick up the half of a spiral. 'It's a snakestone, or at least half of one. Josh used to have hundreds of fragments all laid out on his chest of drawers in our bedroom.'

He handed it to Annabelle, who tested its weight in her hand, running her fingers over the ridges.

'When you find a complete one it is very impressive.'

'It looks like an ancient snail shell.'

'You're right.'

They continued their search, Leo picking out a few examples of witch's fingers and snakestones before his eyes fell on the glint of fairy's money.

'Josh always wanted to find one of these,' he said as he wiped the little stack of star shapes with his finger, gently trying to dislodge the mud.

'You'll have to give it to him as a gift,' Annabelle suggested.

Leo nodded, although he didn't know when he would see his brother again. The fossil was too delicate to send in a package.

'Perhaps one day…' he said, but caught himself. He'd just been about to suggest one day they might be able to make the trip to India. It was a long voyage and he doubted he would be able to leave his responsibilities for some time yet, but one day maybe he would be able to find someone he could leave in charge for a while and take the trip to see his brother. Even though it was something he wanted dearly, he stopped himself from saying any more. Who knew how he and Annabelle would be living in a couple of years' time? It would be cruel to promise her a trip to see her sister and then not go through with it.

Annabelle sensed his hesitation and sighed, sitting down on a sizeable rock a little distance from the cliff.

'I think we need to talk, Leo,' she said quietly,

biting her lip and showing just how nervous those words made her.

'What do you want to talk about?'

'About us, about what we're doing here. About our future.'

'Do we need to? We've only been married a few weeks, everything is still fresh, still malleable—do we really need to decide on everything right now?'

Annabelle regarded him for a long moment and then shook her head. 'You're right,' she said with a tight smile. 'Of course you're right. Let's just enjoy what we have.'

He knew it was not fair on Annabelle, his not wanting to discuss the future. He held all the cards, was the one who ultimately would make all the decisions. If he decided to carry on as he had initially planned, living a life separate to Annabelle, then she would have no choice in the matter. Equally, if he proposed they live a more conventional married life, sharing their time, allowing them to care for one another, it would be him leading that.

Leo blew out a deep breath. He couldn't deny he was starting to care for Annabelle. He enjoyed her company, desired her physically and keenly anticipated every moment they spent together. For the first time in a very long time he actually felt happy, but lying underneath that, creeping to the surface, was a tendril of doubt. It was when he allowed himself to care for someone that their loss was much harder to bear. He'd told himself over and over he didn't want to love someone again, didn't want to put himself in that precarious position. He glanced across at Annabelle. She was young, healthy, there was nothing to say he was going to lose her, but life had taught him it wasn't only the old and infirm who were taken away from him.

'I'm sorry,' he said. 'This is all very new to me. I never expected any of this. I suppose I'm still adjusting, but you are right we need to discuss things. Perhaps tonight, over dinner?'

She nodded and squeezed his hand and together they continued their amble along the beach. Leo was lost in thought, trying to work out exactly what it was he wanted from his wife, aware that it wouldn't be fair to agree to one course and then want to change yet again further down the path.

'Mr Ashburton.' Leo heard his name being called from a distance and both he and Annabelle spun, squinting into the sun to see Michaels hurrying towards him.

'Michaels, what is wrong?' He knew it must

be something serious. His young valet was an excellent judge of when was and wasn't appropriate to disturb Leo and he wouldn't follow him on an intimate walk without good reason.

'There is some news, sir. A letter arrived a few minutes ago—the rider has been chasing us around Dorset, by all accounts.'

Leo took hold of the proffered letter, recognising the handwriting of Mrs Westcott, his great-uncle's longstanding housekeeper. With a heavy heart he opened it and read the short note.

'Lord Abbingdon is dead,' he said, feeling a flicker of guilt that he hadn't been there at the time of his great-uncle's passing. 'He took a turn for the worse a week ago and passed away soon after.'

Annabelle was immediately by his side, taking the letter from him as he shook his head in astonishment. His great-uncle had been an invalid for a long time, bed bound for almost two years and weak of body for much longer than that. Even so, it had seemed as though the old man would go on for ever.

'Do you need to sit?' Annabelle asked, her voice gentle.

He shook his head. He was shaken, but he felt no real sadness and that was a shock. Lord

Abbingdon had never been a particularly pleasant man and they had always focused on discussing business matters when Leo visited. Even so the old man had been part of Leo's life for a long time—surely he should feel some emotion at his passing?

Not knowing what else to do, he reread the letter, the words blurring in front of him as he tried to process the enormity of the moment.

'I need to get back to Kent.'

'Of course. We'll head back straight away.'

'The rider is waiting at the inn in case you want to send any reply, sir. I took the liberty of buying him lunch, but he is ready to depart at a moment's notice.'

'Thank you, Michaels.'

He felt Annabelle's and Michaels's wary eyes on him and wondered if he was behaving strangely. In truth, he felt numb, dazed, as if he were in a half-sleep, stumbling through the world.

'Let's get you back to the inn,' Annabelle said, her hand on his arm, guiding him.

'Yes. Good idea.'

They walked in silence, Michaels hurrying ahead to start readying the carriage and Leo silently gave thanks that he had decided to bring the carriage on their trip and not just rely on the horses they rode. It would mean they could set off straight away and not worry about stopping as much.

As they hurried along the beach he felt some of the initial panic leave him. In truth, he had been preparing for this moment for a long time. Lord Abbingdon had first handed over the reins of running everything from the estate accounts to dealing with the tenants' issues seven years earlier and, as time passed, Lord Abbingdon's input had become less and less as the old man's body had started to fail him.

They were just walking back along the short promenade to the inn when Leo was hit by another memory. Hidden and suppressed for so long, but so painful that it almost made him cry out as he remembered it.

'Leo?' Annabelle was looking at him with concern. He must have made a sound after all.

'I'm fine,' he said, not wanting to share the memory. It was just too painful. The news of another death, all those years ago. He and Josh already in pieces with the news of their mother's death just a few days earlier, petrified when their kindly housekeeper had drawn them to her and whispered that she was so sorry, but their father had gone to join their mother in heaven.

He felt his heart rip anew in his chest, felt the pain of the loss all over again. It was so raw, so real, that he struggled to breathe.

'Sit,' Annabelle commanded, pushing him to a bench. He took great gasping gulps of air, his head spinning.

'Slow down, just breathe normally.' Her voice was calm and instructive and he couldn't help but obey,

'That's it, nice and slow. In and out.' Her hand made circles on his back, rubbing round in one direction, then the other. The memory of finding out both his parents had died had taken him by surprise, suppressed for so long in his subconscious. It made him remember the pain of the loss, the horror of mourning, of feeling as if he would never be whole again.

'I'm not whole,' he murmured.

'Pardon?'

He just shook his head, closing his eyes as some of the panic and crushing emotion receded.

'I'm sorry,' he said stiffly when he had recovered enough to speak.

'Please don't apologise. You've just had a shock.'

He couldn't bring himself to explain that it wasn't Lord Abbingdon's death that was affecting him, that his pain and panic were resurfacing from years earlier, over two decades ago. It sounded ridiculous, he was a grown man, not a little child missing his mother and father.

'We should go.'

He stood up, offering Annabelle his arm out of habit, not noticing the worried look on her face as together they started back to the inn.

Chapter Nineteen

Dear Beth,
I wish I knew how to support Leo better.
He's been so quiet and withdrawn since
the news of his great-uncle's death.

Annabelle had never been so happy to see a house as she was to set eyes upon Five Oaks as they swept up the drive. The journey had been exhausting even though all they had done was sit in the carriage for days on end. Sensing her husband's agitation over how long the return trip was taking, she had urged him to make the stops shorter and even push through the night last night. She had dozed in the carriage, waking up with a stiff neck and cramp in her legs and felt as though she had been walking for days on end rather than sitting doing nothing.

Leo had been oddly quiet and she felt as

though they had lost much of the closeness they'd shared on honeymoon. It made her feel so sad and fearful for the future, but she kept telling herself that it was just circumstantial. Once he had sorted the practicalities and started to mourn his great-uncle then surely there was no reason for them not to return to the happiness they had found in the last few weeks.

He jumped down before the carriage had even rolled to a stop, striding inside and letting a footman hurry forward and help her down from the carriage. Mrs Barnes was waiting at the threshold to welcome her with a friendly smile and to usher her into the drawing room.

'I thought you might have travelled through the night,' she said, leading Annabelle to a chair by the window. 'I've told Kitty to make a cup of tea and I'll organise some toast and jam. You must be exhausted. Will you want to go straight to bed after some food?'

'I wouldn't mind a bath,' Annabelle said, touching her hair and face. Everything felt heavy from the toils of travelling and she wanted to wash any grime away before climbing between the sheets of her bed.

'Very good. We will set to heating the water and I'll send Kitty in when it is ready.'

'Thank you.'

Annabelle sat back and closed her eyes when Mrs Barnes left the room, thankful the housekeeper was so friendly and organised. She was almost dozing off when she heard Leo's voice in the hall, although couldn't quite make out the words. For a moment she deliberated, wondering whether to go and join him, to see whether he was a little more settled now he was home, but before she had even got out of her seat she heard the front door being opened and footsteps on the drive. In surprise she looked out of the window and saw Leo already mounting his horse and riding off without a backward glance.

Something shrivelled inside Annabelle. She had been afraid it would be this way anyway—even before their early recall due to Lord Abbingdon's death Annabelle had been worried about how their newfound closeness might suffer when they were back in a familiar environment. She knew it was easier for Leo to let go of any preconceptions of what their relationship should be when it was just the two of them in their own little world. Now real life was beckoning again, and her husband had just ridden off without even thinking of telling her where he was going or when he might return.

'Here's your tea and jam, my lady,' Kitty said as she came into the room with a smile.

'Thank you, Kitty.' Annabelle swallowed, wondering if it was too embarrassing to ask the maid if she knew where Leo had gone. 'I don't suppose you know where Mr Ashburton is heading?'

'Sorry, my lady, I don't. Michaels will probably know if you'd like me to ask him?'

'Will you send him in here?'

'Of course.' Kitty bobbed and hurried out the door, and a moment later Michaels entered.

'Kitty said you wanted to see me.'

'Mr Ashburton left in a hurry. I wondered if you know where he was going?'

'He wanted to head straight to Willow House, to make the arrangements for Lord Abbingdon's funeral and make a start on sorting through the documents needed for the next few weeks.'

'Did he give any indication when he might return?'

'He said he wasn't sure. He has a change of clothes and all his essentials at Willow House, seeing as he stays there so frequently, so he doesn't need to come back before nightfall, but past that I don't know.'

'Thank you, Michaels. You must be exhausted, too, after the journey. Please feel free to rest this afternoon.'

'That's very kind of you, my lady.'

When she was alone again Annabelle closed her eyes and tried not to let the maudlin thoughts overcome her. Leo was entitled to be shaken by the news of Lord Abbingdon's death. He had told her he was not close to the man, but he had spent much of the past decade by his side, running one of the wealthiest estates in England. Even if they did not share confidences and closeness Lord Abbingdon had still been a big part of Leo's life. None of it had to mean he had changed his mind about her, about their relationship. She had to give him space to mourn, to put his thoughts in order. Had to ensure she was there, quietly supportive, but not pushy or overwhelming.

'Don't fade into the background,' she murmured to herself, knowing she was all too good at that. Stepping back, being unobtrusive. It would be easy, but it wouldn't get her the life she wanted.

No, she would make sure Leo remembered

the strength they could draw for one another, how they were better together.

Leo buried his head in his hands and let out a low groan of frustration. He was exhausted. After travelling for four days solidly with barely any stops his body had been ready to do something more active, but instead he had ridden straight to Willow House and now he'd been sat at this desk for almost five hours straight.

Even though he had been running the estates for the last few years there was a lot to get in order. Two solicitors had been waiting for him on his return and, before he had sat down with them to discuss Lord Abbingdon's will and the practicalities of the inheritance, he'd had to send word to the relevant parties to arrange a funeral. Lord Abbingdon had been dead for just over a week so the funeral was a pressing matter, especially in the summer heat. Luckily Mrs Westcott had anticipated what needed to be done and had all but arranged the practicalities of the funeral to happen the next day, but he had to confirm the details.

Now he was finally alone, sitting with his eyes drooping and a deep desire to collapse into bed.

For the first time since their return to Kent he thought of his wife. He'd left Five Oaks without even saying goodbye or letting her know how long he'd be gone. Leo knew he'd been distant on the journey home as well. It was unfair on Annabelle, but he'd been unable to force himself to act any differently.

His great-uncle's death had shaken him more than he cared to admit. The old man had been cantankerous and rude, but he was still family, still had been part of Leo's life for a long time. Leo had worked hard for him, taking on more and more responsibility, but the old man had recognised it and even though he had never voiced his thanks he had made sure Leo had a comfortable home and a good income.

At first Leo had thought he wasn't mourning his great-uncle, that they weren't close enough for that, but as the days ticked by he realised he felt a sorrow at the old man's passing. It made him realise that he hadn't shut himself off from emotion as much as he had thought.

That worried him. Lord Abbingdon had been old and infirm. He'd lived a good life, longer than most of his peers, and his mind had remained active even when his body was failing. It was not a shock that he had passed away and in many ways Leo had been preparing for this moment for at least two years, ever since Lord Abbingdon had stopped getting out of bed, but he felt off centre and wrong-footed all the same. It had made all the awful memories of his parents' deaths and Emily's death come crashing back and he was worried how he would cope if he lost someone he actually cared a lot for if this was how he felt when a man he respected, but didn't much like, passed away.

He couldn't deny it any longer, Annabelle was creeping into his heart. Soon she would take up residence there and the desire and regard he felt for her would merge into love. He didn't want to love her; he didn't want to love anyone. Lord Abbingdon's death had just served to remind him that life was fragile and could be cut short at any time. He would protect himself better if he shielded his heart from Annabelle.

'Too late,' he murmured, shaking his head. It might well be too late and it would be cruel to Annabelle, too, to change so suddenly. He needed to be sure, needed to decide exactly what he wanted from his wife.

He knew if he returned home she would draw him into her arms and he would push all these doubts from his mind. That might make him happy in the short term, but he would only be postponing the inevitable. He needed to make a decision and that would be impossible with Annabelle there drawing him to her.

With pen in hand he started jotting down some notes, deciding on his plan, writing it down to solidify it in his mind. Tomorrow would be the funeral. He would send word for Annabelle to attend. There he would inform her he needed to travel to London to sort out his great-uncle's affairs. He would take a week, perhaps two, to think through his predicament, before returning to Kent, hopefully knowing what he wanted from his wife once and for all.

Chapter Twenty

Dear Beth,
I wish you were here to take my hand
and tell me everything will work out in
the end.

Annabelle straightened the veil over her face, feeling as if all eyes were on her. It had been a while since she had worn one, her confidence soaring during the trip to Dorset, but the thought of standing by Leo's side with everyone at the funeral staring at her had made her feel sick and so she'd donned a veil, but now she felt like a coward.

It wasn't a bad turn out to the funeral, especially as it had been arranged at the very last minute. As well as the staff from Willow House there were a number of people from the local village. Leo had murmured that he wasn't sure if they actually knew his uncle or had just come out of respect for the old Viscount, but it was good to see the church half-full even for a man who hadn't left his bed for years.

After the short service Annabelle stayed by Leo's side as he thanked the mourners for coming, murmuring her own thanks and trying to fade into the background. She felt inconsequential, insignificant and was fast realising the idea of being a partner to Leo was nothing more than an illusion. Her presence by his side did not make his day any easier. She didn't have the social skills to guide away anyone asking difficult questions or adding to her husband's burden. On a couple of occasions she suspected he forgot she was actually there.

Once the other mourners had left Annabelle excused herself for a moment, retreating round the side of the church and leaning her head against the smooth stone. She closed her eyes, forcing her thoughts to slow down. All she needed to do was be supportive. Doubting whether she was making a difference wouldn't do any good.

'Annabelle?' Leo sounded concerned as he came up behind her.

She turned round too quickly, scraping her arms against the wall and tearing the material of her dress. Silently she cursed, but tried not to react outwardly, even though the scratch of the wall on her skin smarted and she wondered if she had grazed it.

'Are you unwell?'

'No, I'm sorry. I just needed a moment. The heat…' She gestured vaguely to the sky, hoping he would think she had been overcome by the unrelenting high temperatures rather than the realisation there was a gulf between them that she was doubting she could ever cross.

'Come sit in the shade for a moment.' He led her over to a low wall in the shade of the church and Annabelle sat.

'How are you?' she asked, peering up at her husband. He had looked blank most of the day, hardly acknowledging her presence, hardly acknowledging much at all.

'I'm fine. At least I will be once today is over. I hate funerals.'

Annabelle doubted many people enjoyed them, but for Leo she was sure it would dredge up the memories of the funerals of his parents.

'Are they always so quiet?'

Leo frowned at her. 'You have been to a funeral before?'

Shaking her head, Annabelle looked down at her hands.

'No.'

'But your father…?'

The memory was painful and she felt the tears that she had been holding back all day threaten to spill on to her cheeks.

'Died when I was fifteen. I can remember Beth lacing me into this mourning dress that was far too small for me, but there wasn't anything else appropriate and no money for any new dresses.' She paused and shook her head, suddenly angry at her mother even though so many years had passed. 'I came downstairs and my mother told me in no uncertain terms I wouldn't be going to the funeral. She sent me back upstairs.'

'She wouldn't let you attend your own father's funeral?'

'No. She said everyone would stare at me, that it was for my own good, that I had been shut away and kept a secret for too long to just appear in the church now.'

'That's cruel. Not letting you say goodbye to your father.'

'Beth pleaded with her for me, but she wouldn't be moved. She said she would arrange for me to visit the church after dark if I so wished, but that I wasn't going with them for the actual funeral.'

'Your mother was cruel.'

Annabelle let out an involuntary laugh. 'The longer I am away from her the more I realise how extreme and selfish she was. I know much of what she did was out of a desire to protect me from the taunts she thought would come my way, but I feel as though I've missed out on so much in my life.'

'There would have been better ways to protect you. She taught you your scars are something to be ashamed of, to hide away. A mother should teach you to walk with confidence, to hold your head high and realise your beauty inside and out.'

For the first time in days she caught a glimpse of the Leo she had come to know on their honeymoon and she wondered if maybe there was a way back to that. He was allowed to be shaken by his great-uncle's death. Leo had hardly any relatives and even though the late Lord Abbingdon hadn't been warm or loving towards him, it didn't mean he hadn't grown attached to the older man. Added to that were his new responsibilities that came with the land he had inherited and the title. Perhaps as things settled they, too, could return to what they had before.

'What now?' Annabelle asked.

Grimacing, Leo patted her hand. 'I need to go to London. There are some things I need to sort out. It shouldn't be for more than a couple of weeks.' He didn't look at her as he spoke and she had the sense he wasn't being entirely honest with her.

'Would you like me to accompany you?'

'No,' he said just a little too quickly. 'It'll be tedious business. Mainly meetings with my solicitor to sort out the details of the will. And it will be unbearably hot in London in this weather. You'll be more comfortable here in Kent.'

'I really don't mind.'

He leaned across and kissed her lightly on the forehead. 'It'll be two weeks, no more. You use that time to become accustomed to being the mistress of Five Oaks. I'll be back before you know it.'

She didn't argue any more, pushing away her uneasiness and instead lacing her fingers through Leo's. It wouldn't do to moan or beg, instead she would do better to remind him what there was between them.

'Can we return home, or do you have any other duties here?'

'No, all the mourners have left. I've thanked the vicar and the carriage is waiting at the front of the church.'

Arm in arm they returned to the carriage and Leo gave the instructions to take them home.

'Everything is packed, my lord,' Michaels said, picking up the trunk ready to take it from the room and store it for Leo's departure in the morning.

'Thank you, Michaels.'

'Is there anything else you need this evening?'

'No. Get some rest, Michaels. We've got an early start in the morning.'

Leo knew he should follow his own advice and retire to bed. The journey to London would take much of the day and he would need to be fresh for dealing with the solicitors he had arranged to meet in the late afternoon. Still, he felt restless, unsettled. He was acutely aware that Annabelle was just down the hall, probably with her nose in a book reading about crop rotations or Spanish royalty or the life cycle of a frog.

He desperately wanted to go to her, to fall into bed beside her and lose himself in her body. Then after they would lie side by side and talk until the small hours of the morning and all would seem right with the world.

Decisively he stood—one night in his wife's bed wouldn't do any harm. Tomorrow he would still be going to London, he would still have space to consider what he wanted from their marriage. He would have time to order his thoughts, to work out how he felt about Annabelle and whether he could allow her to infiltrate his heart as he had a suspicion she would if they spent much more time together.

The upstairs hallway was dark, but he didn't bother taking a candle, instead trailing his fingertips along the walls and counting the doors until he came to Annabelle's bedroom. Again he felt guilty for not moving her to the room that adjoined his. Perhaps after he returned from London he would broach the subject of her moving. It would certainly make nocturnal trips like this easier.

He paused just as he raised his knuckles to tap against the door. He had promised himself to stay away, to keep his distance until he had properly decided what sort of marriage theirs was going to be. It was unfair to Annabelle to tell her one thing and then not stick to it. Silently, knowing he was going to curse himself as soon as he got back to his bedroom, he dropped his fist from the door and turned to walk back along the corridor.

'Leo.' Annabelle opened the door and peered out.

'I just wanted to say goodbye. You might not be awake in the morning when I leave. I'm planning on an early start.'

She opened the door wider and even in the darkness he saw the vulnerability in her face as she looked up at him.

Without saying a word she held out a hand and waited patiently for him to take it. He couldn't resist for long, slipping his fingers between hers and allowing her to draw him into her room.

'I don't want you to leave without saying goodbye tomorrow,' she said quietly. 'I will miss you.' The statement should sound needy, the last thing he had wanted in a wife, but Leo realised that even though it was his own idea to go he was going to miss Annabelle, too.

'I will miss you, too.'

He could tell she wanted to say more, perhaps to ask him if he really needed to go or to request again that he let her join him, but she held back, instead drawing him over to her bed. For a long time they just lay in one another's arms, Annabelle trailing her fingers over his back and him kissing her forehead, her cheeks, anywhere he could reach. It felt intimate, a shift even from the languid lovemaking on their honeymoon to something deeper, but at the same time comfortable. When Annabelle moved a little and kissed him deeply he couldn't help but grin and the smile remained on his face long after their bodies were sated and they were lying pressed against one another again.

Chapter Twenty-One

Dear Beth,
Is there anywhere in the world where ma-
tricide is legal?

'Really, Annabelle, you need to take more care over your appearance. I know nothing can be done about your face, but you're getting chubby. And a short woman cannot afford to get chubby.'

Annabelle gritted her teeth and counted to ten before giving her mother a serene smile. This had to be one of the worst weeks of her life. Not only had Leo been gone for three weeks with nothing more than a brief note to explain his extended absence, but her mother had turned up unannounced four days ago and showed no sign of ever leaving.

'Shall we go for a walk, Mother?' Annabelle suggested. Anything to get out of the stifling drawing room where the only activity on offer seemed to be listening to her mother criticise her.

'I suppose a turn about the grounds would be agreeable. Not that the grounds here are very extensive.'

Standing abruptly, Annabelle bit back the reply that she was perfectly happy with the grounds at Five Oaks. Her mother had made it abundantly clear that she was not impressed with the house, the grounds, the room that had been assigned to her, the servants, the food and, probably most importantly, Annabelle. These opinions had been voiced over and over again since she had arrived.

'I wonder when you will move to Willow House. That is a much more suitable property for a viscount.'

'I don't know, Mother.'

'You should write to your husband and tell him you plan to organise the moving of your household.'

'Leo will return to Kent soon. There is no need to rush any decisions before he gets home.'

'Has he said he is returning?'

Annabelle walked over to the window and

looked out at the garden. In the three weeks he'd been gone Leo had sent her two letters. The first had been short and to the point, letting her know he had reached London safely and planned to stay for a week while his solicitor sorted the finer details of the late Lord Abbingdon's will out.

The second letter had come a week later. This had been even shorter, with no endearments or sign he thought of her as anything more than a glorified housekeeper. He told her he was staying on for another couple of weeks and he would write to let her know when he was coming back.

Since then there had only been silence. No letters, no messages, nothing. Each day Annabelle watched out for a rider, for some sign that her husband hadn't forgotten her completely the moment he set foot in London, but nothing had come. She felt stupid for feeling so lonely, so abandoned.

'Not yet, but he will,' she said with more conviction than she felt.

'I will move in with you.'

Annabelle just about managed to stop herself from shouting a deafening no to her mother and instead turned and smiled sweetly.

'You know I miss you, Mother,' she said in

her most placating voice, 'but my husband has just lost his great-uncle. This is not the time to make additional changes to our lives.'

'Nonsense. He isn't here and I doubt he's planning on returning any time soon. This is what he wanted, isn't it? A life for him in London and you in the country.'

Her mother's words struck a nerve and Annabelle realised this was what she was worrying about. A few weeks ago they'd spent a blissful few days in Dorset. They'd grown close, become lovers, but it had only been a few days. Leo had planned the details of their marriage for much longer than that. What if this trip to London was to allow him to regain some of that emotional distance between them?

Annabelle forced the idea from her mind. His great-uncle had just died, he had a lot to sort out with his inheritance, that was all.

'Even so, perhaps we can discuss it in a few months.'

'Meanwhile I'm left to rot in that ridiculous cottage in Eastbourne.'

Annabelle stayed quiet, knowing it was better not to argue with her mother and just allow her to rant when she was in one of these moods.

'It's demeaning for a woman of my status

to be forced to live in something you wouldn't force your housekeeper to reside in. I haven't been able to face my friends for weeks—what would they say knowing my daughter has left me in a place like that?'

'I'm sure your friends would be very understanding.'

'Nonsense. They would be appalled. Your husband has just come into how many properties? And I'm left in a pauper's cottage.'

Wondering where the furthest of Leo's new properties were, she didn't even feel her usual guilt at wanting to push her mother as far away as possible.

'I think I need to go and lie down, Mother. I've got the start of a headache coming on. Perhaps when Leo has returned from London we can visit you in Eastbourne and discuss your accommodation then.'

'You need exercise, Annabelle, not to lounge around doing nothing.'

Annabelle pretended she hadn't heard her mother and hurried from the room, feeling a roil of nausea as she fled up the stairs. In her bedroom she smiled wryly to herself. A married woman and she was still hiding behind her bedroom door to escape her mother.

Flopping back on the bed, she thought of the

last night she and Leo had spent here together, lying in one another's arms. When they were close, when they were touching, it was as if the barriers Leo's mind put up to stop them from being together were easy to overcome. The physical distance between them meant he wasn't remembering each day how much better things were when they were together.

'We're better together,' Annabelle murmured. She knew it was true. For a few wonderful days in Dorset she had felt truly happy, a happiness she had never thought she deserved, but Leo had given it to her anyway. It was addictive and now she was craving that same feeling again and again.

She knew Leo had felt it, too, seen how his step was lighter, his lips quicker to smile, his demeanour happier. If he allowed it, they could enrich each other's lives.

'I need to go to London,' she said to herself. The idea filled her with dread. She'd only visited London once before in her life, for Beth's wedding and then to wave her sister off at the docks. Everything had been arranged by Beth, the transport, the accommodation, and Annabelle had barely stepped out on to a street, instead being whisked everywhere in her own private carriage.

She also felt apprehensive about Leo's reaction. She would be impinging on his world, a world she hadn't been invited into. By turning up unannounced she would be putting him on the spot and he might not want to share this other part of himself with her.

With a stronger resolve than she had ever felt before she shook her head. She *would* go to London. She would remind Leo what they could have together. She would fight for the life she wanted for herself.

Knowing if she delayed too long the doubts would start to creep in, she rang the bell and waited for Kitty to appear.

'I am going to London, to join Mr Ash… Lord Abbingdon,' she corrected herself, still not used to her husband's new title.

'Yes, my lady,' Kitty said, unruffled by Annabelle's sudden announcement. 'When do you plan to leave?'

'Today. This afternoon.'

'Shall I start packing for you, my lady? How long do you plan to stay?'

Annabelle hesitated. It would depend on her reception. There was a chance Leo might catch sight of her and send her back home straight away. He wouldn't be cruel in his manner, but he would gently remind her that her place was in Kent. She felt her cheeks begin to flush at the prospect and had to tell herself it was only her suppositions. Equally he might welcome her with open arms and berate himself for staying away for so long.

'A week.'

'Will you need just your mourning clothes, my lady?'

'Pack my two black mourning dresses and the lilac one, too.'

Kitty bustled out, ready to pack Annabelle's trunk.

'Can you let the grooms know to ready the carriage?'

'Of course, my lady.' Kitty hesitated, 'What about your mother?'

Annabelle couldn't hide the grimace. She would have to speak to her mother and send her back to Sussex, even though it would not be a pleasant task. If she didn't expressly tell her mother to leave, Lady Hummingford would still be in residence when she returned and Annabelle didn't want that. She hoped to be coming home with her husband and they would want privacy when they returned, but Annabelle was also aware she might be returning home upset and she didn't want her mother seeing that either.

With a few deep breaths she balled up her courage and then hurried back downstairs to see her mother.

Lady Hummingford had the glass door of one of the display cabinets open and was inspecting a miniature statue, picking it up and running her fingers over it in a predatory fashion.

'Mother.' Annabelle smiled, trying to forget her earlier irritation with Lady Hummingford.

'Good, you're back up.' Lady Hummingford replaced the statue without comment, seemingly unabashed to have been caught so openly inspecting it.

'I have received a letter from my husband,' Annabelle fibbed. 'He has asked me to join him in London.'

'When?'

'I will leave today.'

'No, when did you receive the letter? I didn't see a rider.'

'Oh, earlier. It was placed in my room so I have only just opened it.'

Lady Hummingford eyed her suspiciously.

'You can't go to London.'

'Why not?'

Her mother gestured at her face. 'Your scars. You stay inside.'

Annabelle felt the pain and hurt from the last few years begin to bubble to the surface.

'Not any more,' she said firmly. 'Leo has been encouraging me to get out and socialise a little more.'

'Ridiculous. They will laugh at you in London, Annabelle. They will stare and laugh and talk about you behind your back.'

'They might,' Annabelle said slowly, 'But I cannot stop them from doing that. I can control how I react to them.'

'You're being stupid.'

'I'm not stupid, Mother.'

'Has Lord Abbingdon really asked you to go? I can't see he would want to show his new wife off at the dinner parties and balls of London.'

'He's in mourning, Mother. We would hardly be attending balls.'

'Even so, he will be embarrassed by you.'

Annabelle felt the familiar niggle of doubt. Somehow her mother always managed to get inside her head, managed to make her doubt herself even when five minutes ago her resolve had been absolute.

Drawing herself up, Annabelle reminded herself of Leo's words, of the way he had looked at her, of his desire to show her she was not worthless, not something to be ashamed of.

'Leo is not embarrassed by me. *You* are the only person who is ashamed of me and over the years I have allowed you to make me feel inferior, to make me feel as though I am worth less than everyone else. I may have these scars, Mother, but they do not make me any less of a person.' She exhaled and then pushed off before she could regret any of her words. 'I think it best you leave. Leo and I will not want you here when we return.'

She left her mother with an open mouth, speechless, hurrying out before Lady Hummingford could recover enough to reply.

Annabelle felt sick. She loved her mother, despite the years Lady Hummingford had kept her hidden away, despite the fact the older woman had made her feel ashamed of her appearance. There had been good times, happy memories, and she didn't want to push away her mother entirely, but she did need to make sure Lady Hummingford understood Annabelle had her own life now and would not be controlled by her mother or her fears any longer.

Quickly she hurried back upstairs, hoping she wouldn't have to see her mother again before leaving. Kitty was almost finished with the trunk and as she closed the lid Mrs Barnes knocked lightly on the door.

'I understand you're going to London, my lady,' Mrs Barnes said with a soft smile. 'What a lovely idea.'

'Yes, I know Mr Ashburton—I mean, Lord Abbingdon wasn't planning on being away so long so thought I would surprise him.'

'I have packed you lunch and the grooms know which inn Lord Abbingdon normally stops at when he travels to London. I am sure they can secure you a room. Will you want to take Kitty with you?'

'Yes, if that is acceptable to you, Kitty?'

'Of course, my lady.'

'Good. Will you want to leave immediately?'

'Yes. My mother will be departing today as well.'

'Very good.' Annabelle thought she saw the relief in the housekeeper's eyes and suppressed a smile. At least it wasn't just she who found Lady Hummingford wearing.

Quickly she gathered a few personal belongings and a couple of books to keep her entertained on the journey, her hand hovering over the bonnet with a veil attached before resolutely pushing it away. This was her new start, her chance to show Leo she could be a part of his world, wherever that was and whatever she had to do.

Chapter Twenty-Two

Dear Josh,
I never thought I was the sort of man who
just buried his head in the sand instead
of making a decision, but these last few
weeks I've done nothing but procrastinate.

Leo sat back and loosened his cravat, taking a sip of the whisky in front of him. It was smooth and delicious and just what he needed.

'Is everything sorted?' Wilbersmythe asked as he sat down in the chair opposite Leo.

'More or less. I've signed everything I need to. I had most of the papers anyway, all the details on the tenants and rents. It is all pretty straightforward.' He should thank his great-uncle—the man had left him in a good position. Leo was the only beneficiary of the will and it had been laid out in painstaking detail. Everything was accounted for, everything written down in ink and indisputable. The old man had been organised until the end, even when Leo had taken over the day-to-day running of the estates.

'No surprises, then?'

'No, no surprises.' There hadn't even been the clause about Leo needing to be married to inherit everything. The wily old man had been cunning until the very last. Leo allowed himself a smile at the memory of him.

'Are you planning on staying in London?'

Leo contemplated the question before answering. It was his least favourite time to be in London, the middle of summer, everything was stuffy and even the streets smelled in the oppressive heat. He longed for the rolling hills of Kent, for long rides and beautiful sunsets over the fields. Normally he wouldn't linger in London—normally he left as soon as whatever essential business was complete.

'Perhaps for a few more days.' The truth was he still hadn't worked out how he felt about Annabelle. The main point of this trip had been to get some perspective, to put some physical distance between himself and his wife so he could decide how he wanted their marriage to be going forward. He knew he cared

for Annabelle in a way he never had anticipated, never wanted even, but there was caring for a sister or a cousin and then there was
caring for a lover. He wasn't sure which cat-
egory Annabelle should fall into.

'You'll be keen to get home to your wife,
no doubt.'

'Yes,' Leo murmured, unable to stop himself from thinking about her soft lips and the
sparkle in her eyes when he kissed her. He
wanted so badly to return to Annabelle, to
give himself over to the desire he could barely
hold suppressed. Perhaps that was his answer
right there, perhaps he should stop resisting
it, should accept that despite his best efforts
not to let anyone else into his heart and into
his life Annabelle had found her way in. Perhaps he should just embrace that, allow himself to enjoy it.

Still, though, there was a niggling doubt.
Lord Abbingdon's death had brought back
the memories of both his parents' deaths and
Emily's. Although he didn't feel the same
heartbreaking grief, he did feel a sadness at
the loss of the old man and he felt cautious
about letting anyone else in.

He was just about to excuse himself from
Wilbersmythe, to head home for an early night,

when one of serving staff hurried over to him and bent down to whisper in his ear.

'There is a young woman outside, my lord, she is insisting she sees you.'

Leo frowned, wondering who it could be. Women weren't permitted in the gentlemen's club and never before had anyone waited outside for him. There wasn't anyone he was expecting to hear from, anyone he had unfinished business with.

'I'll be right out.' He excused himself from Wilbersmythe, shrugged on his jacket and straightened his cravat before heading to the big doors that lead out on to the street.

Standing at the bottom of the steps, head bowed and in shadow, was the unmistakable form of his wife. For a moment he was so shocked he couldn't move. Annabelle should be in Kent, safe and comfortable, awaiting his return.

'Annabelle,' he said, hurrying down the steps as soon as he'd recovered. 'Is something wrong?'

'Something wrong?' She shook her head, puzzled, 'No, there's nothing wrong.'

'Why are you here?' The question came out more abruptly than he had planned, but he was shaken by her appearance here where he least expected to see her.

She looked momentarily taken aback, but then seemed to rally.

'I wanted to see you. Your butler told me where you were. Was I wrong to come here?'

He didn't answer, instead taking her by the arm and starting to lead her away from his club.

'I thought something must be wrong. I didn't expect you to be here. Not at the club and not in London.'

'Oh. I'm sorry. I shouldn't have come.'

He knew he should reassure her, should tell her he was pleased she was here, tell her he'd missed her, but something caught his tongue and tied it in knots.

'Let's get you back home. It is late. We can talk in the morning.'

Briskly he marched her through the streets, feeling the tension in her body and not able to quite explain to himself the deep unease he was feeling. It shouldn't matter she had come without informing him. It wasn't the done thing to just appear at a gentlemen's club, but Annabelle wasn't to know that and he certainly couldn't hold it against her.

They hardly saw anyone as they walked

back to his town house, but the couple of acquaintances they did pass looked at them with curiosity as Leo hurried Annabelle on by. He was sure the news of his marriage had reached London by now and no doubt people were speculating about the speed behind the wedding and the nature of the marriage when they gossiped in ballrooms and at dinner tables. None of that bothered him. He didn't see the appeal in being so interested in the private lives of others, but he knew it occurred and after his recent inheritance he was more than ever going to be the subject of such scrutiny. What he didn't want was for anyone to say anything unkind *to* Annabelle. He knew how much that would hurt her, even though she tried to act as though she didn't care.

'I'm sorry,' Annabelle mumbled again as they reached the steps of his town house and the front door was opened by a footman.

'There really is nothing to apologise for.'

'I shouldn't have come to your club, should I?'

'It is a little unorthodox, but there was no harm in it.'

'People will talk.'

'People will talk whatever.'

Annabelle pressed her lips together and he

realised she must have thought he was ashamed of her, hurrying her through the streets like that.

Gently he raised a hand and tucked a stray strand of hair behind her ear.

'It's good to see you,' he said, leaning in to kiss her.

'It's good to see you, too.'

With a jolt he realised he had missed her. The unsettled feeling he'd had over the last few weeks had been down to feeling incomplete without her. Married for less than two months and he was already feeling restless when away from her.

'I missed you.'

'You sound surprised,' she said with a half-smile, but her eyes were searching his face for answers.

'It's only been a few weeks,' he said with a shrug, 'I thought I would cope for a few weeks.'

'I missed you, too.'

'I'm glad you came,' he said, surprised to find it was the truth. London wasn't ever where he had imagined Annabelle, but now she was here it felt good to be holding her again.

'Really? I was worried you would think it an imposition.'

'No.' He kissed her, aiming to show her quite how much he appreciated her being here. 'Not an imposition,' he murmured when he pulled away. 'A pleasant surprise.'

'Pleasant?'

He nodded.

'That sounds a little mundane. How you might react to an aunt dropping in on you.'

'Not my aunt.' He nibbled her earlobe and made her shiver. 'Perhaps pleasant is the wrong word.' Gripping her by the hand, he ignored the footman who was standing discreetly to one side and pulled her towards the stairs. 'I think I should give you a tour of the house. Perhaps we could start in the bedroom.'

Annabelle laughed and he felt himself lighten instantly. These last few weeks had felt empty and hollow. He'd thought it was because he was finally mourning his great-uncle and coming to terms with all the responsibility of his inheritance, and he was sure there was an element of that in his melancholy, but missing Annabelle had certainly been a part of it, too.

'Nice hall.' Annabelle giggled as he hurried her through the upstairs hall, barely allowing her to catch a glimpse of anything before they stumbled into the bedroom.

'I'll give you a full tour later,' he said and then they collapsed on to the bed.

Annabelle smiled as she rolled over and collided with Leo's firm body as she slowly woke from sleep. He flung out an arm and brought her to him, but soon his breathing deepened again as he settled back into a deeper slumber. Light was streaming in through the window where they hadn't properly pulled the curtains the evening before and already the room felt hot, but despite all this she felt happy.

Coming to London had been risky, she knew that. There had been a chance Leo would send her straight back to Kent, annoyed that she would encroach on his life here in the city. When she had first turned up at his gentlemen's club he'd looked shocked and for a moment she'd thought he was unhappy to see her. As he'd hurried her through the streets it had been as if he was embarrassed by her.

No, she told herself, *not embarrassed*. Just eager to get her home. Shifting in bed, she looked across at her husband. Last night he'd shown her how much he'd missed her. Although…

She tried to push the doubts from her mind, but it was undeniable that he had only relaxed once they were in the privacy of his house. When that door had closed behind them Leo had returned to being attentive and affectionate, but outside his club he'd been brusque and he'd hardly uttered a word all the way home, ducking his head whenever they passed anyone as if in a bid to remain unseen.

Annabelle wriggled out from under his arm and slipped out of bed, going to sit on the wide windowsill and looking at the street below. It was still quiet, only the odd servant hurrying by on a morning errand.

She didn't want Leo to be embarrassed to be seen with her and she hadn't ever thought it would be an issue. He wasn't the sort of man who cared what other people thought of him, he did what he wanted without thinking about whether people would gossip or not.

'You're overthinking it,' she murmured to herself.

'Overthinking what?' Leo asked from the bed, his voice heavy with sleep.

'Nothing.'

Even though his eyes were barely open, he still managed to give her a disbelieving look.

'I'm sorry for turning up unannounced last night.'

'Don't apologise. It was a good surprise.'

He reached out a hand and wiggled his fingers, tempting her back. 'Come back to bed, it must still be early.'

It was so tempting to slip back into bed next to him and forget all her doubts and worries. He wasn't trying to hurry her back to Kent, hadn't even mentioned her leaving London, so perhaps she was just overthinking things and his reaction the evening before had been nothing more than shock.

She slipped from the windowsill and joined him again in bed, her body fitting against his as if they were made for each other.

It must have been an hour later when there was a light tap on the door, followed by a long pause. Annabelle grabbed the sheets, making sure she was fully covered, before Leo called out that the person at the door could enter.

Leo's servants were very discreet and never just walked into a room like Annabelle knew was the norm in some households. Their lack of funds when she was a young woman at home had meant they'd never had more than a housekeeper/cook and one maid and that maid had been far too busy to occupy herself with Annabelle or Beth. It meant she found it strange to have servants present all the time, present and privy to all the secrets of hers and Leo's relationship.

'I'm sorry to disturb you, my lord,' Michaels said as he padded quietly into the room, staying close to the door, but closing it softly behind him. 'Miss Culpepper is downstairs and is insisting she sees you and meets your new wife. I did try to gently suggest she could leave a note and you would respond later, but I'm afraid the suggestion didn't go down well.'

'I applaud your attempt,' Leo said with a smile. 'I shall come down and see her, but I am not going to rush. Damn stubborn woman.'

'Very good, my lord. I've put her in the drawing room.' Michaels left the room as quietly as he had entered and Leo reclined back on the pillows and groaned.

'I can't believe she's come so early. Or that she got wind so quickly that you had arrived in London.'

'Is that why she's here?'

'Yes. She will want to meet you, to cast her eye over the woman I have chosen for my wife.'

'Should I start getting dressed?'

'Good lord, no. It's barely eight in the morning Annabelle. She knows it's unacceptable to make a house call at this time in the morning and we will not pander to her.' He kissed her firmly on the forehead before getting out of bed. 'She will not, however, leave without firm orders to do so. I will go and see her and arrange a more sociable time for a visit.'

She watched as he pulled on his trousers and shirt, making himself presentable in just a few minutes.

'Stay in bed,' he ordered with a wicked smile, 'I will be ten minutes.'

Chapter Twenty-Three

Dear Beth,
I can remember once you said that some-
times we have to step away from the
easy path to get what we want in life.
I'm trying...but, gosh, it is hard.

'Fifteen minutes now,' Leo murmured into her ear as they sipped tea from delicate cups. They were sitting in Miss Culpepper's drawing room, waiting for Leo's great-aunt to make an appearance. Annabelle could tell Leo thought his great-aunt was being difficult just because they had made her wait this morning. Beth had met Miss Culpepper a few months earlier when she was still considering marrying Leo, before she had admitted her feelings for Josh. She'd described the older woman as a dragon, a stickler for propriety and rules and unpleasant with it. From the brief insights into Leo's childhood it hadn't sounded as if she had been warm or loving towards the boy in her charge, so Annabelle was expecting someone severe and unlikeable when Miss Culpepper did finally grace them with her company.

'Leonard,' the older woman said stiffly as she marched into the room. Leo stood and greeted her and then turned to introduce Annabelle, but before he could say anything Miss Culpepper put a hand up to stop him.

'It is worse than I thought,' she said abruptly. 'Much worse.'

Annabelle blinked, taken aback by the lack of greeting and not initially understanding what Leo's great-aunt was saying.

'Aunt…' Leo growled, his voice full of warning.

'What have you done, Leonard? You could have had the pick of the debutantes—any of them would have been lucky to have the Abbingdon name.'

'I chose Lady Annabelle.'

'A recluse who no one knows, who has no standing in society, she will not be able to be the wife you need in your new role.'

'She's the daughter of an earl.'

'A destitute earl.'

Annabelle felt so shocked she could barely move. All her life people had been whispering behind their hands at her, pointing and giggling, looking at her with pity, but she had never encountered such open and vicious insults.

She stood and without a word began to walk to the door. Behind her Leo and Miss Culpepper fell quiet.

'Annabelle?' Leo called.

She spun and smiled serenely at him. 'I don't have to listen to this.' She quite enjoyed the shock on both their faces as she turned back to the door and walked out. It was liberating and satisfying and deep down she knew she was doing this for herself for all the times her mother had hidden her or belittled her. Never again would she let another person make her feel less than them.

Leo caught up with her on the doorstep and fell into step beside her. She loved that he didn't try to excuse Miss Culpepper's behaviour or persuade her to go back. Instead he quietly took her arm and accompanied her down the street, waiting for her to be ready to talk.

'How did you survive?' she asked eventually, glancing up into her husband's eyes. 'How did you survive when *that* was the woman who raised you?'

'I honestly don't know.'

'I'm sorry if I have put you in an awkward position.'

'Don't apologise. She was unforgivably rude. I should never have taken you there. I just thought...' He trailed off.

'Apart from Josh she's your only family now. I understand.'

'Yes. No.' He shook his head and then took her hand. 'You're my family now.'

Annabelle nearly cried on the spot, but managed to hold back the show of emotion, knowing it would not be the right place to start sobbing with joy in the middle of a London street. She allowed herself a little smile and revelled in the warmth flooding through her body. He cared for her, despite how their marriage had started, despite both of their intentions for this to be nothing more than a convenient arrangement. He cared for her and she realised that she felt even more than that. She loved him.

'You're smiling.'

'Yes. I like the sound of that. Family.'

'You and me.' They walked down the street in silence for a few minutes and Annabelle contemplated whether she should tell Leo that she loved him. Perhaps not yet, there was no rush and she didn't want to make him feel as though their regard for one another was unequal. In a few weeks, maybe a month or two, she would be ready to tell him she loved him and he would be ready to hear it.

'What would you like to do today?' Leo guided her through the decorative gates at the entrance to the park and they strolled at a sedate pace under the shade of the trees. 'It is going to be unbearably hot, so I suggest we avoid the main shopping streets or any activity that requires much exertion. Although…' He looked at her and gave her a salacious wink more suited to a sailor than a viscount.

'We can't do that all day.' Annabelle laughed.

'Is that a challenge?'

'I would love to go for a ride, although again perhaps that is better saved for a cooler day.'

'This is why everyone flees London in the summer. It is unbearable and the parks are very nice, but there is only so much time you can spend strolling in the shade.'

'I really do not mind what we do, I'm happy just to be here with you. Do you have business to see to today?'

'There are a couple of things I need to finalise with the solicitors, but most does not require my presence in London. Anything that needs a signature can be sent to Kent. Do you want to return to Five Oaks?'

'I have no wish to rush you. I'm happy to be with you here or in Kent, whatever is easiest.'

'I tire of London at the best of times. Let us plan to leave tomorrow. I cannot see this hot weather breaking any time soon and I would much rather be in the country where we can take a dip in the lake or find shade in the woods.'

'That sounds wonderful.'

Annabelle felt content. She had risked pushing Leo away by coming to London if he had truly wanted them to keep their lives separate, but it had been a gamble worth taking. Now they felt like a proper married couple, discussing their plans and deciding on where they wanted to be together.

As they reached one of the main paths they started to encounter more people out for an early afternoon stroll. Annabelle toyed with the edge of her bonnet, wishing she could pull it forward so it would shade her face completely.

Gently Leo took her hand and pressed it back to her side. 'You don't need to hide.'

'People will look at me.'

'Yes, they will and as my wife they will look at you more than they would if you had stayed an unmarried woman in Eastbourne. You will be in more social situations, under more scrutiny.' He paused as he regarded her. 'If you want them to, they will get used to it.'

'What do you mean?'

'The first time you meet people they will look and afterwards they will talk. Perhaps even the second or third time, but after that it will cease to be the focus of people's conversation. They will find more interesting things to gossip about. Especially if you do not show them you care what they think. Society will accept you, if that is what you want.'

Annabelle was stunned into silence, unable to utter a single word. She had lived for so long on the peripheries, always hearing about dances and dinner parties second-hand, always being told it was not her place to expect anything out of life, and here was Leo saying none of that was true. She could see the logic behind his words, she wasn't so self-centred to think that people's worlds would revolve around her looks indefinitely. Of course people would talk when they first laid eyes on Leo's scarred and reclusive wife, but he was right, even the most shocking became mundane on repeated exposure. The fifth or sixth time she was introduced to anyone it wouldn't be that they didn't see her scars, just that it wouldn't register as something worth taking much note of at that stage.

Annabelle felt as if a chasm had opened up before her and she was afraid to take a step forward. For so long she had hidden at Birling View. At first it had been at her mother's insistence, but as the years had passed she had become quite comfortable with avoiding the company of others. In the past few months she had ventured out more than she had ever imagined, mixed with more people than she had in the previous decade, but the idea of socialising properly, of accepting invitations to society events, felt overwhelming.

'Let's go back home,' Leo said, seeming to sense her unease. 'You don't need to decide now about attending the social events. You don't need to decide at all if you don't wish to, I just wanted to show you that the option is there if you wish to consider it.'

Annabelle forced herself to lift her head as she walked through the park, aware of people's eyes upon her, but steadfastly trying to ignore any curious stares. She was sure she was imagining people's interest in her—most of the well-dressed men and women strolling through the park had better things to do than wonder about her, even if she was on the arm of a newly wealthy and influential man.

She tried to clear her head, to work out what she actually wanted. Inside she was screaming to persuade Leo back to the countryside where they could pick up on the idyllic life they had left behind in Dorset on their honeymoon, but she knew she couldn't keep him cloistered in Kent for ever. Perhaps he was right, perhaps there was a way she could be his companion in town as well as the country.

Chapter Twenty-Four

Dear Josh,
When did you realise you were besotted
with your wife?

'Are you certain there is no other way?' Leo ran a hand through his hair and looked down at the pile of papers in front of him.

'Thoday is making the journey to London. He should arrive tomorrow or the day after. I know he is keen to speak to you.'

Leo knew he would have to stay. Thoday was the very capable man he had appointed two years ago to look after his great-uncle's extensive estate in Cornwall. It was one of the most profitable and over the last couple of years the income from that estate had only grown. Thoday was industrious and innova-tive and had thus far solved all problems with the estate himself without having to bring anything to Leo. If the estate manager was spending a week travelling to London, it would be for a good reason. He owed it to the man to at least hear what was troubling him.

It ruined his plans. He'd been looking forward to returning to Five Oaks with Annabelle. She had mentioned redecorating a few of the rooms and they would have to make the decision whether they were going to stay in the smaller property or make Willow House, his great-uncle's main residence, their home. He was actually excited to make these domestic decisions, to make plans for the future with his wife.

'You're besotted,' he murmured to himself, but found he had a smile on his face. He felt happier with Annabelle by his side. The last few weeks had been grey and flat, and now suddenly with her back in his life he felt happy.

'Pardon?' Hayes, his solicitor, said, looking up from the stack of papers.

'I'll stay for a few more days to hear what Thoday says.'

'Good, I will let you know if he contacts me first.'

Hayes stood and gave a formal little bow, then spun and left the room, carrying a huge stack of papers with him. The prim little man always seemed to be in a hurry, but Leo couldn't fault his efficiency.

He waited until he heard the front door close behind the solicitor and then went to follow him out of the study, meaning to look for Annabelle and tell her they would have to spend a few more days in London. Of course she could go ahead to Kent and he would suggest it, but he was hoping she would decide to stay with him here for a few more days.

Before he could make it out of the study one of the maids knocked quietly on the door before entering.

'There's a Mrs Harrison to see you, my lord.'

'Thank you, show her in.'

Mrs Phillipa Harrison, a striking woman in her mid-twenties, swept into the room and held her hand out for Leo to kiss. He bowed over it and then gestured for her to have a seat.

'What can I do for you, Mrs Harrison?' He forced a smile. It wasn't that he didn't like Mrs Harrison—he barely knew the woman. He vaguely remembered her being one of the most sought-after debutantes five or six years ago, creating a flurry of excitement in the ballrooms and at dinner parties. She had married Mr John Harrison, not the sparkling match everyone had expected of her, but there had been no rumours of unhappiness or unfaithfulness since. What he couldn't work out was why Mrs Harrison was sitting in his study, looking at him expectantly.

'I've come to introduce myself to your wife, Lord Abbingdon.'

'Ah.'

'You may or may not know there is a small group of us who stay in London the whole year round, and although the social Season is still a few months away we like to get together for an afternoon ride in the park or an evening of cards.'

Leo waited for her to continue, but she seemed to expect something from him.

'Oh?'

She was still looking at him expectantly, but eventually continued. 'I saw you in the park earlier, walking with your wife.'

'Yes.'

'I thought Lady Abbingdon might like to join our small group one evening.'

'That is very kind.' Leo glanced at the window, wondering if he could decline on Annabelle's behalf, but realised this was exactly what he had been urging her to do earlier in the day. To consider her options for socialising. Perhaps an intimate group like this one would be the perfect way to get her introduced to society. 'When are you planning on meeting next?'

'We are having a music recital at my house tomorrow evening. Just myself and four other ladies. Lady Abbingdon is most welcome to join us.'

He knew he shouldn't accept plans for Annabelle, but he could see this as being the perfect way of boosting her confidence, to show her she could have a life with him here in London as well as in Kent.

'I'm sure she would be delighted.'

'Eight o'clock.'

Leo nodded, hesitating as Mrs Harrison stood to take her leave.

'You may have heard, Mrs Harrison, that Lady Abbingdon sometimes wears a veil,' he said, feeling as though he were somehow betraying Annabelle by mentioning it.

'Oh?'

'She has some scars on her face from childhood. She is a little sensitive about them. I know it is a lot to ask, but if you could have a word with the other ladies and just warn them, so they do not stare too much.'

Mrs Harrison smiled and touched his arm

lightly. 'Of course. I'm so looking forward to meeting her.'

Leo smiled back, wondering why he felt as though he'd just betrayed Annabelle.

Outside the window Annabelle stifled a sob. She had been sitting on the bench just to the left of the study window, enjoying a spot in the shade while she sipped on her lukewarm cup of tea. Her mother had always insisted a hot drink cooled you down in the heat of the summer and, although Annabelle wasn't convinced, it had become a habit to drink tea even when the weather was sweltering.

She'd actually had her eyes closed and was close to drifting off, lulled by the low murmuring of voices between Leo and his solicitor in the study behind her. She could hear what was being said if she strained her ears, but mostly the words just wafted over her.

Once the solicitor had left Annabelle had begun to rouse herself, eager to go and see Leo now his business was done for the day. She'd stretched and shaken her limbs awake when she heard a new voice in the study, a woman's voice.

Her intention had never been to eavesdrop, but she had been unable to pull herself away.

Warn the others not to stare—that was what he'd asked of Mrs Harrison when he'd accepted the invitation on Annabelle's behalf. As if she were some freak in the sideshow at a circus.

She felt as though she couldn't breathe, as if her chest were being squeezed by an unknown hand, tight and unrelenting. He'd always said he hardly noticed her scars, that they were not her defining feature. Annabelle half scoffed, half choked back the tears, wanting to bury her head in a soft pillow, crawl under the bedcovers and never come out.

'Annabelle,' she heard Leo calling her, no doubt wanting to tell her about the pity social invitation she had received. *Poor Lord Abbingdon's wife.*

Somewhere deep down she knew she was being a little irrational, but the hurt was too much, too overwhelming. If she were anyone else, Leo wouldn't feel the need to warn her dinner companions, to plead with them not to stare.

'Annabelle.'

She couldn't face him right now so hurried around the corner of the house, pressing herself against the wall. Hot tears streamed down her cheeks and for the first time since she'd married Leo she wished she was back at Birling

View, locked in her sanctuary away from the cruelty of the world.

Leo moved away from the back door, but she knew he wouldn't give up. The town house was large for London standards, but hardly a sprawling mansion. Once he'd checked the bedroom and the downstairs rooms it would be obvious she was avoiding him.

With great effort she composed herself. She didn't want to confront him, all she wanted was to get as far away as possible as fast as possible. She wanted to go where she would see no one, where no one would have to be warned not to stare at her scars.

'There you are,' Leo said, the smile dropping from his face as she came in through the back door. 'Whatever is the matter?'

'Nothing,' she said, trying to make her voice sound as bright as possible. 'I think it is just the flowers making my eyes water. Sometimes they do in summer.'

'Oh.' He didn't look convinced. 'Mr Hayes has just informed me the estate manager from our Cornwall estate is on his way to London. I will have to remain in London a few days longer than planned to meet with him.'

'Very well.'

'I was hoping you would stay with me.'

'No,' Annabelle said a little sharper than intended. 'I will go back to Kent as planned. I am going to tell Kitty to start packing now.'

'Is something wrong, Annabelle?'

'What would be wrong?' She looked at him with a challenge in her eye.

'I've got no idea, but you're acting rather strangely.'

'All I have said is I will return to Kent as we had planned. That's hardly strange.' Before he could question her any more she swept past him and hurried up the stairs, calling out for Kitty as she went and making sure she closed the bedroom door firmly behind her.

The rest of the day had dragged. She had claimed she had a headache and Leo had dutifully come and checked on her every hour. Each time she had pretended to be asleep and each time she had heard him pause by the door as if he didn't quite believe her ruse. Lying in bed most of the afternoon meant she had slept poorly that night and the next morning she did wake with a headache.

'You look pale,' Leo said with concern as she shuffled away from him in bed in the morning.

'I feel a little queasy,' she said, this time not having to lie. 'And my head still hurts.'

'Stay,' Leo said, reaching out for her. 'Stay here and rest. My business will be finished in a few days, then we can travel back to Kent together.'

He looked so earnest, so honest, that she could almost convince herself she had misheard his words the day before. *Warn the others so they do not stare too much.* Silently she reminded herself of his words and the implication. That he *did* think her scars hideous, that they were all anyone would see when they looked at her.

'No,' she said sharply, pulling away further. 'I'm going back to Kent.'

He tried once more to reach for her, but she pretended not to notice, standing and starting to rifle through the wardrobe as if choosing her dress for travelling.

Chapter Twenty-Five

Dear Beth,
I think I might have overreacted. I just find
it so hard to think people are talking about
my appearance when I wish sometimes I
could just fade into the background.

Back at Five Oaks Annabelle felt restless and
low. She tried going for a ride, but couldn't
concentrate enough and found herself slipping once or twice in the saddle. Knowing the
dangers of falling from a horse, she returned
home, only to find herself wandering the house
aimlessly again. Even reading held no great appeal for her. She was moping, feeling sorry for
herself, and even though she knew she needed
to shake herself up, she couldn't summon the
energy or will to do so.

Each night when she slipped into bed she

would remember Leo's arm snaking around her waist, pulling her to him, his lips on the back of her neck making her go wild with desire. She missed him and she wondered if she had been too quick to react. His words hadn't been spoken out of malice, she could see he might argue he spoke to protect her, to prevent any of the ladies in Mrs Harrison's social group from staring at her in a manner that would upset her. It still hurt, though. He had worked so hard to make her believe her scars were not her defining feature, but then still went behind her back to warn other people not to make a fuss.

She had resolved to talk to him about it when he returned, knowing that running away from London had been cowardly and unfair on Leo. He had hurt her, but she had abandoned him, and he deserved a chance to explain why he had said what he had.

Annabelle slept better the third night back at Five Oaks, more at peace with what had happened in London now she had decided she would discuss it with Leo. Hopefully he would return to Kent soon and they could find their way back to how they'd been on honeymoon.

She half expected Leo to stride through the

door on her fourth day back in Kent. He had promised only a few more days in London, and with a day travelling added on she had hoped that he would make it back to her before the weekend. Late in the afternoon she heard the sound of hooves approaching the house and felt her pulse quicken in anticipation. Annabelle was in the hall when one of the footmen opened the door and felt her body sag when she realised it was only a messenger.

'A letter for you, my lady.'

It was in Leo's hand and she knew immediately he had been delayed longer than expected.

Dear Annabelle,

I send my apologies. The business with Mr Thoday is taking longer than expected. I hope to be finished and returned to Kent within a few more days.

I write to ask you a favour. Upstairs in the attic there is a room where I store the papers and correspondence that do not fit in my study. I need a paper with a map drawn on it, headed 'Abbingdon Estate, Cornwall'. I think it should be in one of the chests closest to the door.

If you could find it for me and send it

*on to London, this business should be re-
solved much more quickly and I will be
able to return to you.*
Warmest regards,
Leo

Annabelle read the letter through twice,
wondering if she was imagining the formal
tone. There were no words of endearment, but
she had run from him in London without an
explanation and it did sound as though he were
anticipating his return.

'Stop worrying,' she told herself. Leo was
formal in his correspondence and she knew he
felt a keen sense of responsibility to the estate
he had inherited, the estate that had been in
his family for generations. That was why his
letter was so formal, his mind was on business.

Deciding there was no time like the present, she climbed to the top of the house. She'd
only been up here once, when Mrs Barnes had
shown her around her new home while Leo
was lying sick in bed just after their wedding.
They'd spent a grand total of four minutes in
the attic rooms which comprised of four rooms
for servants and two used for storage. It was
one of these that Annabelle headed to now.

Like the rest of the house it was meticulously

maintained with no dust in sight even though the room was rarely used. Annabelle was grateful, shuddering at the thought of the attic rooms at Birling View. Some of those had been so thick with cobwebs and dust you would leave footprints on the floor when you entered.

Crouching down, she looked at the two chests closest to the door. They were huge and heavy, made of thick wood with brass fastenings. They looked as though they had been passed down through the centuries, the wood getting more battered and scarred with each owner.

Inside the first chest were neat stacks of letters, row upon row almost identical. She lifted a stack out, frowning at the childish handwriting, before looking at the writing on the next few piles. The letters were obviously organised in chronological order, the handwriting developing and becoming more mature, more formed, as time passed. Annabelle felt a lump grow in her throat as she realised this chest contained all of Leo's correspondence with his brother from over the years. Every letter he'd received from Josh, every drawing, all kept pristinely in this chest as if it were an important document.

She hesitated, knowing she should put the letters back, knowing they were private, but a flash of colour caught her eye. She unfolded a piece of paper from the bottom of the first stack and smiled at the childish painting of rolling green hills backed by a brilliant blue sea. The writing that accompanied the picture was large and curvy, no doubt from Josh at the age of seven or eight, soon after his arrival in India. It was a few lines only, detailing his new home. Annabelle carefully flicked through the letters, smiling as the handwriting became more formed, the letters longer. The brothers might have been young when they were separated, but by the looks of it they had written often, although the delay in receiving the communication from the other side of the world must have been hard.

Knowing she shouldn't pry, Annabelle replaced the stack, but curiosity got the better of her and before moving away she took out the next stack. From the dates at the top of the letters it seemed these were from late adolescent and early adulthood. In one she saw a line about Josh finishing school and starting to work in his guardian's business.

She wished she could see Leo's replies, see his half of the treasured correspondence. The way the letters were stored so carefully, so lovingly, showed what they meant to her husband.

'Put them away,' she murmured to herself. They were private. She didn't think Leo would actually mind her looking, but she owed it to him to ask first.

Carefully she tucked the second stack back in the trunk, but as she did so she dislodged a letter from the middle which floated out of place. As she picked it up she realised it was written in a different hand on thicker paper. Her curiosity won over her ethics and she unfolded it, gasping when a charcoal drawing fell out of the middle of the letter.

The drawing was of a stunningly beautiful young woman. She was half smiling, looking down in a coy way that only the truly ravishing could pull off. Her hair cascaded over her bare shoulders and she was biting her bottom lip in a way that seemed both innocent and provocative.

Instantly Annabelle knew this was Emily. It was unclear who had made the drawing, Leo or Emily herself, although it looked more like someone looking on rather than a self-portrait. No wonder Leo had fallen for her so fast and so hard. She was captivating even just on paper.

With her hand shaking she reached for the letter. She was surprised to find it was written in Leo's hand, not Emily's as she had first thought, although the writing was curvier, more flamboyant than his writing now.

My darling love,
It has been three months since I last set eyes upon you and my heart dies a little more each day we are apart. I long to run my fingers through your hair, to taste the sweetness of your lips, to look upon your perfect face and just take you all in.

I return to Cambridge for Lent Term tomorrow, but I do so with a heavy heart. For in Cambridge I am even further from you than I am here.

I know it is difficult, my darling, but if you can send me a note, even just a single word, to show me you haven't forgotten our time together...

I long for the day we can be with one another properly.
Keep safe, my sweet.
All my love,
L.

Annabelle felt as though she had been punched in the gut. There was nothing unexpected in the letter, nothing Leo hadn't told her himself. It must have been written at the height of their entanglement, but before Emily's husband found out about the affair. Her eyes flicked again to the picture.

'Don't compare yourself,' she told herself harshly, feeling sickened that she felt jealous of a dead woman. Leo had said he had loved Emily, but that he had mourned her and moved on. She should believe him. She did believe him. What she couldn't believe was that he would ever find her attractive if *this* was the woman he had lost his heart to.

All the platitudes people had uttered over the years started swirling around in her head: *Beauty is on the inside. Beauty is in the eye of the beholder. Looks are only skin-deep...a person's true worth is in their heart.*

With shaking hands she folded up the letters and put them carefully back in the trunk. Scrabbling in the second trunk as she felt the tears start to form in her eyes, she finally found the map Leo wanted, pulling it out and slamming the lid down with a crash.

She sank back against the wall, wishing she could just disappear, wishing that she could free Leo from this marriage to her. He deserved someone like Emily, someone beautiful, someone whom he didn't have to warn the other society ladies about, someone he could walk into a ballroom with and not have to be subject to whispers and stares.

Closing her eyes, she tried to tell herself to calm down, that she was overreacting, but all she could see in the darkness was Emily's portrait, her perfect face.

After a few minutes she staggered downstairs, knowing she shouldn't act rashly, but feeling trapped and upset. She loved Leo and realised she secretly hoped that one day he might love her back. Despite going into this union as a way to get away from her oppressive life and her mother, despite promising it was a marriage of convenience only, it had become so much more than that. Leo had been attentive on their honeymoon, and she knew he enjoyed her company, even enjoyed her in bed, but she was beginning to realise he would never love her. It was nothing to him to spend time apart from her, she was the one who had followed him to London, who had foisted herself on him. There would never be any of the adoration she had seen in the letter to Emily directed to her.

It shouldn't matter. She had a lovely home and a kind husband, but Annabelle knew her heart would break if she stayed too long in Leo's company, her love unrequited. Perhaps a few weeks away would help her to decide what to do. Perhaps with some time and some distance she would be able to persuade herself that it didn't matter, that she could just quietly live her life loving Leo, knowing he cared for her, but would never return her love.

He had plenty of properties and as his wife she could make any of them her home for a few weeks. She had the desire to be alone, to find her peace with her lot. Throughout her formative years she had often been left on her own at Birling View while her parents and Beth visited friends or went on little trips.

'Just a few weeks,' she murmured to herself.

She glanced down at the map in her hands. Cornwall seemed a long way away, but perhaps that was what she needed. Time and distance. Time to think and distance to accept her lot, to accept that her marriage might be more than Leo had first promised her, but it would never be exactly what she wanted. As she looked at the map she shook her head—Cornwall was perhaps too far. Surely somewhere closer would give her the space she needed.

'Mrs Barnes,' she called as she hurried down the stairs to the kitchen. 'I'm going on a little trip.'

Chapter Twenty-Six

Dear Josh,
I think I've ruined everything.

Leo was weary. He'd ridden from London, having sent the carriage on with Annabelle a week earlier. It was getting dark and he probably should have stopped overnight to break up his journey, but he had decided to push on and just get home. Michaels was riding beside him, the valet half-asleep in the saddle, but he roused at the sight of Five Oaks in the dusk.

The house was quiet as they dismounted. He had planned on sending a note to say he was returning home, but had only finalised his plans the night before so it felt a bit unnecessary. A rider would only arrive a few hours before him and he didn't need a fanfare to announce his arrival.

The door opened as he and Michaels dismounted and Leo handed his reins to his valet who started to walk the horses round to the back of the house where the stables were situated.

'Good evening, my lord,' the footman said, taking Leo's jacket.

'Good evening. Do you know where Lady Abbingdon is?'

He had hoped she would be up to meet him, had been imagining the moment of their reunion for the past week, but perhaps it was too much to ask. He had arrived unannounced and Annabelle might have already retired to bed. Suppressing a smile, he decided he didn't mind having to seek her out in the bedroom.

'Lord Abbingdon, how lovely to have you home,' Mrs Barnes said as she hurried up from the kitchen. 'I have a note from your wife.'

'A note?'

Surely she didn't need to send him a note when she was just upstairs.

'Is something amiss?' He tore open the seal with trepidation and unfolded the small square of paper. Perhaps her mother had been taken ill and she'd had to journey down to Sussex. He couldn't think of any other reason she wouldn't be here waiting for him.

As he skimmed over the words he started to frown, then folded up the paper and strode to his study. Brown, the young footman, followed him and lit a candle, then discreetly slipped away, closing the door behind him. Slowly Leo unfolded the note again.

Dear Leo,
  I have gone away.
  Please do not follow me. I need time to think.
Love,
Annabelle

That was all it said, short and brutal. Leo sagged back in his chair, reading and rereading the note, trying to find some scrap of information to put the words in context. When they had parted in London Annabelle had been a little quiet, keen to leave the capital, but he had thought that was because it was her first time in the city and she had become a little overwhelmed. He couldn't think of anything he had done to upset her.

As the minutes ticked past the feeling of confusion was slowly replaced by the familiar sensation of abandonment. She'd left him. Without a proper explanation, without a proper plan on when she was coming back. She'd crept away while he was still in London and left him.

Leo felt sick. The feeling of abandonment conjured up all the horrible memories from childhood, the awful sensation of being left on his own. Annabelle knew all about that, yet still she had left. With shaking hands he rose and poured himself a glass of brandy from the decanter on the shelf, but it tasted bitter on his tongue and he set the glass down after just one mouthful.

She'd left him. Perhaps not for ever, but she'd left all the same.

Letting his head sink into his hands, he tried to think logically, tried to work out why she had gone so abruptly. Until the day before she had left him in London everything had been wonderful. Then she had become a little more distant, but nothing that he would have thought would cause her to run away from her home.

Standing, he went over to the corner of the room and rang the bell, asking Brown to fetch Mrs Barnes when he appeared at the door.

She came in a minute later, a look of concern on her face.

'My wife,' he barked, knowing it was unfair to take his foul mood out on his housekeeper.

She didn't even blink, the expression of concern never wavering on her face.

'Lady Abbingdon left four days ago, she took the carriage and a few changes of clothes.'

'Did she say where she was going?'

'No, my lord…' Mrs Barnes hesitated. 'Although she did seem to make up her mind after she had been up in the attic looking for the documents you asked her to find. And I got the impression she was planning for a long journey.'

'Surely not Cornwall. What would possess her?'

'Can I get you anything, my lord?' Mrs Barnes looked at him with an air of motherly concern.

'No. I think I will retire to bed soon. I'm weary from travelling and I need a clear head to decide what to do in the morning.' He had another thought. 'The carriage hasn't returned?'

'No, my lord.' She smiled at him and started to move away, but seemed to want to say something more, hesitating by the door.

'What is it, Mrs Barnes?'

'I hope Lady Abbingdon is safe, my lord. She may be new, but she is very well liked by the servants. She is kind.'

Leo inclined his head. Annabelle might only have been mistress of Five Oaks for a short time, but it would seem his servants were good judges of character.

When his housekeeper had closed the door behind her he flopped back in his chair and rubbed his brow with one hand. He felt worried, wanting to know that Annabelle was safe, but he couldn't deny the feeling that she had abandoned him overshadowed everything else. Surely she wasn't so unhappy she felt the need to flee right to the other end of the country.

The next morning things were no clearer to him. He had hoped a good night's sleep would clarify how he felt and illuminate the course of action he should take. If anything, this morning he felt less sure about anything. Surely he hadn't imagined the way she looked at him, the way she responded to him. She'd come all the way to London to just be with him, to the city where she was completely out of her area of comfort.

Once he was dressed and had gulped down some scorching hot coffee, he abandoned the rest of his breakfast and stomped up to the attic, wondering if there were any clues up there as to why Annabelle had left so suddenly.

There was nothing, just the trunk of old letters from Josh, kept meticulously in date order from the very first letter received when Leo was eight and Josh had first left for India with his new guardian right up until the letter that Josh had written from France, informing Leo he would be back in England in just a few short days. The letters spanned twenty-five years, a brotherly relationship almost entirely made out of pen and ink. Soon the letters would start arriving again from India, once Josh was back home with his new wife.

He couldn't see anything here that would upset Annabelle, except perhaps for the reminder that her sister was on that same boat bound for India, but that shouldn't make her want to run away. If anything, the shared loss of their siblings should bring them closer together, not rip them apart.

He moved on to the next chest, but in there were just official documents, maps of the estates, deeds of ownership, old contracts.

Sitting back, he closed his eyes for a moment. She'd left him, by the sounds of it had travelled to Cornwall, to the other end of the country, to get away from him and he had no idea why.

He could choose to wallow, to let the pain

of her leaving build up inside him, to conjure up all the old feelings of being left alone, being abandoned and unloved. Or he could go and find her, bring her home and work out exactly why she had felt the need to run from him.

'If you let her go, she might not ever come back,' he murmured to himself. The idea of losing her, even after such a short time together, was more painful than he had expected. Over the past couple of months he had grown to first respect and like Annabelle, then to care for her. Now...well, now it was feeling even more than that.

'You don't love her.' As soon as he said the words he knew it was a lie. He *did* love her. It might not be the sudden, destructive love he had felt for Emily, but it was love all the same, warm and completing. As soon as he realised it, it was as if a peace descended on him. He loved his wife, he loved her and he needed her, and he needed to make things right with her, whatever had happened to make her feel as though she did not want to be here.

Standing, he packed away the contents of the chests and pushed them back to where they had been stored, then hurried back downstairs to instruct Michaels to prepare for a trip to Cornwall.

* * *

The journey to Cornwall was arduous even at the best of times, but in a hired carriage with hard seats and a faint musty smell about the fabric it was anything but comfortable. Even with changing the horses it took three days to get to Exeter, then the poor condition of the roads slowed everything even more. All in all the journey took over a week and Leo had been pressing for early starts to make the most of the travelling time.

It was mid-afternoon when he hopped down from the carriage, his legs stiff and his body in need of exercise. The last time he had visited the estate in Cornwall had been over a year earlier. Mr Thoday ran everything so well he didn't need to visit any more regularly and, although it was in a beautiful part of the country, his schedule hadn't allowed him time to just come and enjoy it.

'Lord Abbingdon,' Mr Thoday said, hurrying out of a side door of the main house. 'Is something amiss? I didn't expect to see you so soon after our meeting in London.'

'My wife,' Leo said, looking up at the windows and wondering if she was up there looking down at him.

'Lady Abbingdon,' Mr Thoday supplied helpfully.

'Where is she?' A look of puzzlement crossed Thoday's face and Leo paused. 'Lady Abbingdon is here, isn't she?'

'Please excuse my ignorance, my lord, but why would she be here?'

'She hasn't arrived to stay?'

'No, my lord. I haven't ever met your wife.'

Leo felt the ground shift underneath his feet and he reached out for the wall of the house to steady himself.

'She's not here?'

'No.'

He'd come all this way, rushed off from Five Oaks, without even bothering to clarify this was where she was. For a moment he closed his eyes, thinking of all the properties he owned. She could be at any one of them, or she could have gone home to her mother in Eastbourne. Quickly he dismissed the idea. However bad things were, he didn't think she would return to Lady Hummingford.

'Will you be staying, my lord?'

Leo looked at the carriage. He'd already spent far too long inside it, he longed to stretch his legs, go for a bracing walk along the clifftop, to ride out on horseback, but he knew he wouldn't.

'No. I'm not staying.' He would visit all his estates one by one if necessary until he found Annabelle and made things right between them.

'Can I at least offer you a meal, Lord Abbingdon, while your man sees to the horses?'

Leo thought for a moment, then acquiesced. It would mean they wouldn't have to stop for dinner and the horses could be fed and watered before starting on the return journey.

Annabelle sat in the sunshine with her eyes closed, not caring for once that the sun would colour her skin. It was too glorious a day to be hiding in the shade, cool, almost cold, but the sun was just warm enough to allow her to sit for a few minutes outside. She loved the month of October; she loved watching the leaves turn and fall from the trees and nature begin all its preparations for the hard winter ahead.

She placed a hand on her belly, knowing she was imagining the fluttering inside her. It was far too early for her baby to be anything more than the size of a walnut she knew, having read a book on the development of the foetus a few years earlier. She was two, perhaps three months pregnant, depending on when she had conceived, and as yet the only outward sign was her constant and debilitating nausea.

It had been six weeks since she had left Five Oaks. Six weeks of solitude, six weeks of reflecting on where she was in her life and what she wanted. Initially she had thought she might only stay a few days, keeping the carriage with her rather than sending it back to Five Oaks in case she wanted to return. After two weeks she had secretly hoped Leo might come after her, that he might make the trip an hour down the road to Willow House, but she couldn't begrudge him staying put, she had asked him to in her letter. In those six weeks she had realised she needed to make peace with her lot. A few months ago she had been completely happy with the prospect of a loveless marriage. The opportunity to run her own household, to get away from her mother's influence, had been enough to propel her into marrying a man she barely knew. Love was too much to ask for. Leo cared for her, even if he went about showing it in the wrong way as he had in London with the comment to Mrs Harrison about her scars.

Now there was also their unborn baby to take into consideration. She had decided she would allow herself to love Leo without asking for any love in return. In time she would learn how to wave him off without her heart feeling as though it were breaking each time. She would become the wife he wanted—affectionate, but not overbearing—and she would take pleasure in raising the child she never thought she would get to have.

Annabelle knew she had taken too long to reach this decision, to come to peace with her lot. She probably should have returned to Five Oaks weeks ago, but she felt better having had some time and space to consider her options.

The heat was making her doze off, so at first she didn't register the sound of hooves on the driveway, it was only when they stopped and she heard Leo's voice float into her consciousness that she realised he was here.

'Annabelle,' he said, as he rounded the corner of the house.

She stood, wondering if he was pleased to see her, wondering if he remembered the tense way they had parted in London all those weeks ago.

As she scrutinised him she realised he looked tired and dishevelled, his clothes were dusty from the road and he looked thinner than he had when she had left him.

He looked as though he were going to say

something more, but then he just strode over to her and took her into his arms.

'You don't know how long I've been looking for you,' he murmured into her hair.

'Looking for me?'

'It's a long story. Are you well?' He pulled away slightly, his eyes roaming over her face, searching for some sign of how she had fared these weeks they had been apart.

'Ye…yes,' she said falteringly.

For a moment she forgot all her deliberations and decisions of the last few weeks as Leo kissed her, cupping her face in his hands and kissing her until they were both gasping for breath.

'I've been wanting to do that for such a long while.' He frowned, then led her back over to the bench where she had been sitting. 'Tell me, Annabelle, why did you leave? I've been racking my brain, but I cannot make myself understand.'

She looked down at her hands. Now he was here, happy to see her, his thumb caressing the back of her hand and his eyes searching hers, all her resolve to rise above everything, to float along loving him but not minding when he didn't love her back, seemed impossible.

'I needed time to think.'

'What about, my love?'

She blinked. It was the first time he had called her *my love*. It sounded casual, but her heart began to race all the same.

'In London,' she said slowly, gathering her thoughts, 'I was outside the window when Mrs Harrison came to call.' She watched as he frowned as he tried to remember. 'She came to invite me to one of her social soirées.'

'Oh, yes.' He was still looking puzzled and Annabelle knew she was going to have to decide to let this go or explain in detail why it had upset her.

'I heard you say something to her that upset me very much. I heard you tell her to warn the other ladies about my scars, so they wouldn't stare.' She looked down at her hands for a moment before returning her eyes to his.

'I just wanted to make it as painless as possible for you.'

'I know. I know there was no malice in it...' She paused as she tried to find the words to explain why it had hurt so much. 'I suppose it just hurt that, despite telling me otherwise, you see my scars as so bad that people need warning about them.'

'Annabelle, no,' Leo said, looking shocked. 'That's not true.'

She raised her fingers to touch the scars that had marred so much of her life. 'I know they're awful, but I think I had allowed myself to forget a little just how prominent they are. When you spoke to Mrs Harrison you reminded me.'

'That was never my intention. I just wanted you to be able to go to a social event and enjoy yourself.' He took her hand and squeezed it. 'Once people get to know you they hardly see your scars—they see you. Wonderful, interesting, beautiful you. But of course the first time they meet you they will look, it is human nature to look at things that are different, I just wanted you to be spared that.' Leo leaned in and kissed her gently on the forehead. 'I'm sorry. Is that why you left?'

'It's why I left London.'

'I could tell you were upset about something, but I thought we would talk it through when I got back to Five Oaks. Then when I got home you were gone.'

Annabelle bit her lip. At the time she had just needed to get away, but since she had been at Willow House she had realised she'd just abandoned Leo. She'd thought solely about herself. She had been hurting, but she hadn't considered how Leo would feel to return to Five Oaks and find her gone, with just the perfunctory note to tell him she was taking some time to think and not to follow her.

'I'm sorry I just left,' she said, realising that Leo, although a man who valued his independence above most other things, could have felt as though she had abandoned him without good explanation.

'Why did you leave Five Oaks? Why come here?'

'I saw something that upset me when I went into the attic to find that map you asked for.'

'Oh?'

'I saw a letter you had written to Emily and with it a charcoal drawing of her.'

'Ah. Yes, I'd forgotten my letters to her were up there.' He frowned again, 'But I told you I was over her, that I loved her once, but had mourned and moved on.'

'And I believe you—it wasn't that. It isn't that.' She shook her head, wondering if she would be able to explain how inadequate, how inconsequential the letter had made her feel. She wasn't even sure she wanted to. It made her sound like a jealous woman, jealous of someone who was long dead. Feeling something settle inside her she took a deep breath before speaking again. 'Leo, I love you.' His eyebrows shot up in surprise, but she gently placed a hand on his to stop him from saying anything. 'I know love isn't what we were thinking of when we married, it isn't what we agreed on, but I can't help it. Somewhere along the way I fell in love with you.' She knew exactly when it had been: that night on their honeymoon when they had walked back through the woods in the dark together. Something had shifted then and her world hadn't been the same since.

'I read the letter you had written to Emily and there is so much love there in every word, you adored her, and the picture, I'm assuming you drew it?' She waited for him to nod. 'I can see how much she meant to you, how much you cared for her. She was beautiful, too.'

'Annabelle...'

'No, let me say this—please let me finish. I read that letter and I realised you would never love me like that.' She smiled sadly. 'You may never love me at all. It hurt, that realisation that I loved you, but it may never be reciprocated. With the picture and the letter I could see the sort of woman you could love and I am nothing like her. I needed some time to make my peace with that.'

Leo was looking at her as though she were a little crazy.

'Do you know where I've been the last six weeks?' he asked eventually.

'At home?'

'No. In fact, the only night I've spent at home since returning from London is last night. I've been travelling. To Cornwall. To find you.'

'Cornwall?'

Leo smiled, but she could see the tiredness there around his eyes.

'You'd left, with no clue from your letter where you were. Mrs Barnes told me you'd announced you were leaving just as soon as you came down from the attic holding the map of the Cornwall estate. I panicked and set off without actually thinking things through.'

Annabelle pressed her lips together to try to stop herself from laughing.

'Go on, laugh. It is laughable. If I'd just stopped and thought for a moment, I would have realised you wouldn't have chosen to go somewhere you'd never been before, not when there was an empty property sitting fifteen miles down the road.'

'You travelled all the way to Cornwall and back?'

'Yes. Didn't even spend the night there when I realised my error. I think if I ever have to sit in a hired carriage again I will not be responsible for the cursing that comes out of my mouth.'

'You must be tired.'

'Do you know why I did it? Why I travelled that distance as quickly as I possibly could?'

She shook her head.

'I couldn't bear to think of you alone and hurting. I didn't know why you had gone, but I knew you weren't happy and that made me want to find you, to gather you in my arms and do *anything* to make it right.'

Annabelle blinked. He'd done all that for her, the travelling, the putting aside any hurt he was feeling at her just leaving without an explanation. All of it was done to find her, to be with her.

'I realised something a few weeks ago,' he said quietly, looking into her eyes. 'I love you, Annabelle. I never set out to love you, I never set out to be your husband in anything more than name, but you have completely bewitched me. I, a man who has never spent more than an hour or two happily in anyone else's company, hate to be apart from you. I miss you even when you're just in the next room. I want to share everything with you.'

She couldn't believe what she was hearing

and searched his face for the lie. There was nothing there she could doubt, nothing but honesty and love in his eyes.

'You love me?'

'I love you.'

'Really, truly, honestly?'

'Really, truly, honestly.'

Annabelle launched herself at Leo, wondering how she had ever thought she could live without his love. She kissed him, for a moment forgetting where they were, forgetting everything but the man before her.

'I love you,' she murmured as they pulled apart. 'And I have something else to tell you.' She bit her lip, remembering Leo's declaration that he didn't want children, that he was happy for his brother and future nephews to be his heirs. Surely things had changed since then. 'I think I am pregnant.' Annabelle held her breath after her announcement, searching her husband's face for his initial reaction.

Leo smiled, the smile growing wider as he reached out tentatively and placed a hand on her belly.

'Are you sure?'

'Not sure, no, but I feel absolutely terrible with sickness most of the day and I've missed at least one of my monthly courses.'

'That is amazing.'

'Do you mean that?'

'Yes. I mean I never thought I'd have children, but then I never thought I would have you.' He kissed her again and Annabelle sank into his arms, wondering how her life had changed so much in such a short time, all thanks to the man who once she had thought of as stiff and insufferable.

Epilogue

❦

September 1822

Annabelle ran along the rail of the ship, shading her eyes with one hand and gripping her daughter's pudgy little fingers with her other.

'I can see them,' she cried, turning to face Leo. He grinned, as excited as she, then leaned in to kiss her.

'Urgh, Papa is kissing Mama again.' Edward sighed dramatically, making his little sister burst into a fit of laughter.

It seemed to take an eternity for the ship to dock and for the wooden gangplank to be lowered to allow the passengers to step off on to the dock. Annabelle was one of the first off, an excited Lucy skipping beside her, her long blonde hair flowing behind in the hot breeze.

'Annabelle,' Beth shouted so loudly a few people took a step away out of surprise.

Annabelle broke into a run and threw herself into her sister's arms, not knowing if she was laughing or crying. Somewhere beside her she was vaguely aware of Leo's reunion with his brother.

After a long embrace Annabelle broke away to take in the two little boys standing on either side of her sister. Her nephews, Robert and Joseph, now six and three, stood there shyly eyeing her and the rest of their family up.

'This is Edward and Lucy.' Annabelle placed a hand on each of her children's shoulders and watched as Beth crouched to say hello. In turn she embraced her nephews, wondering how almost seven years had passed since she'd last set eyes upon Beth. She and Leo had planned to visit sooner, but first there had been Edward, their surprise baby, now six years old and already looking like a little version of his father. Once he had been old enough to travel they had started planning their trip to India, only to find that Annabelle was pregnant with Lucy. More delays, but now Lucy was three they had decided they could wait no longer.

Leo had spent the time in the interim well, training up Mr Thoday, his capable estate manager in Cornwall, to take on more and more responsibility. Now he was Leo's second-in-command, entirely capable of looking after everything while Leo was away on an extended trip. It meant they would be able to stay longer than Annabelle would ever have imagined would be possible.

'Let's get you home,' Josh said, embracing her. She marvelled at how well her sister and brother-in-law looked, their skin bronzed from the sun, their faces aglow with the joy of the reunion.

Josh led the way to two large carriages and organised their luggage to be loaded on to the back of both. Then he motioned for them to get in. Annabelle climbed in with Beth and the younger children, while Leo went with his brother and the two elder boys.

'It isn't very far to the house and there are lovely views,' Beth said as she settled in the seat across from Annabelle, her younger son Joseph nestled in the crook of her arm. The hustle and bustle of the docks was soon replaced by a dusty town that soon dwindled to the odd dwelling in the beautiful countryside. After a few minutes they began to climb, the carriages slowing as the incline got steeper. Annabelle gasped at the raw beauty of the view, the hills a lusher green than she had ever seen before, rolling away to a sparkling blue sea fringed by a narrow strip of golden yellow sand.

'You look happy,' she said to her sister. 'You look as though life here suits you, Beth.'

'It does. I'm very happy. It feels as though this is where I am meant to be. The only thing that has been missing is you.'

Annabelle wrote to her sister every week and received a similar volume of post in return. Everything was at least nine months out of date by the time it had travelled across the oceans, but Annabelle loved receiving her letters from Beth. It was no substitute for sitting with her, for hearing her voice and her laugh, but at least it was something.

'I had hoped it wouldn't be so long,' Annabelle said.

'Me, too. We planned to come and visit England after Robert was old enough, but then I was pregnant with Joseph.' Beth shrugged, but Annabelle could see the tears in her sister's eyes.

'We're here now.'

'I'm so glad, I've missed you so much.'

The carriage drew to a stop in front of a magnificent white mansion, with a trickling fountain in the middle of the drive and perfectly manicured lawns to either side. It looked so exotic that Annabelle couldn't believe her sister actually lived here.

'This is our home, come and let's get you settled.'

Already Leo was stepping down from the other carriage, laughing at something Josh had said and looking up at his brother's house. He crossed over to her, making sure she was steady on her feet, before ushering the children inside.

'I'll show you your rooms, then perhaps once you've had a chance to freshen up we can have lunch on the veranda.'

When Beth and Josh had closed the door behind them, Annabelle turned to Leo and gave a little excited squeal of delight.

'I can't believe we're actually here.'

'I know. I'm sorry it has taken so long.'

'It feels as though not a day has passed since I saw Beth, yet it has been seven years.'

'She's still your sister, no matter how much distance there is between you.'

'Mama, look at this massive bed,' Edward called, pushing off his shoes and jumping on top of it.

'Edward,' Annabelle said admonishingly, leaning over and tickling him so he collapsed into a giggling heap.

Their rooms were spacious, a set of four rooms set in their own wing. Leo and Annabelle had a large and airy bedroom, with a door leading through to a slightly smaller room with two beds for the children. There was also a prettily decorated room that looked out over the rolling hills set with comfortable chairs and a little writing desk, and then a small bathroom off to one side.

'Can you believe seven years ago we had just waved off Josh and Beth on their wedding day and I was nothing more to you than your grumpy brother-in-law?'

Annabelle smiled. 'You were very grumpy. Do you remember the day my mother and I moved out of Birling View and you found me hanging out of the window? I've never known someone so annoyed at having to witness another's predicament.'

'I was worried you would hurt yourself.'

'You barely knew me.'

'Josh had asked me to look out for you and you know I take my responsibilities *very* seriously.' He leaned in and kissed her and for a moment Annabelle forgot where she was. Even almost seven years after she had first kissed Leo, he still made her feel as though she were floating on air.

* * *

Once they had freshened up and changed their clothes which were dusty and creased from travelling, they made their way downstairs, to find Beth and Josh on the veranda.

'Your cousins are playing in the garden, you can join them if you like,' Beth said to Edward and Lucy, calling over Robert to show his cousins around.

Annabelle settled back in a comfortable chair and sipped at the drink one of the servants handed her once she was settled.

'How was the voyage?'

'Long, especially for the children, but so worth it,' Annabelle said, starting to relax. It had been arduous at times to keep the children entertained while cooped up in such a small space, but the alternative—leaving them at home—had been unthinkable. They had loved stopping at the different ports, exploring a bit of the world and learning about the ship from the friendly crew.

'I can remember the first time I did that trip,' Josh said quietly. 'I was only a little older than Edward. It seemed as though it lasted for ever.'

'You'll just have to stay longer so it makes

the journey worthwhile,' Beth said with a smile. 'How long are you planning on staying?'

'Well...' Leo glanced at Annabelle who gave a discreet nod. 'We had planned on four months, but we think it might have to be a little longer if it is not too much of an imposition?'

'You know we'd have you stay for ever if we could.'

'Why longer?' Beth asked, her eyes skimming over Annabelle's body. Annabelle grinned.

'I never could keep a secret from you, Beth.'

'You're pregnant?'

'Yes. About four months, we think. I don't fancy having a baby on board the ship, so I was hoping we could stay until after the birth, then perhaps a couple more months to let the little one grow to be a bit more robust.'

Beth launched herself at Annabelle and squealed in excitement.

'This is the best news ever. And in that time perhaps we can work on persuading you both to stay for ever. I've got so much planned for your visit and we've got seven years to catch up on. I'm so excited.'

'We thought in a month or so we could take you on a little tour of India. We have a couple of small properties dotted around that we use when we need to travel for the business. Beth has to be here for the next few weeks to sign the contracts for her book that should be arriving from the publisher, but after that I can hand the running of the transport business over to my managers for a few weeks.'

'That sounds delightful. I would love to see as much as possible while we're here.' Annabelle leaned over and squeezed her sister's hand. 'I'm so proud of you.' Beth had always wanted to travel the world and write about her experiences, even as a child it had been one of her dreams. A year ago Annabelle had received a letter telling her that Beth's ambition had been realised—a publisher in London wanted to publish her account of an Englishwoman travelling around India.

'And I of you, little sister. I can't believe how much you've changed since I last saw you. It is so lovely to see you so confident, so at ease with the world.'

Annabelle took a sip of her drink as she remembered all those years she had spent locked away at Birling View, never socialising, too scared to be part of the wider world.

'It's been a long road,' she said, taking Leo's hand, 'But little by little I realised how much I was missing out on.'

'Thank you for looking after my sister so well,' Beth said to Leo.

'She's the one who deserves the praise,' he said quietly. 'She is the strongest person I know.'

'It is easy to be strong when you are right next to me.'

Leo leaned over and kissed her and Annabelle felt as though everything was right in the world. She was here with the people she loved the most, with a long trip stretching out before her, and who knew, after a few months she might even be able to persuade Leo that they could make their home here, especially if Mr Thoday proved to be as capable as Annabelle hoped at running everything back home. Whatever their future held she didn't mind, as long as she had her family around her.

* * * * *

COMING SOON!

We really hope you enjoyed reading this book.
If you're looking for more romance, be sure to
head to the shops when new books are
available on

Thursday 19th
August

To see which titles are coming soon, please visit
millsandboon.co.uk/nextmonth

MILLS & BOON

THE HEART OF ROMANCE

A ROMANCE FOR EVERY READER

MODERN

Prepare to be swept off your feet by sophisticated, sexy and seductive heroes, in some of the world's most glamourous and romantic locations, where power and passion collide.

HISTORICAL

Escape with historical heroes from time gone by. Whether your passion is for wicked Regency Rakes, muscled Vikings or rugged Highlanders, awake the romance of the past.

MEDICAL

Set your pulse racing with dedicated, delectable doctors in the high-pressure world of medicine, where emotions run high and passion, comfort and love are the best medicine.

True Love

Celebrate true love with tender stories of heartfelt romance, from the rush of falling in love to the joy a new baby can bring, and a focus on the emotional heart of a relationship.

Desire

Indulge in secrets and scandal, intense drama and plenty of sizzling hot action with powerful and passionate heroes who have it all: wealth, status, good looks…everything but the right woman.

HEROES

Experience all the excitement of a gripping thriller, with an intense romance at its heart. Resourceful, true-to-life women and strong, fearless m face danger and desire - a killer combination!

To see which titles are coming soon, please visit

millsandboon.co.uk/nextmonth

MILLS & BOON

Coming next month

A SCANDAL AT MIDNIGHT
Annie Burrows

'Oh stop arguing Ben. I am sure you have had to do all sorts of unpleasant things when you were in the thick of a campaign. But the point is you are not on campaign now. You are staying at your friend's house, where you ought to be able to have a bed with blankets and sheets and a hot breakfast in the morning. And no matter what you have done, I could not possibly sleep myself, knowing you were out here, shivering and naked in the rain all night.'

'That's very good of you my...Daisy.' And so typical of her. Others might think she was cold, but beneath her outer reserve, beat a heart that was good, and kind, and compassionate. 'But look, you really don't need to row me back across the lake yourself. Couldn't you just go across and then...send a message to my manservant to row over with some dry clothes?'

She glanced up at the sky. 'I could, I suppose, but it would be quicker to just row you across myself. And then you could shelter in the boathouse while I go and fetch your manservant. Because it is going to rain soon. Can't you feel it in the air?'

'I can, yes, but a little rain won't do me any harm. Not English rain. Summer rain.'

She stuck her fists on her hips. 'I see. You would

rather do anything than get into a boat with me, wouldn't you? Would it damage your masculine pride so much to allow a mere female to help you out? Yes, it would. Hah! I didn't think it of you, Ben. I thought at least you were...' She pulled herself up to her full height. 'But I see I was wrong. You despise me just as much as...'

'No!' He couldn't let her think that of him. 'Daisy, that isn't true! I don't despise you! I...'

Instinctively he darted forward.

'You would, in fact, rather freeze out here than be forced to sit within one foot of me for the short duration of the boat ride back to the mainland.'

'No, Daisy...' He strode across the gravel to where she was standing. 'You haven't considered...if anyone were to see you, and me, like this in a boat, in the dead of night...'

'Yes. You would risk being compromised into marrying me, wouldn't you?'

Continue reading
A SCANDAL AT MIDNIGHT
Annie Burrows

Available next month
www.millsandboon.co.uk